Mrs. R. Pacheco

The Untold Story of Playwright and California First Lady Mary McIntyre

Rose Ann Woolpert

HISTORIUM PRESS U.S.A.

HARDCOVER ISBN 979-8-950078-97-2
PAPERBACK ISBN 979-8-950078-98-9
EBOOK ISBN 979-8-950078-99-6

First edition
Printed in the United States of America

Edited by Sheila Bender, Patti Trimble, Rachel Santino

Cover photo of Mary McIntyre Pacheco, in formal bust pose, age about 30; hair parted in middle and in bun, broach at throat, white at collar. Courtesy of the History Center of San Luis Obispo County

Woodcut photo of Romualdo Pacheco, Hutchings' Illustrated California Magazine, Volume II, No. 10. Hutchings & Rosenfield (San Francisco), "Members of the California Senate." April 1858, p. 435

Hand-drawn sketch maps of Cañada de los Osos y Pecho y Islae boundaries. Volume 2, page 183 Courtesy of the California State Archives

This novel is a work of fiction based on the lives of real individuals and actual events. While many of the characters and circumstances are drawn from historical records, many of the names, details, and dialogues have been adapted or dramatized for narrative purposes. Any departures from documented history are the author's own.

www.roseannwoolpert.com

For my granddaughters

Mary Catherine Pacheco, circa 1872

Romualdo Pacheco, 1858

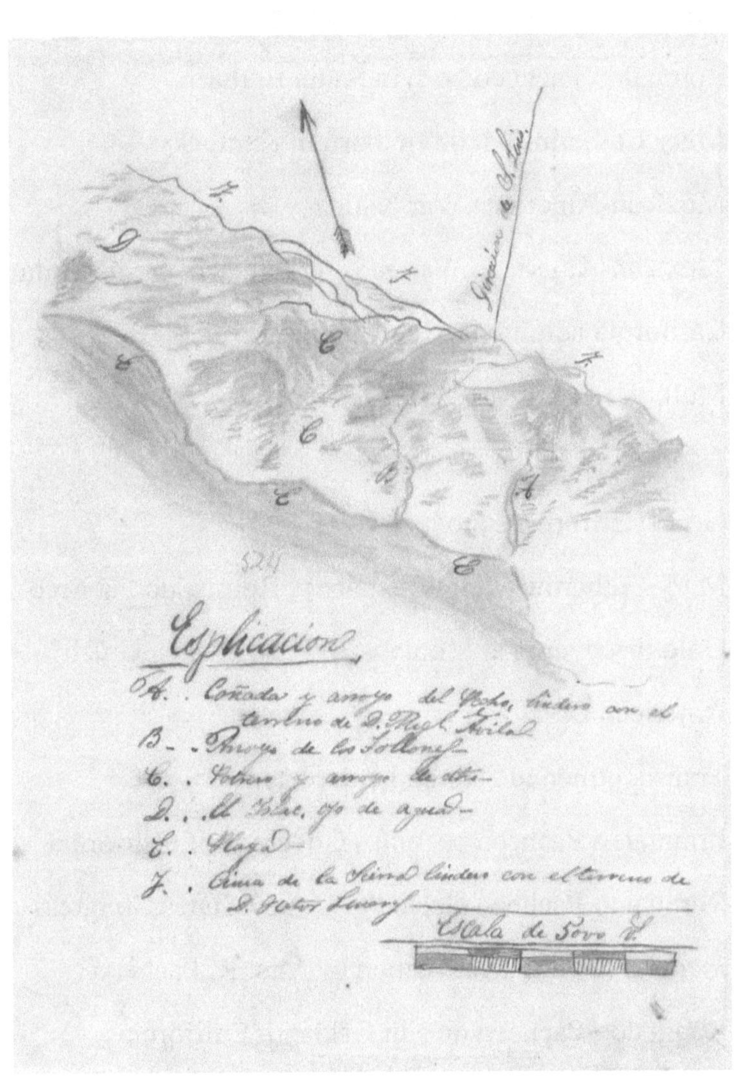

Rancho de los Osos, 1843

Chronology of Events

1812 - María Ramona Carrillo born in San Diego

1821 - Mexican independence from Spain

1831 - Romualdo Pacheco born in Santa Barbara

1842 - Mary Catherine McIntyre born in Kentucky

1846 - Mexican-American War begins

1848 - Mexican-American War ends; gold discovered at Sutter's Mill

1850 - California admitted to the Union

1859 - McIntyre family arrives in Sacramento

1861 - American Civil War begins

1862 - Great California Flood

1863 - Mary Catherine McIntyre marries Romualdo Pacheco

1864 - Gold discovered at Montana's "Last Chance Gulch"

1865 - American Civil War ends

1869 - Transcontinental Railroad completed

1875 - Romualdo Pacheco becomes Governor of California

1876 - Romualdo Pacheco elected to United States Congress

1880 - *Incog*, a comic farce, written by Mrs. R. Pacheco

1899 - Romualdo Pacheco dies in Oakland, California

1908 - *Three Twins,* a musical based on *Incog,* opens on Broadway

1914 - Mary Catherine Pacheco dies in Oakland, Californi

Table of Contents

Chapter One

Stagecoach to Lexington

June 1857

Everyone in Danville knew everyone else's business, or at least thought they did, and Molly could easily guess what Mother's friends would be saying. Hal Lucas, the station agent, would likely tell his wife Margaret, who'd tell Phoebe Springer, and quick as a blink, it'd be all over town. By Sunday's service, every church pew would be buzzing with the news.

"Have you heard?" Margaret Lucas would whisper to Phoebe from behind her hymnal. "Sarah's taken Mary Catherine and left the younger girls with David. I suppose they'll be obliged to fend for themselves while she's away."

"You can never tell what Sarah might do," was Phoebe's likely reply, her lips pursed prim as a prayer book.

"That's a true fact, if ever there was."

"She's always been a free spirit," Phoebe would add, part admiring and part disapproving.

Margaret would sigh and say, "I suppose she had no other choice. Who else is there to help Louis and Mary, what with Caleb off chasing gold in California?"

"California, of all the places!"

That was Danville, Molly figured—tidy as Mother's sewing basket and lacking the least bit of imagination. The thought of spending her entire life in such a narrow, uninspired town almost made her want to follow Cousin Caleb out west.

"Come along, Mary Catherine! We haven't time to dawdle."

They'd reached the station, so Molly put away her musings, checked to be sure the strings securing the box she carried hadn't come loose, and followed Mother inside.

Mr. Lucas sat behind the ticket counter tallying up the day's tickets. He stopped to look up.

"Morning, Sarah, off to Lexington, are you?"

"We are indeed, Hal, but only for a short visit. My brother's wife Mary is feeling poorly, and Molly and I are going to help her out for a few days."

Raising one eyebrow, the agent lowered his chin and peered through his sadly smudged spectacles.

"Just the two of you? That'll be three dollars apiece."

Mother paid for the tickets and turned toward the door.

"You'll give Mary my best, won't you?"

"Bless you, Hal, we surely will," she said. "And would you be a dear? I'm sure I won't be able to find a place for this bag."

Tapestry carpetbags were big and heavy, and Mother's was thoroughly stuffed, bulging with bundles of medicinal herbs and teas and small stoppered jars of healing salves. Molly had added her journals and pencils and a stack of magazines, and they both required at least one change of clean clothes.

"Let me help you there, Sarah."

"Oh, thank you, Hal. I so appreciate a man's assistance."

Molly smiled to herself. She knew it would never have crossed Mother's mind to lift the heavy load on her own, at least not when there was a man nearby to help.

Mr. Lucas somehow found a way to shove the bag into the last available space inside the coach. It was already packed with parcels, mail, luggage, and a dozen travelers laden with assorted personal belongings.

Molly sighed. Though there'd been lots of talk about building a railroad between Danville and northern Kentucky, so far it was just talk. For now, the Lexington stage was their only option.

She gathered her skirts, climbed inside the coach, and looked around for a good place to sit. Unfortunately, the quiet corner next to Mother had already been claimed.

A friendly, high-pitched voice floated from behind a large, round hatbox, then a sweet face popped up from beneath the brim of an oversized traveling bonnet.

"I'm happy to move over for you, dear."

The hat itself was pretty enough, but it was crowned with a riot of rosy satin and butter-yellow silk flowers, then trimmed with ten times the ribbons and bows any sensible woman would wear.

"Thank you kindly, ma'am."

The lady scooted across the coach seat, leaving the strong scent of lavender water and just enough space for her to sit next to Mother.

Molly carefully tucked her cakebox under the seat and leaned back against the cushions. Now, with any luck, she'd be able to look through her magazines without very many interruptions.

She was glad to be the one chosen to go on this trip with Mother. Earlier that morning, both her sisters had strongly protested the decision to leave them home in Danville.

"I don't understand why I can't come," Lizzie had said. "It's not fair."

"You may accompany me next time," Mother had said.

"But why does Molly get to go?"

"Because she's the oldest, Elizabeth," Mother said, slightly raising her voice. "I can depend on her to help with the shopping and baking, and whatever else Aunt Mary may require."

Molly could tell Mother was exasperated. Everyone called her youngest sister Lizzie, except their parents, and then only when she was particularly annoying. In Molly's opinion, Lizzie was nearly as spoiled as Peony, the family's lazy calico housecat, who acted as if she owned the world. Like Peony, Lizzie almost always got her way.

Joanna had also begged Mother to let her come. This was surprising, because she usually preferred to stay home, curled up in a quiet corner with whatever reading material could be found. But today was different.

"Please," Joanna had said, "I was hoping to look for a novel in Lexington. I've already read and reread *Moby-Dick*. I simply have to have something new!"

Mother was not in the mood to patronize Lizzie or argue with Joanna. They'd have to leave soon or be late for the stagecoach. So, she ignored their long faces, tightened the ribbons of her hat, and pulled on her black kid gloves, then started toward the door.

"You girls are quite capable of getting by on your own for a day or two. Remember, you are not to disturb your father without a very, very good reason. You know how he hates to have his work interrupted."

Professor McIntyre had morning classes to teach and did not want to be late. He was waiting for them on the porch, drumming his fingers in brisk, impatient bursts against the railing, checking and rechecking his silver pocket watch.

"Ah, there you are, Sarah."

He lowered his eyes at Molly.

"Have you remembered everything?"

"Yes, Father."

"What about the jam cake you baked for Mary?"

"It's here. Carefully wrapped. I will guard it with my life."

He gave her a warm, indulgent smile.

"I am sure you will, Molly."

Turning to his wife, he said, "Will you be home by the end of the week?"

Mother set dainty gloved hands on her ample hips, tilted up her chin, and planted a little kiss on his cheek.

"We won't stay a moment longer than is absolutely necessary. You'll find plenty of food in the pantry. Oh, and Lucinda promised to bring you a pan of chicken and dumplings for tonight's supper."

"All right, then," he said with a little half smile. "Will you give the Handleys my regards?"

"I surely will. Come along now, Molly."

With a quick turn, Mother swept her full skirts down the front steps.

Molly hurried after her, down the path in front of the house and around the corner of the boxwood hedge. There was no time to talk about it now, but she would stop at a bookstore for Joanna if she had the chance.

***

The air inside the coach was thick, close, and heavy with damp wool and dusty leather. The hatbox lady tilted forward in her seat and pointed her chin toward Molly.

"I do declare, this weather is unseasonably warm. Not what you'd expect so early in the summer."

"Yes, ma'am."

Molly noticed the loose, beige linen duster the woman wore. Layered over the usual skirts, petticoats, and other ladies' garments, it was no surprise she was feeling the heat.

"I find it necessary to wear excessive amounts of clothing when I travel," the lady went on. "I always strive to arrive at my destination as clean as humanly possible. Soiled clothing is so disagreeable."

"Yes, ma'am," Molly said again.

She glanced down at her own long-sleeved indigo cotton dress. It, too, was needlessly warm, but the dark, sober blue color was meant to hide the dirt and grime of travel. At least her lightweight straw was cooler than this woman's elaborate traveling bonnet.

A short, barrel-chested fellow on the opposite bench tipped his brown felt bowler and gave Mother a friendly smile.

"Morning, ma'am. Pardon my interruption, but I wonder if you'd care for my window seat?"

"Thank you, sir, you are most kind. I prefer this quiet corner. I like to avoid the noisy horses and carriage wheels."

"Absolutely understandable," he said with a little sniff. "Travel can be exceedingly bothersome. I sometimes ask myself why I ever leave home."

Shifting his considerable weight, he pulled a crumpled linen handkerchief from his breast pocket, wiped his nose vigorously, and nodded at Molly.

"How 'bout you, miss? It's all of four hours to Lexington. I warrant the trip will be hot and bumpy."

Molly smiled and shook her head.

"Much obliged, sir, but I don't mind the ride."

She wasn't just being polite, she wanted to go to Lexington. Her aunt and uncle's front porch featured a wide, wooden swing that was perfect for reading a good book on a sultry summer afternoon. She loved how the white gardenias outside the bedroom windows scented the house with sweet, fragrant perfume, and always liked hearing Uncle Louis talk about the happenings around town.

Hal Lucas poked his head back inside the coach. "Everyone settled in there?"

Hearing no objections, he signaled to the driver, and the stagecoach lurched away from the Danville station.

The road led straight out of town, past the tall, slim spires of Trinity Episcopal Church and the white Grecian columns of Centre College. Molly leaned forward to get a better look at the boys lounging around on the school's grassy front yard. They were not much older than her, and as usual, she found herself wondering what their classes were like.

"Mother," she said, "do you see those students out on the lawn? I wonder if they're waiting for Father. Do you think I could sit in on his lectures someday? You never know, I might want to become an astronomy professor like him. Or maybe I'll be a lawyer like Cousin Caleb."

Mother reached over to pat her hand.

"Wouldn't that be nice, dear? Unfortunately, as you very well know, girls may not attend Centre College."

"I don't see why not. Girls can learn just as well as boys. Besides, most of those boys would rather be home asleep in bed."

Mother obviously did not understand her frustration. Yes, of course she knew that women were not supposed to become astronomy professors. Clearly, they couldn't be lawyers. But she was already fifteen years old. Molly needed to decide what to do with her life, and it had better be something interesting.

The old wagon road stretched due north, past the pioneer graveyard and through a wide grove of tall yellow poplars. The stagecoach jolted, rattled, and wobbled over the deeply rutted road. Molly braced herself against the wall and tried not to bump into anyone.

It was really getting hot now, and the man in the bowler hat began to perspire heavily. He removed his hat, started fanning his face with a rolled-up newspaper, and leaned over to tap Molly's arm.

"Mind if I push this curtain back a bit further, miss? I'd appreciate just a little more air. 'Sides, this view of the woods is mighty enjoyable, don't you agree? They say the road through southern Kentucky was once a Shawnee foot trail. Course, that was nearly a hundred years ago, back in the days of pioneers like Daniel Boone. I'm told there used to be quite a large forest beyond here. But it's been gone for years. After we round the next bend, you'll see little more than endless acres of corn and tobacco."

Molly was still irritated about the matter of college and wasn't interested in hearing a lecture about Kentucky's countryside. She nodded as courteously as she could manage and reached down to rummage around in her bag for a magazine. Pulling out a copy of *Godey's Lady's Book,* she began leafing through the well-worn pages.

Mother had been watching the world go by without a word, but now she looked over at her daughter.

"Haven't you read and reread every one of those articles by now? You must know them all by heart."

"I still enjoy them."

Molly opened to a page with an illustration of city buildings and ladies strolling along tree-lined paths.

"Have you seen this piece about the new Central Park they're building in New York? Oh, and here's one describing the amazing exhibits in P.T. Barnum's museum."

"Yes, dear, it's all very interesting."

"I'm going to go there one of these days. I intend to visit art galleries and promenade with the Broadway shoppers. I may even stop for a look inside Tiffany's Fancy Goods Emporium."

"You have quite the imagination, my dear."

"It's more than just my imagination. I will get there someday. And when I do, I plan to attend a show at one of the theaters. Maybe more than one. Oh, Mother, doesn't New York sound exciting to you? It has to be far more interesting than Danville."

Her mother only went on smiling, so Molly shrugged and returned to her reading. She flipped through the pages, scanned recommended book lists, noted recipes to try, and read and reread every article she could find on writing techniques.

Newspapers and magazines were the only way she had to learn about the outside world, and there was so much she longed to know. Maybe she'd become a writer herself. It was one of the few respectable options open to a girl who wanted something beyond marriage and motherhood.

She drew out her journal to make a brief entry:

It would be thrilling to live in a city like New York. Mother and Father might be satisfied with Danville, Kentucky, but it feels too small and ordinary for me. They take it for gospel truth that every girl is satisfied with the simple joys of marriage. But I want art and beauty and adventure, and one day I shall have it all. Somewhere, in some other place. I'm absolutely sure of it.

Chapter Two

Lexington, Kentucky

June 1857

Molly returned to reading her magazines and imagining life in New York City. This helped the time pass quickly, and soon they'd left the cornfields far behind. The stagecoach crossed the Kentucky River and started the climb into Lexington's rolling bluegrass hills. By and by, sprawling horse farms and neat white fences came into view, and then rows of red brick buildings and elegant three-story houses began to appear.

It was only a short walk from the stage depot to Maple Avenue.

"We're almost there," Molly said.

They were so close, in fact, that the tulip trees towering over the Handleys' white-frame house were clearly visible from the depot. When they reached the front fence, Mother stopped to admire the cottage roses in bloom, then continued up the gravel path to the front porch.

Aunt Mary waited for them just inside the house, with one hand braced against the doorframe for support.

"Sarah, Mary Catherine! You're here! My land, it's good to see the two of you. Come in now, come right on in."

Mother gave her a warm embrace.

"How are you, Mary? Molly and I had to come and see if we could help."

"Oh, that brother of yours troubles over me far too much. It's true, I have been under the weather, but it's nothing serious, just a touch of the ague. Still, I must say, it does raise a body's spirits to see the two of you!"

Pale and hesitant, she began to cough.

"You poor thing, you are very congested," Mother said. "I'm sure your skin is too delicate to tolerate a mustard plaster. But I've brought along my goose grease and turpentine rub. If it doesn't fix you right up, one of my herb teas will surely do the trick."

"Oh Sarah, you are dear to come all this way for me!"

"Don't say another word, Mary. We are here to help with whatever is needed."

Mary waved vaguely toward the kitchen.

"Well, we are short a few sundries. Louis loves his cornbread, but I'm almost out of molasses and Indian meal...."

"I've brought you a cake," Molly said. "And I can shop for you. Just let me know what I should buy."

"I'll put the teakettle on," Mother said. "Molly will help you back to bed."

Molly made sure her aunt was comfortable, then went into the kitchen, where Mother was murmuring quietly to herself.

"Chamomile, sarsaparilla, mint, horsetail, snakeroot... ah, here's what we need—licorice root, skunk cabbage, and lobelia powder. With a bit of honey, that should do the job nicely."

She filled a blue-flowered porcelain teapot with hot water, added the dried herbs, and mixed in a spoonful of honey.

Molly took a china cup and saucer out of the cupboard and set them on the sideboard.

"Mother, how do you think she looks?"

"Oh, Mary will be fine, though she does fall sick more often ever since Caleb left for California."

"California is a far distance from here."

Mother gave the tea another slow stir.

"That's sure and certain."

Aunt Mary's heart is heavy, Molly thought. *Caleb's close to broken her heart. Still, he's trying to find his fortune in California. Who can blame him for wanting a better life?*

***

Early the next morning, Aunt Mary gave Molly a list of items to fetch downtown.

"Be careful you don't get lost," Mother said. "Lexington may not be the size of Louisville or Cincinnati, but it's a sight bigger than Danville."

"I know, Mother. It's not my first time in town. Bodley's Mercantile sells books, so after I've bought everything on Aunt Mary's list, I'll try to find a novel for Joanna."

Mother shook her head and gave her daughter a wry smile. Such an independent child!

"If I'm not back in an hour or two," Molly said with a laugh, "you might find me at the State Theater auditioning for a part in a show."

She slipped the list into her skirt pocket and headed quickly out the door. Molly knew exactly where the State Theatre was, and that it sometimes featured plays straight from New York City. Not that she'd ever been to the theater. At least not yet.

On her way down Maple Street, she tried to imagine what it would be like to see a real theater performance. Lights, music, colorful costumes—it must be something very special indeed. Reaching Main Street, she stopped for a moment to survey the downtown scene.

It was still early, and the muffled morning sounds of creaking carts and snorting mules were somehow warm and comforting. She saw a pair of young girls walking together arm and arm, giggling as they strolled the boardwalk. A white-aproned shopkeeper swept the dust from his doorway—*swish, whisk, swish, whisk.* The day felt fresh and new, and Molly was happy to be alive.

The shopkeeper paused to lean on his broom and greet a passing neighbor.

"Morning, Hiram. Looks to be a passable good day."

"Could be. Cornfields looking mighty dry. We'll be needing rain soon. If it don't—whoa! Look out there, you!"

A child darted across the street and barely missed a serious collision with the wheels of a speeding delivery wagon.

"Who's that ragmuffin belong to?" the shopkeeper yelled, looking sharply around for someone to blame.

Close behind the boy was his owner, who grabbed him by the collar and gave him a rough shaking. The girls were fully occupied with admiring one another's finery, and they kept on walking. A shoeshine boy looked up from his work, wagged his head, and went back to polishing his customers' boots.

Molly shuddered and tried not to think of the lashing the poor child would soon be getting. She wished she could do more than glower disapprovingly, but Kentucky was a slave state. She'd seen far worse.

The interior of Bodley's Mercantile smelled of cider vinegar and brown sugar. The place was packed with all sorts of goods for sale.

Molly ticked off each item on her shopping list, then looked around to see what else she could find. There was a small bookshelf tucked behind some flour barrels and it held a gently used copy of *The Wide, Wide World* on sale for only twenty cents. This she could afford.

She had a little time to wander before heading home with her purchases, so she left Bodley's and continued down the boardwalk. There was a long line of patrons queued up in front of Roberts' Bakery. No wonder—the irresistible aromas of fresh-baked cinnamon twists and sweet, eggy Sally Lunn bread flowed out the door and halfway down the street.

Passing a tall, wooden office building, she stopped to read several brightly colored billboards pasted on the outside wall. One poster advertised an upcoming show at the State Theatre.

This Friday Evening
June 26, 1857
Uncle Tom's Cabin
by Harriet Beecher Stowe
A Drama in Six Acts

How she'd love to see *Uncle Tom's Cabin* performed on stage! There'd be romantic heroes, innocent heroines, and nasty villains. There was the noble and steadfast Uncle Tom, the angelic Little Eva, and the evil, brutal Simon Legree. But the show might be hard to watch. Having just finished Mrs. Stowe's novel, she knew quite well what the famous author had to say about the horrors of slavery.

Nevertheless, Molly might have been of a notion to go if the prices weren't quite so exorbitant. Even the least expensive ticket cost twenty-five cents, and she'd already spent her last penny on Joanna's novel. Besides, her parents disapproved of theaters.

Then another poster caught her eye, and despite the heat of the day she felt a deep, sudden chill.

A Large Number of Negroes Wanted!
Sound and Healthy Negroes of Both Sexes
for which
The Highest Price in Cash Will Be Paid
Opposite the County Jail

The cruelty was there for all to see. Lexington's Cheapside auction block was where thousands of enslaved African Americans were bought and sold, where husbands and wives were separated, where children were sent off to the highest bidder. Molly turned quickly away, but the joys of the day had vanished.

Chapter Three

Uncle Tom's Cabin

1857

Aunt Mary felt much better after a few days under Mother's care. On Friday morning, she pointed to a wicker basket hanging on a hook near the garden door.

"Molly darlin,' would you be willing to go outside and pick us some berries for breakfast? There's nothin' I like better than fresh red raspberries doused with sweet cream."

Molly loved berries too. The bushes were heavy with fruit, and it took little time at all to gather a good-sized basketful.

Back inside the kitchen, the others were chatting over their coffee cups.

"Louis," Mother said, "you seem to be spending more hours than usual at the bank. Tell me, is everything all right?"

Her brother leaned an elbow on the table, rubbed his forehead, and frowned.

"Times are uncertain, Sarah. When the future's unsettled like it is, it's hard for people to calm down. Nobody knows what the politicians will decide to do about slavery, and folks are just plain nervous."

Molly rinsed the dust off the raspberries and put them in an earthenware serving bowl. "But Uncle Louis," she said, "How can anyone believe slavery is anything but evil?"

He shook his head.

"I can't answer that, Molly, truly I can't. And so far as I see, there's no middle ground. It doesn't bode well for the country's future."

"It's the same in Danville," Mother said. "People don't agree, and they are at each other's throats."

Listening to the grownups talk, Molly doubted whether anything could be done to fix the mess the country was in. If only adults were better at solving problems!

Aunt Mary brought over a large, fragrant platter of baking powder biscuits still warm from the oven, then took a cold pitcher of cream out of the icebox and set it on the table next to the berries.

"It's an awful shame," she said. "But I must change the subject. Sarah, your remedies have worked their magic. My aches and pains have almost vanished."

"David is likely anxious to have us back in Danville," Mother said. "We should head home tomorrow."

That evening, Molly helped Aunt Mary prepare supper.

"Molly dear," Mary said, "would you reach the honey jar down from the cupboard? I do love a little glaze on my baked ham."

"Would you like me to bake a pan of cornbread?"

"That would be lovely, but don't count on your uncle joining us. We can't be sure what hour he'll be home."

By the time Uncle Louis walked in the door, Mother was already washing up the supper dishes and handing them one by one for Molly to dry.

Aunt Mary stopped stacking her flowered china in the sideboard cabinet and looked up.

"Oh, there you are, darlin.' We saved a few slices of ham and some cornbread for you. There's a little of Molly's blackberry jam cake left, too."

Louis tossed his hat onto the hallway stand, then went over to his wife and kissed her lightly on the forehead.

"How are you, my dear?"

"I still have a small headache, but it'll surely soon be gone."

He arched his brows and looked at her closely.

"Truly, I'm much better. Now sit yourself down and eat."

"I will. But first..."

He slowly pulled a small brown envelope from his upper vest pocket.

"Can you guess what I have here?"

"Is it tickets for the Independence Day picnic?"

"No, dear. These are for tonight's theater show, and I'm told they're coveted by everyone in town."

"I'm sorry, Louis. I want nothing more than to retire early tonight. Why don't you and Sarah go?"

Mother slowly dried her hands on her apron. Theater patrons were known for heavy drinking, carousing, and other shocking behavior, and everyone suspected that stage actresses were women of loose morals.

She frowned and said, "David considers theater a thoroughly unsuitable pastime. I surely couldn't attend."

Louis tugged at his beard and took a moment to consider.

"I believe I understand. Stage performances are not always respectable. However, they can also teach the values of courage and goodness. Sarah, I believe David might consider this show to be educational."

Molly saw Mother's hesitation. She wouldn't let this chance to see her first play go by without putting up a fight.

"Mother," she said, "I've always wanted to see a stage play, and Father says *Uncle Tom's Cabin* is one of the greatest stories ever written."

Louis wanted to see the play himself and sensed his sister might be open to persuasion, so he put on his most beguiling smile.

"Don't worry, Sarah. The story of a trip to the theater is safe with me, and Molly won't say a word to anyone."

"That's right, Mother. I promise never to speak of it."

Her daughter's hopeful eyes reminded Sarah of how she'd felt at Molly's age, always wanting to try something new. And after all, David did read plays and poetry to the girls, and he loved to recite his favorite quotes from Shakespeare...

"Well," she finally said, "some might consider it sinful to let a costly ticket go to waste."

That rascal Louis. He always had a way of talking her into things.

"Good. It's settled," he said, gulping down a last glass of cider. "Find your bonnet and shawl, Mary Catherine. We are off to the show."

He grabbed his topcoat and hurried Molly out the front door before Mother could change her mind. They nearly ran the few blocks into town and arrived at the State Theatre just as the play was to begin.

The noisy lobby was packed with ticket holders waiting to enter the theater doors. Never in her life had Molly seen so many frothy layers of lace, beads, and silk taffeta flounces. She felt rather out of place in her simple cotton gown. Still, her dress was far easier to wear than a hoop skirt so round it should probably have its own ticket.

Uncle Louis studied the crowd.

"There looks to be some sort of problem here," he said. "I see an acquaintance of mine up ahead. Maybe he can tell us what's wrong."

"Hello, Alfred," he called. "What seems to be the holdup?"

"Hey there, Handley. The entrance is blocked. One of the ladies is wearing a skirt too wide to fit through the door and her companions are attempting to collapse the hoop springs."

"Poor girl!" Uncle Louis said.

"Hmph!" Alfred said. "It's ridiculous."

Molly burst out laughing.

"So hoity-toity! My own outfit may not be fancy, but at least I can get myself through the door!"

The crowd started to move again, but Molly needed some time to take in the grandeur. She stood open-mouthed, gazing at the theatre's high, coffered ceilings, red brocade draperies, and the beautifully painted walls where cherubic angels floated upon a sea of heavenly clouds.

Uncle Louis looked back at her and grinned.

"I almost lost you, Molly. What do you think?"

"Oh, this is absolutely grand!"

"I'm glad you like it."

He pulled the tickets from his front coat pocket.

"Now, where do you suppose these seats could be?"

"In the front row, I hope!"

"Let's find out."

They headed down the middle aisle until Uncle Louis found two unoccupied chairs.

"Here we are, Molly, front and center. Take a seat."

The orchestra began playing "Camptown Races," the hugely popular minstrel song by Stephen Foster, and the audience roared its approval. This was a lively crowd that was ready to be entertained.

The stage crew lowered the lights and drew back a heavy, blue velvet curtain to reveal an immense, colorfully painted canvas. A surprisingly realistic landscape of weeping willows and deeply furrowed cotton fields stretched across the back of the stage. Hay bales and farm implements were stacked next to a tiny, run-down wooden hut, and black-faced actors lingered by the door.

"It's as if we've arrived at an actual plantation," Molly whispered.

"Yes, it almost looks like the real thing, doesn't it?"

The drama unfolded, and Molly was instantly lost in the story. Her heart thrilled at the excitement of Eliza's daring escape from captivity. She almost cried at little Eva's sweet vision of heaven and Tom's deeply moving heroism in the face of evil. The entire experience—the darkened theater, lively music, and skilled acting—was something more than wonderful. Incredibly, it seemed more authentic than life itself, and she was spellbound.

But all too soon, the show was over. The last curtain fell, the room erupted in applause, and the air rang with wild cheers and hurrahs.

Back out on the street and on their way home, Uncle Louis gave Molly an inquisitive look.

"So, did you like it?"

She needed a little time to consider before answering.

"Well, I enjoyed the music and dancing very much. The acting was awfully good too. But here's a question—why wasn't the story more like Mrs. Stowe's novel? This stage version ignored the wickedness of slavery, and that made no sense to me. Even worse, the audience hissed and laughed during some of the sad scenes when I wanted to cry. We all need laughter, but I didn't think those parts were funny at all."

She was quiet for a long moment before going on.

"I guess most folks would rather enjoy themselves than face unpleasant facts, and plays are one way for people to escape their troubles."

"You may be right, Molly," he said softly. "You may be right."

They walked wordlessly for a while. She kept running things over in her mind, and finally said, "I think I'm going to tell stories of my own one day."

"You should, Molly. You'd make a fine writer."

They reached the front porch of the house on Maple Street, and she stopped and said, "Thank you, Uncle Louis. I won't ever forget this night."

Chapter Four

Danville

Summer, 1857

Molly and Mother said their goodbyes the next morning, then headed home under a bank of brooding, threatening clouds. This time the coach wasn't so crowded as before. A white-haired couple in the seats across from them snored much of the way, and Mother dozed a bit too. With the previous evening still heavy on her mind, Molly gazed quietly out the window. She barely noticed when a gentle rain began to dampen the thirsty cornfields.

There was so much to think about—the emotion-filled acting, lively music, gorgeous, colorful costumes, and clever scenery. How did last night's show make her feel happy, angry, and sad, all at the same time? It was as if a spark had been struck deep inside her soul. Could she ever write a play like that?

By the time Danville's orderly wood-shingled rooftops came into view, Molly couldn't keep her thoughts to herself a moment more.

"Mother, are you awake?"

"Yes, dear, what is it?"

"I have made an important decision. I'm going to be a playwright. I can't say today whether my plays will be happy or sad. I only hope they'll be entertaining enough to someday make it onto a Broadway stage."

She yawned and squeezed Molly's hand.

"You may be hoping for too much, my dear."

"But don't you see? Plays can make a difference in the way people look at life. They can show people how to be brave and kind, or maybe even bring folks together to solve their problems."

Mother gave her a little smile.

"It's fine to have big dreams when you're young, my dear. But someday you'll realize there are more important things in life. You'll soon have to become serious about finding a suitable husband. Then, once you marry and start a family, your priorities will change. For now, though, please be sure to remember your promise. You mustn't tell anyone you've been to the theater."

"I know. I promise."

Molly was careful to keep her word. Still, Mother didn't understand how serious she was about becoming a writer, and she never told Molly not to write a play herself. So, a few days later she sat down at her desk, pulled out a fresh piece of paper, and filled her inkwell to the brim. Then she picked up her pen and started in.

THE DASTARDLY DR. DODSWORTH
A Terrifying Tale in One Act
by Molly McIntyre
Scene I
The curtain opens with two men standing center stage.
Father: *No sir, I tell you NO! I forbid you to aspire to the hand of my dear, darling daughter!*
Dodsworth: *I'll have that delicious damsel, I'll have her! Just TRY to stop ME!*
Father: *You'll see me dead first, you villain! Dinah is the light of my life....*

The pen seemed to have a mind of its own, and her words flowed almost faster than she could think them. It became a one-act play, a melodrama like the ones she'd read about in her magazines. This was certain to entertain the neighborhood children, but who should play the parts? After considering all the options, her choices were obvious.

An old, moldy trunk was hidden in a back corner of the hall closet. Though it was long forgotten and smelling of dust, Molly tugged it out and propped open the lid. She dug under a pile of ragged patchwork quilts, pushed aside some worn-out muslin aprons and a few musty calico pinafores, and pulled out a flowery, old-fashioned poke bonnet. Then she summoned her little sister.

"Come here, Lizzie. Let's tie these ribbons under your chin and take a look."

Lizzie batted her lashes and tilted her gently pointed chin in an effort to appear demure. Sure enough, those wide, yellow-green eyes had her looking as sweet as a curled-up kitten.

Molly stepped back with a self-satisfied nod.

"It's a little big, but it still fits. You will have the role of my young, innocent damsel in distress."

Turning to Joanna, she said, "Jo, you are the tallest. You shall play the despicable villain. We will paint a black mustache under your nose and hide your ringlets under one of Father's old hats."

Joanna secretly thought it would be great fun to play the part of a fiendish evildoer, but she felt contrary, so she scowled and said, "And I suppose you will be the director?"

"Of course! Who else would it be? My appearance is less distinctive than yours—ordinary, in fact. So, I'll be the one to play all the extra parts."

In Molly's opinion, her own face was rather plain and unremarkable. Her medium-brown eyes perfectly matched her medium-brown hair, which was only slightly wavy. Her rosy-pink skin burned far too easily. If she forgot to wear a sunbonnet, her nose would turn as red as a summer tomato left out too long in the heat.

Mother often told Molly she didn't realize how pretty she was.

"Don't worry, my dear. You are smart and creative and have an excellent sense of humor. When the time comes, you'll have no trouble attracting a man to marry. Besides, your oval face and delicate, tapered fingers give you a gentle, gracefully feminine appearance."

Ugh. Mother's talk of marriage was so terribly tiresome. She might fall in love, marry, and have children someday, or maybe she wouldn't. Things were different these days, not the same as years ago, when Mother and Father first met. He had just left Scotland, hoping for a better future in America. She was young and high-spirited, but never pictured herself as more than a mother and wife. But Molly wanted a life greater than anything her parents ever imagined for themselves.

* * *

She was convinced her first play would be a tremendous success— and well it might have been, if not for a bit of bad timing.

"I believe we are nearly ready," Molly told her sisters.

"I know my lines by heart," Lizzie said. "Or, almost."

"I have perfected my evil sneer," Joanna said.

"I'm pleased with your progress," Molly said. "Let's try on our costumes and have one final practice in the backyard."

The rehearsal was well underway when their parents quite unexpectedly appeared from around the corner of the house. Father's intense blue eyes were immediately focused on Molly. Wasn't she the one always organizing some sort of silliness?

"Mary Catherine, what's all this?"

She braced herself for a scolding, but then Joanna came to her rescue, and she only stretched the truth a little.

"It's nothing, Father. We are simply playing dress-up."

"Such foolishness! Find a worthwhile book to read. How often must I say it? There is no more valuable activity by which to broaden your mind."

Suddenly, Father was overcome with a violent cough. Mother had a look of alarm. She reached into a pocket hidden deep within her skirts and pulled out a clean cotton handkerchief.

"Here, David, take this."

Her voice may have trembled slightly, but then Father caught his breath, steadied himself, and squared his shoulders. She slipped her hand around his arm. Together, they walked down the path, talking just loud enough to be heard, their voices low but unmistakably firm.

"Sarah, it's time our daughters began behaving like proper young ladies. Especially Mary Catherine. She lacks all self-discipline."

"Yes, dear. You're probably right. We'll discuss it later, after we've seen the doctor."

With Mother's many home remedies, Molly thought it strange that Father should need a doctor. And was that a blood stain she'd seen on the handkerchief? But she wouldn't think about that—not just then anyway. Father would surely disapprove of her plans to write for the stage, and her play was finished, at least for now.

David McIntyre wanted his daughters educated just enough to attract the sort of husbands who were willing and able to provide for them. Mother was more independent than she let on, but even she saw no reason her girls should desire a life different from her own.

Still, Molly couldn't let go of her own visions for the future. She saw it all in her mind's eye—stories coming alive on a Broadway stage, great actors and actresses eager to star in her plays. It was going to happen one of these days, whether her parents approved of it or not.

Chapter Five

Danville

1857-1858

The kitchen was the warmest room in the house, and Molly sat at the table near the oven, peeling apples for a pie. The weather outside was miserably bleak, and no one was in a good mood.

"I'm sorry, girls," Mother said. "I've tried everything I can think of to relieve your father's cough. He is still tired, irritable, and feeling worse than ever. Horehound tea usually helps, but this time it hasn't made the least difference. I don't see how we can manage a trip to Lexington for Christmas."

Peony was rolled up in a ball, snoring softly on Lizzie's lap.

"But I was *so* looking forward to going," Lizzie said. "It isn't Christmas without Uncle Louis and Aunt Mary."

Joanna glanced up from her magazine.

"Have you even bothered to look outside? Last night's snowfall was so heavy that most of the roads are probably closed."

"Complaining won't melt snow," Molly said. "If it did, we'd be halfway to Lexington already."

"I know, but I still wish we could go. I hope Father feels better soon."

"We all do," Molly said. "But Jo's right. The journey would be hard for all of us. We should probably stay home."

"I hate winter. It's so exasperating!"

Lizzie stood abruptly to her feet, and Peony leapt onto the floor with a yowl.

"*Yeeoww.*"

"Poor Peony! You're looking for sympathy, aren't you?"

Molly reached down and scooped the cat up.

"I know, your Majesty, you're the queen of the house. You don't like this weather either, do you?"

Molly was unhappy too. It seemed as though Uncle Louis was the only person she could talk with about her plans and dreams. She'd been hoping to ask him for advice.

Then, a few days before Christmas, Mother said, "Girls, I have a surprise for you. Since your father isn't able to travel, your aunt and uncle are coming to us instead. Weather permitting, they'll come at the end of the month."

***

Louis and Mary arrived on New Year's Eve, which greatly revived their spirits. Father felt much better, and he surprised them all at breakfast the next morning.

"Sarah," he said, "why don't we invite a few neighbors over to help us celebrate the new year?"

She was pleased at the thought of celebrating with friends, yet anxious for her husband's health.

"Oh, David, that would be lovely, but are you sure you feel well enough?"

"Yes. I believe we'd all enjoy a good party."

"Well then, Molly, would you please go around to the Winslows and ask Lucinda and George to come by tonight? And if the Springers are home, you might ask them too."

"What about the Somers? I hope they're invited."

"Well, of course, they're coming," Mother said. "It's not a party without James and Lydia."

This was true. Lydia Somers was about the cheeriest person Molly could imagine. She always wore a cheerful smile, and her infectious laughter never failed to brighten a room.

"I'll set the table," said Joanna. "Should I get out the best china?"

"Why yes, thank you, dear. Goodness, I don't know when we last used my wedding crystal. And don't forget Grandmother's damask tablecloth."

"Happy New Year," Molly said, opening the door for Mr. and Mrs. Somers. "Won't you come in?"

Lydia brushed a light sprinkling of snow off her dark wool cloak and gestured at the pasteboard container her husband held in his hands.

"It's a fresh lemon cake," she said with a light laugh. "I hope y'all like it. We've brought cider for the children, and here is a bottle of James's sour mash whiskey."

The holiday refreshments put everyone in a cheerful mood and the house was filled with warm, friendly conversations. Molly was about to try Lydia's lemon cake, but she spotted Uncle Louis alone in one corner of the parlor and decided there would never be a better time to talk.

"Happy New Year, Uncle Louis."

"Thank you, Molly. Happy New Year to you."

"Mind if I join you? There's something I've been wanting to ask."

"Of course, of course. Just give me a moment here."

He took a pinch of tobacco from a small, brown leather pouch and used a finger to carefully press it into the bowl of his pipe. Striking a match, he held the flame to the leaves and took a few quick puffs.

"There," he said. "Now, how can I help?"

Molly took a sip of apple cider and cleared her throat.

"Here's the thing," she said. "My parents expect me to get married. The problem is, I don't want to live my life according to someone else's wishes. I intend to move to New York City and become a playwright. I may want to marry someday, but if a husband doesn't share my hopes and dreams, is marriage really worth the trouble?"

Louis drew a puff from his pipe and took some time before offering her an answer.

"Finding the right partner may not be easy, Molly. But having someone at your side who believes in you is no small thing. Take your cousin Caleb. He was a troublesome boy, and Mary and I worried he'd never amount to much. But his sweetheart Rebecca never gave up on him."

He lowered his voice as if to share an important secret.

"Caleb's written to say he'll be home this summer. While he's here, he plans to ask Rebecca to be his wife."

Molly wasn't surprised. Caleb lived with their family while he studied law at Centre College, and before setting out for California after graduation, he confided to Molly that he'd asked his sweetheart to wait for him.

"Caleb told me he planned to return for Rebecca once he struck it rich out west."

Uncle Louis nodded.

"Turns out he was better at lawyering than mining. Gold attracts plenty of crooks, but Caleb knew how to deal with claim jumpers who were out to steal from honest miners. Settling nasty arguments made him a wealthy man."

***

In early June, a wedding invitation came from Rebecca's parents. With the spring planting finished and a busy harvest season yet to come, July was the perfect time for a farmer's daughter to be married.

Molly was putting the finishing touches on a sketch of Peony, which she planned to give the bride and groom as a wedding gift. Peony posed beautifully, fast asleep on the window seat, her calico paws tucked sweetly under her chin. Lizzie sat nearby, embroidering a bright, colorful bouquet of flowers on a pair of linen pillowcases.

"I'm looking forward to the wedding," she said. "I can't wait to meet Rebecca."

Joanna, leafing through a copy of *Putnam's Monthly Magazine,* carefully noted the page number of a recent installment of "Bartleby, the Scrivener" before glancing up.

"I hope I like Rebecca. I also hope there aren't too many people at this party."

Molly saw the look on Joanna's face and knew her sister would prefer to stay home.

"Oh, Jo," she said, "It's going to be fun. You can dance with Lizzie and me."

"A wedding is not exactly a party," Mother said. "It's a solemn, important family occasion. Still, I expect there'll be a reception afterward. It will be nice to meet Rebecca and her family, and Mary's sisters are coming over from Shelbyville. It's been forever since I saw them last."

Despite the cheerful talk, Mother was still worried about Father. His cough had worsened, and even on warm spring afternoons he kept a thick wool throw over his knees.

Then, the week before the wedding, he said he wouldn't be coming.

"I do not feel up to it, Sarah. Besides, I have reading to catch up on. You should go. Take the girls with you."

Mother was disappointed, yet she reasoned that a few days of quiet rest might do him good. So, with promises from Lydia and Lucinda to look in on him while they were away, Father stayed home in Danville.

Rebecca's family lived in a two-story clapboard farmhouse on the outskirts of Lexington. Pinewood rocking chairs graced the wide front veranda, red roses climbed the white-painted trellises on either side of the porch, and an old privy sat partially hidden behind a bramble of lilac bushes and honeysuckle vines. Chickens roamed the side yard, and beans, squash, and tall stalks of sweet corn grew in the vegetable garden's neatly tended rows.

When they arrived, Caleb met them at the door.

"Aunt Sarah! How good to see you!"

He embraced Mother, Molly, and Joanna, then lifted Lizzie clear off her feet and swung her, laughing, in the air.

"My, how you've grown! Rebecca can't wait to meet you all. Look, here she comes now."

Rebecca was only a few years older than Molly. She wore a wide, welcoming smile and a flowing, sunshine-yellow dress almost the same color as her curly blond hair.

"Caleb's told me so much about you," she said warmly. "I am so glad to meet y'all."

After a simple wedding ceremony, everyone gathered in the barn. Rebecca's cousins had stacked hay bales in a wide circle to make a dance floor, and a banjo and country fiddle struck up a country tune. Soon everyone was dancing, including the littlest children, who spun and twirled into rolling piles of laughter.

Later, after most of the guests had left and the menfolk were busy caring for the animals, Aunt Mary sat and talked with Mother and the girls about the newlyweds' plans.

"Caleb and Rebecca will make a brand-new home in Sacramento," she said. "Caleb says it's more suitable for young families than San Francisco, and we are not to believe the worrisome stories we hear. He believes California will one day be the greatest of all the states in the Union."

"You must be proud," Mother said. "No doubt they will shine among the brightest stars of the new state."

Before falling asleep that night, Molly and her sisters talked quietly among themselves.

"I thought Aunt Mary sounded awfully sad," Joanna said. "She's probably heartbroken, what with Caleb and Rebecca moving all the way out west."

"I think California sounds exciting," Lizzie said. "If I were Aunt Mary, I'd be happy for them."

Joanna rolled her eyes.

"Don't be silly, Liz. Haven't you read anything? It's an empty wilderness. Moreover, it's so far away, she'll never see her parents again. He may as well be taking her to live in the deepest jungles of Africa."

"California isn't where I would choose to live," Molly said thoughtfully. "But I don't believe Caleb would ask Rebecca to move out there if the situation were half as dire as you say."

She stood up and put her hands on her hips.

"Anyway, we'll soon have family at the far edge of the continent. We ought to wish them well."

Chapter Six

Spring

1859

Winter arrived early that year, lingered longer than usual, and stayed bitterly cold right up to the first months of spring. Molly looked forward to the end of dreary, wet weather. Then, right before Easter, the sun started to thaw the streams around Danville. It would soon be time to put away her warm woolens and bring out her light muslin dresses.

Father had been ill for over a year and still wasn't better. Though the doctors came and went, they could do nothing to help him, and his breathing grew weaker by the day. When he refused to take any food at all, Molly wondered how much longer he could survive.

On Saturday morning she climbed the narrow flight of stairs leading to his room. Mother would be unhappy over any unnecessary disturbance, so she tried to remember which board made that annoying creak.

Creeack. Ugh.

"Is that you, Mary Catherine?"

She slipped through the doorway and saw Father in bed with his head propped on a tall pile of pillows.

"Yes, Mother. I've brought a stack of fresh towels."

"Thank you, dear. You may put them on the table."

Ice frosted the thick panes of the bedroom window. It would be so good to feel warm again.

"Mary Catherine," Mother said, "please open the windows. I believe Father would enjoy some fresh air."

Mother was trying her best to be cheerful, and really, one should never give up.

Joanna sat reading on the bedroom floor, her legs folded under her skirts. At Mother's words, she raised an eyebrow and set down her book.

"I'll help you, Molly."

Working together, they unlatched the locks and threw open the casements. In the yard down below, a clump of purple crocuses was pushing its way through the crusted ice. An early robin studied the softening ground beside a patch of green grass, extracted a fat earthworm, and swallowed it in one greedy gulp. Molly couldn't help but smile. Spring always made her feel hopeful.

Sadly, hope was not enough. Father took his final breath on Easter morning.

Even though she'd known it was coming, his death was a shock. Why did their time together have to be so short? She had hoped to learn more about the stars and the planets, and to listen to her father's favorite lines from Shakespeare. Now he would never know how much she yearned to become a writer.

Their neighbors sent word to Uncle Louis and Aunt Mary and tended to Father's funeral arrangements. They set his dark wooden casket in the front room beneath Mother's lace curtains, and people came to pay their respects with fruit pies, hot dishes, and comforting words.

Joanna stayed with Mother while Molly and Lizzie greeted guests at the door.

"Who's that coming up the walk?" Lizzie asked.

Molly had never met the impressive-looking gentleman, but she recognized the woman at his side.

"It must be the college president, Dr. Young. That's his wife, Frances."

Dr. Young wore a tall black hat and finely tailored waistcoat, carried a brass-handled cane, and leaned on the arm of a plump, middle-aged woman.

"Allow me to offer my sincerest condolences," he said in a low, solemn tone. "Professor McIntyre will be sorely missed."

"You must be beside yourselves with grief," Mrs. Young said. "Your father was a fine man. Even so, as the Bible tells us, he resides now in a better place, finally at rest, may the dear Lord bless him. Now, girls, here is a chess pie baked fresh for you this morning!"

"Thank you, ma'am," Molly said. "Won't you come inside? Everyone's in the parlor."

She felt a sudden rush of pride. Father was a man of importance at the college, admired and respected by Danville's most distinguished citizens. Everyone would miss him. She would miss him too.

Lizzie saw the black-clad mourners crowded inside and began to giggle.

"It looks like a flock of crows has landed in our parlor."

"Hush, Lizzie!"

They were in mourning, and Molly felt she should set a good example. But it was funny. She would note it in her journal later, when this was all over.

"Everyone who's coming must be here," she said. "Let's find Jo."

Menfolk stood in the hallway smoking cigars and drinking Father's best bourbon while the women gathered in the front parlor, chatting and gossiping among themselves. Mother sat on the overstuffed horsehair sofa with Aunt Mary, who patted her hand gently while friends took turns offering what they hoped were comforting words.

"David was a wonderful husband and father."

"You'll always treasure his memory."

"It may be hard to believe now, Sarah dear, but better days lie ahead."

Molly stood with Joanna and Lizzie in one corner of the room, silently watching Mother's friends. Such characters they were! Lydia always ready with a smile, Phoebe constantly glum and fearing the worst. Someday she'd have to write them into a play:

Two women upon a sofa...
Mrs. Springfield (sobbing) I'm never happy unless I'm miserable. Isn't it terrible?
Miss Summer (giggling) Everything makes me laugh! I've even been known to do it in church and at funerals. Funny, isn't it? Ha ha!

The parlor was packed with people, and no one seemed to notice that the sisters could overhear everyone's conversations.

"Listen," Molly whispered, nodding toward a group of ladies near the fireplace.

Lucinda Winslow was talking with Lydia Somers and Phoebe Springer, whose teary-eyed face was nearly hidden under several layers of gauzy black veils. Lydia always looked perfect. She was dressed head to toe in black except for a delicate white lace collar at her throat.

Lucinda leaned toward the other women and inclined her head knowingly.

"I can't begin to imagine what sort of future lies ahead for those children. I'd be surprised if David's illness hasn't left the family penniless. Sarah will have to find boys for them to marry, and the sooner, the better."

"I do believe you're right," Phoebe sniffed. "The way things look to me, it won't be long before all our men are off fighting each other. My husband says if a Northern abolitionist is elected president there is sure to be war between the states."

She reached a handkerchief under her veils and dabbed at her eyes.

"For aught I know," she sobbed, "there won't be a marriageable man left in all of southern Kentucky."

"I understand Sarah has relatives in Sacramento," Lydia said in a sweet, lilting voice. "She may consider joining them in California. Some say our best young men are already there, prospecting for gold."

"Well," Lucinda said, "I will surely miss Sarah if she goes. But I hope for the girls' sake she's able to find them husbands out west."

At this, Lizzie let out a gasp.

"Did you hear that? They want Mother to find us husbands in California!"

Molly shushed her to be quiet, but now the women realized the girls were listening and the conversation turned to predictions for tomorrow's weather.

"Don't mind us," Joanna said under her breath. "We're only the penniless children."

Molly took hold of her sister's arm and said, "Come on, Jo. Let's see if there's any pie left."

The day grew late, the house emptied of guests, and only Uncle Louis and Aunt Mary remained with Mother. Molly heard their soft murmurs coming from the kitchen but was unable to make out the words. She was left to guess how much truth there was to what she and her sisters had heard in the parlor.

At any rate, she knew that Mother would now have to depend heavily on Uncle Louis. Kentucky law did not favor widows and women rarely held property in their own names. Also, since Mother was a widow with daughters not yet eighteen, her brother was now their legal guardian. Like it or not, it was the law.

She lay upstairs in her room for a long while, listening to the gentle hoot of a barn owl outside the window. It had been a hard day, and her heart ached far too much for sleep. Talk of marriage and war and moving to California had put her mind in a spin.

What will become of us now without Father? Will we lose our home and end up in the poorhouse? Or maybe something worse, something I don't dare think about.

The grandfather clock in the downstairs hall sounded eleven, and she heard footsteps pad across the room toward her bed.

"*Pssst*, Molly, are you awake?"

Before she could answer, Joanna dropped into the bedside chair wrapped in a thick woolen blanket. Behind her was Lizzie, who climbed in the bed and covered herself with Molly's patchwork quilt.

"We are all awfully sad," Lizzie said. "Especially Mother. Do you think she'll decide to move us out West?"

Molly gave her a little hug.

"I don't know, Lizzie. Mother will try to decide what's best for us. Cousin Caleb seems happy enough in California. Everyone says it's where people can start new lives for themselves."

"That's all bunkum and bottle wash," Joanna said. "People who try to go to California get themselves lost in the desert. They can be swept away while crossing rivers. There are too many dangers to count, and I, for one, don't want to die on the way. We need to stay in Kentucky."

"Goodness, Jo," Molly said. "Nothing like that is going to happen to us. Let's not trouble ourselves anymore tonight. If Mother plans to move, she will tell us."

She hugged them both and sent them back to bed. Still, it was hard to follow her own advice, and even harder to soothe her aching heart. One thing was certain. Wherever they ended up, she would not stop writing. In fact, she might turn this day into a romantic drama about a fatherless girl forced to marry a stranger in a far-off land.

Hmmm. Should the heroine find happiness or come to a tragic end?

It was well past midnight before she finally slept.

Chapter Seven

An Invitation

1859

Weeks passed without any word of California. Wild violets carpeted the backyard in purple, butterflies drifted through the flower garden, and a pair of Kentucky warblers trilled near their nest down by the creek. Mother kept herself busy cleaning house, washing linens, beating rugs, airing feather pillows, ironing, scrubbing, and mending. There was always something to do, and the work seemed to soothe her grief.

Late in May, Molly was in the kitchen, about to soak a pot of beans for supper, when she heard familiar voices at the door.

"Sarah dear, we reckoned you might fancy some fresh-baked biscuits. I can't say if it's true, but my husband says my baking powder biscuits are the best in Boyle County."

"Lucinda, you are too kind," Mother said with a little laugh. "Won't you and Phoebe come in for a cup of mint tea?"

Molly set out china for the ladies while they sat and talked over Danville's latest news.

"Sarah, have you heard about Minnie Keller's new baby," Phoebe asked breathlessly.

"Why, yes, I understand she's had a little girl."

"It's about time she had a girl," Lucinda said. "With seven boys, Elmer has all the help he needs."

"He's lucky to have them," Phoebe said, producing a handkerchief at the thought of what she was about to say. "You know he hasn't been able to work a lick since that mule kicked him last fall."

Honestly, all the tittle-tattle was a bit much. Phoebe in tears at every hint of sorrow, Lucinda ready to pounce on the tiniest scrap of news. How long could this go on? But then Lucinda paused and inclined her head toward Mother.

"Now, do tell us. How are *you* getting on, Sarah? How do you manage to stay cheerful?"

Mother's cheeks flushed.

"I appreciate your concern, but truly, I have no time to dwell on my sorrows, what with endless things to do around the house."

"The thought of it makes me like to cry," Phoebe said, wiping away a tear. "I couldn't cope a single moment without my Samuel. Still, I suppose there are things to tend to no matter how one feels."

"A thorough cleaning is necessary," Mother said with a little wave of her hand. "And one's home does require minor repairs from time to time. I must ask Louis to help me with them when he's here next week."

"My George is perfect in many ways," Lucinda laughed lightly, "but he is no help whatsoever around the house. Louis must be a great comfort to you."

"Oh, he surely is. Thanks to him, I am doing very well indeed."

Mother talked as though everything was fine. But Molly knew the roof leaked, the front door wouldn't lock properly, and the pantry was half empty. Father's illness had likely drained the family's savings. Still, Mother wasn't one to share her troubles, even if there were troubles aplenty.

A few days later, Molly was in the kitchen buttering a slice of fresh-baked wheat bread and about to use up the final bit of last summer's peach jam.

"I have errands in town, dear," Mother said. "Would you like to come along?"

Molly had been hoping for a good time to ask Mother about her plans. This could be the perfect opportunity.

"I'll get my hat and meet you on the porch."

Mother talked on and on while they walked.

"Have you seen the bluebells in Lucinda's yard? I do wish I had her green thumb. She has the prettiest yellow jonquils in the garden behind her house. Now, when we get to Lyman's, I want you to help me look for percale sheeting. Lydia says they have some fine new bolts of cotton cambric. We are completely out of straight pins, and goodness knows you girls could all use new handkerchiefs…"

Molly only half-listened. She kept wondering how she should bring up the questions on her mind. Eventually she decided there was no better way than to plunge right in.

"Mother," she said, "we're all wondering what will become of us now, with Father gone."

"You shouldn't be concerned, dear. The good Lord will provide."

"But are we leaving Danville?"

Mother pressed her lips together.

"We'll know in good time."

"But, Mother, when will—"

"Mary Catherine, I don't wish to discuss it."

Molly clenched her teeth. Mother was so exasperating! Why did she talk as if nothing was wrong? Why did she treat her like a child, then expect her to act like an adult?

Lyman's Dry Goods Store was the best place in town for goods such as ribbon, thread, and clothing fabric. After a few moments admiring several brilliant bolts of silk yardage on display, Mother went up to the front counter to speak with the proprietor.

"Good morning, Mr. Lyman," she nodded politely. "A paper of straight pins and three cotton handkerchiefs, please."

"Morning, Mrs. McIntyre. Will this be on credit again?"

"Why, yes. I do plan to settle my account at the end of the month."

Molly eyed a tall glass jar filled with striped sticks of green-and-white peppermint, but she knew there wouldn't be any splurging on extras today.

Mother pocketed her purchases and led the way out onto the boardwalk.

"The post office door is open," she said. "Let's go in."

The Danville postmaster was in the back of the mailroom sorting a tall stack of papers. He looked up when he heard them enter.

"Good day, Sarah."

"Hello, Ned. Anything for us today?"

Ned Harper was a wide-waisted man, not tall, but goodly-sized for his age. They had to wait while he huffed and squeezed past a row of hardwood shelves on his way to the front of the office.

"I do believe you had a letter arrive yesterday. Let me see. Ah, here it is."

Ned pulled a slim envelope out from under the counter and handed it to Mother. She examined it closely before tucking it deep inside her purse, then tightened the drawstring as if to cinch the news inside. The way she did it made Molly guess it was really important, not just another newsy letter from her cousin Martha in New Jersey.

Ned had been grinning at Molly, and now he gave her a wink.

"Mary Catherine," he said, "you're gettin' prettier every time I see you. How old are you now, 'bout seventeen? You must have so many beaus your mother has to hide you in the closet."

He seemed to find himself amusing, but Molly didn't think he was funny at all and couldn't manage any sort of smile. If only she'd gotten a glimpse of who sent Mother that letter. Could it be from Cousin Caleb, writing to her from California?

Ned wanted to gossip, and Mother was in the mood to hear the latest goings-on around town. Molly fidgeted impatiently, tapping her foot, waiting for them to finish.

"It's been a pleasure, Ned," Mother said at last, "but we really must be off."

"Take care now, Sarah. Be sure to keep watch on that pretty daughter of yours."

He winked at Molly again, and when they were back outside, Molly rolled her eyes.

"That Ned Harper is so annoying!"

"You should be flattered, dear. You know he means well."

"He's an old flirt, and I hate the way he looks at me."

"I believe Ned would make a good catch for the right girl. But come along, we have one more stop to make."

Molly grimaced. Could Mother really consider a gossip like Ned Harper potential marriage material? She'd rather live in a chicken coop than have a beau like Ned.

Mother continued on past the post office to a small brick office building. Molly followed her inside and down the hallway to a door labeled *Edward Gideon, Attorney at Law*.

"Wait here while I speak with Mr. Gideon," Mother said. "I won't be long."

Molly settled into an uncomfortable, rickety chair outside the law office. She was curious to know what Mother wanted from her lawyer, and the door was left slightly ajar. She moved a little closer and tried to make out Mr. Gideon's words.

"Rough times ahead…John C. Breckinridge said last week… grave situation…trouble around the corner…"

So. Mother was there to ask her lawyer for advice. If he said trouble was coming, the situation must be getting serious.

Several days went by, and Mother seemed even more preoccupied than usual. She took to sitting alone at the kitchen table, gazing into an empty teacup or using a finger to trace and retrace the floral lace patterns on her tablecloth.

Even Lizzie thought she looked distracted.

"Why won't Mother tell us what's on her mind?" she complained. "I wish we knew what she's planning to do."

"Mother doesn't want to worry us," Joanna said. "But I've no doubt that talk about moving west was just idle gossip."

"Maybe," Molly said. "But I'm not so certain."

That evening, she opened her journal and began to write.

Father's death left a wide, gaping hole in our family. I know Mother needs time to grieve. We all do. But I feel sure something else is going on, and it's vexing not knowing what it is.

***

When Uncle Louis arrived for a visit the following week, Molly took the first chance she could to ask him about it.

"Can you tell us what's happening, Uncle Louis? Are we leaving Danville?"

"Kentucky may not be the best place for your family right now," he sighed. "The country is impossibly divided, and Congress can't agree what to do. Tempers are flaring, and the upcoming elections will likely make things worse."

"Do you think John Breckinridge will be elected president?"

"I hope not. I've no doubt he'd lead the nation to tragedy. I plan to vote for Abraham Lincoln, though he doesn't appear to have much of a chance of winning. Either way, the consequences will be serious. A war between the states isn't likely to last long, but if fighting starts, no one is safe."

Goodness, Molly thought. *First, my father dies, and now a war might start. We may not have enough money to live on, and our family could end up moving to California. Can life get any worse?*

Answers came the following week, while the girls were at the kitchen table finishing their morning breakfast.

"You make the best buckwheat cakes, Molly," Joanna said, helping herself to the last golden hotcake on the platter.

She poured warm honey syrup over her plate and added a pat of fresh-churned butter.

"Are there more?"

"No, you've eaten them all," Molly said, "even though I made enough to feed the entire Kentucky Militia."

She looked down at Peony, who was rubbing against her leg and purring loudly.

"Lizzie, if you're not going to finish your milk, I'll give what's left to the kitty."

Mother had been unusually quiet all morning long, but now she pushed back her chair and stood up to speak.

"Girls, I have something important to say before you leave the table."

Molly put down her water glass and shifted in her seat. The envelope Mother held in her hand looked exactly like the one Ned Harper had given her at the post office.

"Do you recall your cousin Caleb, whose wedding we attended last year outside Lexington?"

Joanna raised an eyebrow. Why was Mother asking such a silly question?

"Of course, Mother, you know we do."

"Yes, well then."

She paused and cleared her throat.

"I recently received a letter from Caleb and his wife, Rebecca. They've sent us a generous invitation."

For a long moment, no one spoke. Even the ticking clock seemed to hold its breath. Then Mother drew a paper from the envelope, unfolded it carefully, and read its message out loud.

"Dearest Aunt Sarah,

Rebecca and I have heard the sad news of your beloved husband, Uncle David. It is hard to imagine the grief you must feel. Please accept our deepest condolences. Having one's life so tragically altered brings tremendous uncertainty, but we wish to offer our help. We would like you to consider relocating your family to California.

Hardworking people from all over the world call the Sacramento Valley their home. The future here is full of promise, and in my opinion, ours is the most desirable of all the states of the American Republic. Farmers already harvest more wheat than California can use, and the orchards are full of apple, peach, plum, walnut, and almond trees. Some people even say our farms will one day be more important than our gold mines!

We will be happy to help you get settled and promise to introduce you and your daughters to all our friends. Well-mannered, cultured young women are in great demand in this community. With your girls' many talents, I'm of the opinion that each of them will find an excellent husband.

Once an appropriate time of mourning has passed, I urge you to come to California. Rebecca and I look forward to greeting you at the Golden Gate.

Your loving nephew,
Caleb Handley

Mother set the letter on the table and looked around at each of her daughters.

"I know these past months have been difficult," she said. "You miss your father terribly, and it's hard to think of leaving the only home you've ever known."

"Goodness," Molly said. "It is very kind of Caleb to invite us, but why California? Don't you think we should move to New York?"

"California is the right choice for all of us, Mary Catherine," Mother said with a thin smile. "I am convinced this is the best course of action."

Lizzie squirmed in her seat. She tried to hold her tongue but couldn't keep still for another moment.

"Mother, does Cousin Caleb realize I am only thirteen? Molly may be ready to marry a grizzled old prospector, but I'm not."

"Goodness, Elizabeth. No one will be rushed into marriage. Still, before you know it, you'll be all grown up and ready to marry."

Joanna sat back in her chair and folded her arms.

"Mother," she said, "just how do you expect us to make this journey? Are we crossing the badlands by prairie schooner? Or will we attempt to sail around the southern tip of the Americas through the deadly Strait of Magellan?"

Joanna's reaction was overly dramatic, yet Molly's imagination flew in nearly as many directions. Most people took a wagon train across the continent but traveling in a Conestoga wagon behind a team of oxen didn't seem possible without Father.

"We are truly among the fortunate," Mother said, her voice faltering ever so slightly. "Your uncle has offered us the means to travel west in comfort and safety. We'll go by riverboat and steamship to meet the railroad across the Isthmus of Panama, then sail north to San Francisco. His generosity allows us to afford the price of upper-class tickets."

Molly had known something was afoot, but the announcement was still a shock. She wanted more excitement in her life, yes. But California? It was on the opposite side of the continent, the very edge of the world! How would she ever make it to Broadway now?

Mother tried to appear confident, but Molly understood the truth. Danville had closed in on them, and California offered a promise for the future. She walked over to Mother and gave her a hug.

Then to her sisters she said, "Let's all start packing. We're off to Sacramento!"

Chapter Eight

Leaving Home

1859

Now that her mind was made up, Mother saw no reason for delay. She set to work sorting household belongings and finding buyers for whatever could be sold. Centre College gladly accepted Father's leather-bound volumes of science books, but her fine crystal and delicate porcelain dishes were harder to give up.

"They were wedding gifts," she told the girls, carefully wrapping each piece in a scrap of soft linen. "I hate to let them go, but it's not likely they'd survive the journey."

Mother's friends came by clucking like hens, curious to hear their plans.

"Can it be true?" Lucinda exclaimed. "Are you really leaving us?"

"Yes, I am sorry to say goodbye, but I must think of my girls' futures."

Phoebe dabbed at the tears filling her eyes.

"I hope it's the right decision. California is so very far away!"

"I sincerely appreciate your concern, but with David gone there's little reason to stay. My nephew Caleb has promised to make our introductions in Sacramento."

"Oh, Sarah! How we shall miss you!"

While Mother went in the kitchen to make a pot of tea, Molly overheard the women talking quietly to one another.

"Sarah has always been adventurous," Lucinda said. "But this time may be too much. Can you imagine? Traveling to California without a husband!"

"I only pray for their safety," Phoebe sniffed. "One hears of terrible tragedies encountered by those who attempt the journey. Still, I suppose she must escape her sorrowful memories."

"Well, those girls need to find husbands soon. They say California is full of wealthy bachelors. I hope it's worth the risk."

Such fretful hand-wringers, Molly thought. *I only hope California is full of interesting stories. If not, I'll just have to find a way to get back to New York.*

***

As moving day approached, the girls spent their time cleaning and repairing the clothing they'd need on their journey. Molly looked at her small leather valise with dismay. Clearly, there wasn't room for everything.

"Mother, how should I decide what to bring?"

"Pack your warmest wool shawl and a few cotton frocks. They'll do until we reach Sacramento."

A few frocks? Did Mother expect her to start dressing like a mountain woman in buckskin and bear grease? She tried to see a suitable spot to tuck away her folded undergarments but found barely enough room for her pantalettes, much less her journals.

"I'm not at all convinced we should be making this move," grumbled Joanna. "Immigrants die from thirst in the Nevada desert. They're attacked by bandits or hostile natives, then left for dead. And let's not forget the dreadful fate of the Donner Party!"

"Trust me, dear," Mother said. "Ours is the safest possible route. We'll be in California in only six weeks."

Joanna looked down at Peony, who was curled into a ball in her lap. "What about our sweet Peony? What's to become of her?"

"Lydia needs a new mouser, and knowing her as I do, Peony will end up more spoiled than ever."

Molly understood Joanna's unhappiness. They would be leaving friends, neighbors, and everything familiar. Despite all the misgivings, she'd seen Mother's letter to Cousin Caleb and knew there was no turning back.

We will soon depart Kentucky...We meet the boat in Louisville... All is packed but for our shoestrings....

Uncle Louis arrived at the end of August to see them off.

"I've found a trustworthy wagoner, an Irishman named Taaffe," he told Mother. "He'll carry you from here to the Louisville waterfront. I reckon it'll take all of eight hours, even with a fresh team of horses and a reliable rig."

"Well then," said Mother, "there won't be much sleep for us tonight. We'll be ready to leave before dawn."

Molly was too excited to sleep, so she wrote one final entry in her journal.

I'm beginning to realize all I'm leaving behind. My room, my desk, my friends at school. The swing Father hung for us on the old sycamore down by the creek. Fireflies, whippoorwills, long summer evenings—do they have any of these in California?

She tucked the journal back into her traveling bag, then lay awake reviewing items in her head. She'd remembered to pack a pair of scissors. What about a thimble, or a needle and thread for fixing loose buttons and hems?

Just before dawn, Molly was awakened by the muted sounds of rustling harnesses and creaking wagon wheels. She peered from her window to the street down below and saw Uncle Louis and the wagoner talking as they carried the cases out to the road.

"So, Mr. Handley, your sister's leaving these parts behind?"

"Yes, Mr. Taaffe. They're beginning new lives out West."

The man scratched his neck and looked concerned. He hefted a large leather trunk onto the wagon.

"All on her own with three young girls? She's a brave 'un, then."

Uncle Louis added another bag to the load.

"Brave and determined. She wants the best for her daughters, and California looks like a golden opportunity."

Mr. Taaffe straightened his back and took a moment to stretch.

"Aye, perchance it's better out there."

He paused to tug at his curly beard.

"Could go meself one day. Too much talk of fightin' round here."

Sometime later, Mother emerged from the house and walked down the front stairs with a firm, determined step. Joanna and Lizzie followed after her, yawning and blinking half-closed eyes in the soft lantern light.

Molly stopped a moment to gaze at the vacant hallway, the closed shutters, and the rooms empty but for childhood memories and the sweet smell of lavender-scented dust. Taking a deep breath, she turned and stepped out onto the porch.

A wisp of chimney smoke hung in the chill morning air and a dog in a neighbor's yard barked a faint farewell. Otherwise, the streets were empty and eerily quiet.

I was never meant for Danville, she thought. *An exciting life waits for me somewhere and I intend to live it. Maybe I'll find it in California...*

"Mornin', miss," Mr. Taaffe said. "All set to go?"

"Yes, sir. I believe I am."

Mother hugged Uncle Louis and said, "I will miss you very much."

"Take care now, Sarah," he said with a catch in his throat. "Give my love to Caleb and Rebecca."

He kissed Joanna and Lizzie, then turned to Molly.

"Keep after your dreams, my dear. Your father once said to me, 'Mary Catherine will never settle for anything ordinary.' Remember those words and don't ever give up."

"I believe we're ready now," Mother said, and she bustled Molly into the wagon next to her sisters before she could even think of starting to cry.

"Be careful with them, Mr. Taaffe," Uncle Louis said.

"Aye, Mr. Handley, to be sure."

"Hi ya, g'long."

The wagoner flicked his reins and began whistling a haunting Irish tune.

"Good luck," Uncle Louis called after them. "God bless!"

The wagon rolled down Walnut Street past Danville's church spires, columns, and familiar storefronts. As pale morning light eased the darkness, they reached the outskirts of town and the buildings faded into the horizon. Molly sat firmly back against the wagon seat and turned her face to the west.

Chapter Nine

The Way West

1859

Mr. Taaffe drove his team of bay geldings right through the crowded streets of downtown Louisville. The high-pitched whistle of calliope music met Molly's ears long before they reached the waterfront. Then she caught sight of the fancy gold lettering on a magnificent multi-story paddleboat tethered next to the wharf.

"There she is!" she cried. "It's our ship!"

The *Cumberland* floated like a huge white wedding cake, beautifully decorated and ready to begin the journey downstream to the Mississippi River and on to the great city of New Orleans. On the nearby docks, muscular, dark-skinned laborers were hard at work. Some loaded and stacked wood to feed the steamship's boilers, others lifted and shoved heavy barrels and crates into place below deck.

Mr. Taaffe skillfully maneuvered his team through the crowd and stopped as close as he could to the Ohio River. One of the crewmen helped him unload the family's belongings and add their cases to an already towering stack of bags. Then, after checking to be sure nothing had been left behind, the wagoner climbed back onto his wagon and picked up the reins.

"Farewell, Mrs. McIntyre. Good luck to ye."

"Thank you, sir, and God bless you."

As the girls watched him go, Mother went to introduce herself to the purser.

"Afternoon, Missus, four to New Orleans?"

The man lowered the reading glasses perched on his forehead to the bridge of his nose and carefully checked his register.

"First class, on the left, ready to board."

Handsomely dressed travelers milled about, talking and laughing among themselves. Little groups of ragtag below-deck passengers waited to one side. They'd be allowed to board once everyone else had found their quarters.

"Come along, girls," Mother said.

A porter escorted them to their stateroom and swung open the door. The cabin was quite small, furnished with a tiny bureau and an oval wall mirror barely big enough to fit one's reflection.

"Lizzie, you and I will share the larger bed," Mother said. "Molly and Jo may each take one of the cots."

"There's not much room for the four of us," said Joanna.

"Look on the bright side," Molly said. "We won't get lost while we're in here. Besides, I plan to spend most of my time in the parlors or out on the decks."

"Let's go explore the ship," Lizzie said.

"Wait just a moment."

Mother had spotted a slight, dark-skinned young woman standing outside their doorway.

The girl stepped forward and said, "Beg your pardon, Missus. I'm Delia, your chambermaid. Would you like me to help organize your things?"

"Why, yes, I would. And I understand you are to wake us each morning?"

"Yes, ma'am, and I'll bring fresh water and clean towels and tidy your cabin. You'll have plenty of time to freshen up before the breakfast bell."

Molly suspected Delia was close to her own age, but what a different life she led. Her own paltry worries shrank in comparison.

Once they were settled in the room, the sisters ventured out onto the promenade deck to see the happenings down below. Roustabouts had finished loading the cargo, and now the lower-class passengers started to come aboard. The girls watched as people tried to squeeze themselves and their meager belongings around stacked crates filled with squawking chickens, squealing pigs, and tightly packed freight.

Lizzie leaned over the upper railings and craned her neck for a better view.

"I'm glad we don't have to make our beds on top of lumpy old grain sacks. How can they sleep next to those hot, noisy boilers and smelly old animals?"

Molly glanced sideways at her sister.

"Really, Lizzie? If not for Uncle Louis's help, we might have been below deck ourselves."

Lizzie obviously didn't know how close their own family had once come to the poorhouse. One could never tell what a turn of luck might bring.

Once the crew finished their preparations, the boilers were stoked, and black, sooty clouds began to billow from the *Cumberland's* towering smokestacks. The whistles screeched a warning signal, the wooden wheel churned the waters, and the boat pushed out into the Ohio River. It met the current, gained momentum, and they were off.

At nearly nine that evening Mother found Molly and her sisters lounging on plush velvet sofas outside the main dining room.

"I was wondering where you were," she said. "It's nearly time for supper to be served."

"Finally," Lizzie said. "We've finished exploring and I'm starved."

Just then a porter threw open the blue-and-gold-painted doors of the Grand Saloon. Uniformed waiters stationed around the room stood silent and attentive, ready to meet every request. Blue velvet chairs lined tables draped in crisp white linen and set with shining sterling silver utensils. Faceted crystal chandeliers hung the entire length of the room and candlelight sparkled off the mirror-lined walls, making it look as if there were two saloons instead of one.

"Oh my!" Mother said. "Look, girls, isn't it marvelous?"

"If this is a dream," Lizzie said, "don't wake me up!"

Engraved cards at each place setting listed the evening's offerings —turtle soup, several kinds of baked and broiled fish, cold roast beef, mutton, pork, and turkey, and a wide variety of vegetables, sauces, puddings, pastries, fruits, and nuts.

"Look at this menu," Molly said. "If I ate half of what they show here I'd end up with a nightmare from the indigestion!"

The assortment was overwhelming. In fact, everything on board the *Cumberland* was inordinately luxurious. Travelers in elegant silks and velvets dined, gambled, and frequented the lively saloon. Glowing cigars and pungent tobacco smoke filled the public areas no matter the hour, and twinkling lanterns lit the dance hall right through the night.

Everything was lovely except for one deeply disturbing fact. The porters, cooks, chambermaids, and waiters, the laundry workers, boilermen, and the roustabouts who loaded and unloaded cargo, all those who made this trip possible had no choice in the matter. Every one of them was a riverboat slave.

Molly could not shake off her discomfort. She chose to avoid the noisy gaming tables and party rooms. Instead, she spent the time reading and observing, and as they traveled, she wrote about the river.

At night, all is empty and quiet, but when the morning fog breaks life is everywhere. Deer, mink, otter, and other wild creatures show themselves along the bank, then quickly disappear. We pass hundreds of shallow, sandy islands covered with tall, grassy reeds that hide unknowable numbers of water birds. They startle, and masses of softly flapping wings darken the sky. Hawks, osprey, and eagles circle overhead hunting for a meal. Other birds travel in immense, weaving flocks that cloud the horizon...

At Cairo, Illinois, the Ohio spilled into the Mississippi River. Now, entering a wide plain of water, they met boats loaded with cotton bales, rum barrels, and heavy sacks of tobacco, sugar, and coffee. Long flatboats drifted nearby, laden with whiskey kegs, pork barrels, stacked animal furs, and cowhides.

Molly got up from her chair on the upper deck and went to join her sisters.

"So many different kinds of boats there are," she said. "And look at how those men use poles to guide their rafts."

"Captain Smith says the cigar-shaped ones are keelboats."

Molly looked at her sister with surprise.

"You're acquainted with the captain of our boat?"

"Of course," Lizzie said with a smug grin. "How else do you expect to know anything?"

Molly shook her head. How could sisters be any more different? Jo rarely risked speaking to a stranger while Lizzie constantly made new friends.

"Goodness, look over there!"

Joanna pointed to a low plume of smoke billowing from a boat docked close to shore. Men with buckets and hand-pumps were trying to contain the blaze, but the wooden barge carried a highly flammable load of cotton.

"I wish them luck," Molly said, and felt an uncomfortable knot unsettling her stomach.

She remembered hearing about the terrible riverboat blaze that had devastated St. Louis, Missouri. Flames from one waterfront steamer had leapt to another, and dozens of steamboats, flatboats, and barges were set on fire. The embers spread to nearby buildings and entire city blocks were left in ashes.

Like Lizzie, Mother spent much of her time visiting with fellow travelers. One of the women she met was Katerina Bockrath, a double-chinned, dumpling-shaped farmwife from Cincinnati. Katerina's smooth pink cheeks and pleasant smell of fresh-baked bread were warm and welcoming, and she had plenty of information to share.

"The mister and I go to see my sister in Indiana," Mrs. Bockrath offered kindly. "And you? Where do you go?"

Mother explained the reason for their journey and Mrs. Bockrath's eyes grew as big and round as apples.

"Poor dear, without a husband to protect you!"

She reached down to lift a white cotton cover off her bulging food hamper. Retrieving a ripe yellow pear, she handed it to her husband.

"Klaus, have you heard this? Missus McIntyre travels alone with three young daughters."

Mr. Bockrath wagged his head sadly. He took a bite from the pear and used his shirtsleeve to wipe juice off his chin while his wife dispensed her helpful advice.

"Mind you, always lock your cabin door and never take your eyes from your belongings. Captains on this river will hire thieves to steal from you."

Mother's dark eyebrows arched into little half-moons.

"Gracious! I suppose one must always be wary, but surely Captain Smith isn't a dishonest man."

Mrs. Bockrath clucked her tongue, sounding exactly like a plump mother hen.

"Oh, Mrs. McIntyre! You never know who might try to take advantage. Especially you, a woman traveling without a husband."

Mother was distressed to think someone might betray her trust. Still, she realized it would be wise to warn her daughters.

"Girls," she said, "we must remain vigilant and always be cautious."

"Everyone I've met is nice," said Lizzie, who had difficulty thinking badly of anyone.

Joanna regularly expected danger and was not one bit surprised.

"Lizzie," Joanna said, "haven't you noticed the unsavory characters on this boat? They drink, play cards, and gamble all night long."

Molly never imagined such things when she lived in Danville. They certainly made life more interesting, and she noted it all in her journal.

***

It was a relief to arrive safely in New Orleans. Though the city was roughly one hundred miles north of the Gulf of Mexico, sailing vessels and ocean-going steamships clogged its banks.

The girls watched Captain Smith skillfully maneuver the *Cumberland* through the congested river traffic. Dock workers waved and whistled directions to the crew until the side-wheeler was lined up and tied securely to the wharf. Then, finally, they were allowed to disembark.

Mother engaged a porter to carry their luggage, but to reach the next ship they'd have to push their way through the sweaty crowd gathered on the hot, humid Louisiana riverfront.

Molly felt as if she'd stepped into another world. Mountains of goods were piled high on the docks. The air was thick with kerosene fumes and sweet with molasses and tobacco smoke.

Vendors cooked and sold unfamiliar foods in open market stalls, where clouds of spicy, pungent aromas filled the air. Some sellers hawked their wares in thickly accented English, while others cried out in languages she did not understand.

"*Beignets, ma chérie,*" sang a beautiful, doe-eyed woman with skin the color of polished mahogany.

Molly gave Mother a questioning look.

"She's speaking French, dear. She wants you to buy her doughnuts, but we have no time to linger."

Molly longed to try one of the woman's sugary treats, but Mother was in too much of a hurry to stop. Further on, another young woman sat beside a tall pile of golden yellow fruit.

"Bananas, come taste, fresh and good," she cried.

"Molly," Lizzie whined, "I want to see what's for sale. Why won't Mother allow us a few minutes to explore?"

"Because we mustn't miss the boat to Panama. It won't wait for us and we don't dare be late."

"Lizzie! Where do you think you're going?"

Her sister had started to head off into the crowd, but Molly lunged forward to grab her wrist before she could be swallowed up in the mob.

"Look over there, Molly! Have you ever seen anything like it?"

Lizzie had caught sight of a street performer who played a hand organ while a monkey did tricks on his shoulder. Now the little animal was bowing and tugging at its cap for coins.

Molly had never seen such a thing. She might have stayed to watch, but Mother and Joanna were waiting up ahead and she didn't dare tarry any longer.

"Elizabeth Leticia!" Mother said in an exasperated voice. "If you don't stay with us, you'll surely be stolen away and sold to the circus."

"I'm of a mind to let them take her," Molly said, only slightly under her breath.

"The *Carolina* should be along here somewhere," Mother said, trying to control her rising frustration. "Now, where did that porter go with our trunks?"

Joanna had been searching the river bank, and now she spotted the man up ahead of them, gesturing toward a wood-sided triple-deck ocean steamer docked at the wharf.

"Be it your pleasure, ma'am," he called, "I'll leave these for the stevedores to load."

Mother hurried over to where he stood and said, "Thank you, sir. Here's a coin for your work."

He promptly pocketed the money, nodded his thanks, and immediately vanished into the crowd.

The *Carolina* had been built to carry mail from New Orleans to Panama. Its quarters were barely adequate for paying passengers, but

Molly curled up on her tiny cot, pulled out a pencil and her journal, and settled in for the next part of the journey.

It wasn't until they were underway again that Mother shared some of the unsettling information she'd learned while aboard the riverboat.

"While aboard the *Cumberland,* a fellow passenger took it upon himself to apprise me of the risks of riverboat travel. According to him, we've been fortunate to arrive safely thus far.

"'Madam,' said he, 'we'll be lucky to make it to New Orleans. Half these steamboats sink. And if a boiler explodes, we'll be blown to bits.'

"I told him I'd been given to understand there was no better way to reach our destination.

"'It is the best choice,' he agreed. 'Stagecoaches take too long and aren't the least bit reliable. Still, it requires an experienced pilot to avoid calamity on the Mississippi. Tree snags, sandbars, boiler explosions. There are unseen perils everywhere.'"

Danger, uncertainty, promise, and adventure were all closely linked. At this point of the journey Molly had no idea how it would all play out.

Chapter Ten

On to Panama

1859

It took several hours for the *Carolina* to reach the Gulf of Mexico, but then the ship picked up steam and set sail for the Caribbean Sea. The Mississippi River's gentle rocking motion hadn't bothered Molly at all, but the rough ocean waves brought on a dizzying headache. Alas, no one remembered to pack the ginger tea. Her nausea led to seasickness, and it took two days for the discomfort to settle so she could safely venture outside.

Molly finally felt well enough to leave the cabin, and she went to meet Joanna on the wide-open upper deck.

"Molly! I'm glad to see you up again."

"Yes, I've gained my sea legs at last. Is my face still green?"

"No, you look much better."

Molly's gut lurched again, but it was not nearly so bad as before.

"I'm starting to wonder if it might not be the waves," she said.

"Maybe you just can't stomach the travel?"

"Me? Remember, Jo, you're the one who couldn't handle the thought of leaving home."

"True. But I must say, I do love the ocean, especially after dark. You should see how lovely it is when the stars are out."

Late that night, Molly joined Joanna on the hurricane deck. The inky-black sky was lit only by a thin crescent moon and the soft glow of the Milky Way, and she craned her neck, trying to make out the patterns of the stars. Just then, a bright, gleaming streak of light shot across the darkness.

"Look, Jo, a falling star," Molly cried. "Do you remember what Father said whenever we saw a meteor?"

"I do remember. It was a line from one of Shakespeare's plays. *Comets, importing change of times and states, brandish your crystal tresses in the sky.*"

Yes, Molly thought. *We are clearly in a change of times and states. Everything will be different in California. Who can know what's waiting for us there?*

After falling asleep that night, she dreamt of floating upon a vast, salty ocean. A sudden, unruly tempest caused her to lose her footing and uncontrollable currents dragged her out to sea. Powerful swells carried her into the deeps, but just before awakening, she landed on the sandy shore of an unfamiliar world.

She lay on her bunk for a long while, moody and unsettled. When morning sunlight finally brightened the room, she opened her journal and picked up her pencil.

New York City is where I'm supposed to live. Not California. I'll have to figure it all out when we get to Sacramento. I know I'll find solid ground again.

***

The *Carolina* continued steaming across the Caribbean toward Central America, and eventually, they reached the Panamanian coastline. The crewmen dropped anchor at Aspinwall, a tiny, waterlogged settlement at the eastern terminus of the Panama Pacific Railroad. Molly stepped out onto the flat, soggy island at the mouth of the Chagres River, and her heart sank. Before her lay a cluster of sorry buildings perched on rotted wood pilings.

"What in the world? Goodness, it smells awful here."

She lifted a hand to cover her nose, but the oppressive heat and humidity made it impossible to escape the stench of mud and decay.

"Oh, what a miserable place," Lizzie said.

"This heat is unbearable," Joanna said. "And can you believe all the insects?"

The air was alive, and the bugs were definitely after blood. Molly tried shooing away clouds of sand flies and mosquitoes, but she met with little success. Thankfully, she'd draped her face and neck with gauze netting so that her long cotton skirt, sunbonnet, gloves, shoes, and thick cotton stockings covered every inch of skin.

Mother pointed toward a small engine at rest on a set of narrow iron rails.

"That must be our train," she said. "Let's hope we board soon."

Rusty tracks led to a tin-roofed depot building situated next to an expanse of wet, marshy mudflats. A few men near the tracks were covered with sweat. They were hard at work transferring heavy bundles of mail while others loaded baggage from the steamship onto the waiting locomotive.

Some of the westbound passengers were growing impatient.

"When will we board our train?" asked a rotund, red-faced fellow. "We deserve better than this, considering the cost of our tickets."

Sweat dripped off his face. His clothes were soaked with perspiration, and he looked extremely uncomfortable.

"We all want to be away from this place," said an older man with a thin, graying beard and droopy white mustache. "It appears there's a shortage of labor. Unless you wish to pitch in and help load the freight, there is nothing to be done for it but to sit and wait."

Another traveler pulled a damp linen kerchief from his pocket and began wiping away water that was beading on his forehead and dripping from his nose.

"Yes, sir," he said. "He's absolutely right. Complaining won't help a bit. Besides, you should be grateful for the train. I reckon you never heard 'bout all it took to cross this isthmus before it was finished."

"Charlie and me, we crossed here in fifty-one," said a man using a ragged canvas hat to swat at a swarm of gnats. "It was risky business back then. All we could think of was getting to the gold, and the only way upriver was to paddle yerself and yer gear in a dugout canoe. Ain't that so, Charlie?"

His companion squinted and spit a mouthful of tobacco juice into a muddy puddle next to his nearly worn-out boots.

"Yep, then 'twas over the mountains on the back of a mule. Had to fight off bandits, didn't we? Barely escaped with our skins."

"'Sides them robbers, poisonous water snakes and hungry gators wanted nothin' more than havin' us for dinner."

Charlie nodded and scratched at his scraggly, juice-stained yellow beard.

"Glad we're goin' through the jungle by daylight this time. Too many ghosts in there. Hundreds, maybe thousands, died puttin' in them rails. Swore I'd never cross through there again. But this train

ain't so bad. It'll get us to Panama City lickety-split. Be there in just a few hours."

He gave a toothless grin and spit again.

Molly turned and went to stand with Mother. She wasn't sure if she believed in ghosts, but the place felt eerie enough to be full of them. Mossy vines draped the mangrove trees like shadowy veils, and the air itself seemed haunted. Seasickness or not, she looked forward to reaching the Pacific Ocean as soon as possible.

Mother was also growing impatient. She decided to go inside the depot to ask when they might expect to board. A few minutes later, she emerged from the building with one of the railroad officials.

"Girls," she said, "we're ready to depart. This gentleman promises to find us a place where we can sit together."

They boarded the train, the conductor showed them their seats, and the family settled in as best they could.

Lizzie was growing peevish.

"This metal bench is not at all comfortable," she said.

"Upholstery would rot in this humidity," Molly snapped irritably. "Be glad you have somewhere to sit."

She considered reminding Lizzie of their good fortune. They could be following a Conestoga wagon across the prairies, blistering the soles of their feet on the Oregon Trail.

Elevated train tracks stretched across a vast, murky swamp, and further on, a tall railroad trestle carried them over an expanse of watery brown goo. Hissing steam fogged the air and the engine sent gray clouds out of its smokestack.

It was hard to tell for sure, but Molly thought she saw something moving in the twisted growth of mangroves. Curiosity overcame her fear of ghosts.

"There's a platform at the rear of the train," she said to her sisters. "Let's try to get a better view of the jungle."

"Are you certain it's safe?"

Joanna was still thinking about the phantoms, or maybe robbers. Having just finished reading *The Adventures of Robinson Crusoe,* she expected something frightening to happen at any moment.

"Come on, Jo," Molly said. "We'll be fine. Don't you want to see monkeys?"

"Well, yes, but we should be careful. Are you aware that venomous frogs inhabit these swamps? And hostile natives might be out there, ready to capture us."

Joanna somehow summoned her courage. The girls made their way to the back of the railcar and out into the open air. Then they heard a howl, and Molly caught a glimpse of movement in the dense forest canopy. A chattering tribe of monkeys was just visible in the leafy green foliage. Next came a high, piercing shriek, and Lizzie jumped back with a frightened cry.

"Watch out, it may be a cougar," yelled Joanna, starting for the door.

"Wait, Jo."

Molly leaned forward to peer into a nearby tree.

"Look up there. If that's a cougar, it's one with wings!"

The monkeys were gone, but two brightly colored tropical birds were partially hidden in the thick vines. One uttered another shrill cry, then flitted out of view.

Not long after the girls returned to their seats, the train left the jungle and began a steep climb into the mountains. After reaching the summit, they began a steep descent, then rounded a sharp turn. Suddenly, the earth seemed to fall away. Panama City's red-tiled roofs and whitewashed bell towers came into view, and beyond the city a wide expanse of brilliant blue stretched on for forever.

"There it is—the Pacific Ocean!" Lizzie cried.

The feat was truly amazing. In one single day, they'd left one great ocean behind and come to meet another. Only two weeks left before the curtain would rise on the next act of their story.

***

"Look at all the people," Molly said, "and all the mail!"

Massive heaps of freight and baggage filled Panama City's railroad depot. Workers loaded stacks of mailbags onto freight cars for the trip back to New Orleans or perhaps even farther, to New York City. Crates filled with furniture, spices, and leather goods spilled from adjacent warehouses. It was truly amazing to see how much cargo passed across this narrow strip of land connecting North and South America.

Mother checked a scrap of paper in her hand.

"Our ship must be somewhere on this wharf," she sighed.

Molly saw a group of travelers crowded around a man in a wide-brimmed *sombrero*. He was talking rapidly and gesturing toward a boat tethered to the pier.

"Mother, that man over there appears to be helping people with directions."

"Yes, I see. You girls wait here. I'll try to speak with him."

Mother waited her turn, then approached the gentleman with a hopeful smile.

"*Buenas tardes, señor.* Would you be so kind as to direct me to the *SS Veracruz*?"

The official tipped his hat and pointed to the nearby waterfront.

"*Sí, señora.* It is here."

Fortunately, they were in the right place. Unfortunately, it would be a while before final fuel and provisions were loaded and the steamer was ready for northbound travelers to board.

"There will be a short delay," said Mother. "Let's look for a shady place to sit."

"It's hot, and I'm tired," complained Lizzie. "I don't think we'll ever make it to California."

Molly sighed. She was tired too.

There was a low adobe wall near the waterfront, and this is where they sat, in the shade of a small fig tree. At last, the purser was ready to inspect and stamp passage documents and a crewman motioned for passengers to come aboard. Mother rose, stretched her tired muscles, and picked up her traveling bag.

"Are you ready, girls? Before you know it, we'll be in San Francisco."

Chapter Eleven

On the SS Veracruz

1859

The *Veracruz* steamed away from the wharf with scores of passengers and tons of freight destined for San Francisco. Molly climbed a set of narrow iron stairs to the upper deck for a last view of Panama City. The sun was about to drop into a distant row of clouds, and the hazy orange-gold light wouldn't last much longer. A brisk ocean breeze brought some relief from the heat and humidity, and Molly reached up to push the stray hairs away from her face. She took a long, deep breath. What a blessing to be on the last leg of this journey!

The way north hugged the long Pacific coastline. She could just make out a series of flat, sandy beaches and one or two fishing boats close to shore, but once they passed Costa Rica, there was nothing to see but endless blue ocean.

Lizzie was bored.

"We've been traveling for so, so long," she said. "Where are we now? Are we ever going to be in California?"

Mother rubbed her forehead.

"Why don't you look for the crewmen, dear? They might be able to answer your questions."

Molly took her sister's hand.

"Come on, Lizzie. We can go together."

Mother gave Molly a grateful smile, settled back in the chair, and closed her eyes.

I suppose this isn't easy for Mother either, Molly thought. *Three daughters, three worries. She has more than enough troubles to keep her awake at night.*

Together, they climbed the steep iron stairs to the upper deck. Other passengers were already there, leaning against the railings, enjoying the sunshine and sea breezes.

A few crewmen were gathered around an officer, presumably the captain. He appeared to have finished giving instructions and was about to return to his quarters, but Lizzie hurried over before he could break away.

"Excuse me, sir," she said. "I have a question."

The captain looked startled, but he managed a small smile.

"Good day, miss, and who might you be?"

"I am Elizabeth Leticia McIntyre, but everyone calls me Lizzie. This is my sister, Mary Catherine. We call her Molly."

He gave them each a slightly formal bow.

"I am very glad to make your acquaintance, Lizzie, and you as well, Mary Catherine. I am Captain Denman Dorr, at your service."

"Captain Dorr," Lizzie said, "could you please tell me when we'll be in California?"

He smiled again and said, "I expect smooth sailing from here on out. We stop briefly to refuel in Nicaragua, then once we've passed the Mexican coastline, we'll cross the Sea of Cortez, round the Baja Peninsula, and head straight up the California coast. If all goes well, we'll be in San Francisco in a fortnight."

"We're not staying in San Francisco," Lizzie said. "We're going to Sacramento where our cousin Caleb lives. I'm only thirteen, but Molly's already seventeen. Caleb and Rebecca—that's his wife—are going to help her find a husband."

The commanding officer threw back his head and gave a hearty laugh. There were wide smiles on the other men's faces. Molly felt her own face turning cherry red. Honestly, she could not believe her sister!

"Lizzie," the captain said good-naturedly, "I'd like you to meet Mr. Biddle, my first mate. He'll be happy to answer all your questions, won't you, Billy?"

"Aye, Captain, pleased to help."

He winked one eye at Molly and gave Lizzie a lopsided grin.

Molly immediately thought of the sea turtles she'd seen on the Panamanian coast. Like the turtles, Mr. Biddle's brown, leathery face was weathered and deeply lined from endless hours on the open ocean. He also had an odd habit of jerking his chin from side to side while he talked, as if checking to see if anyone was actually listening.

Lizzie was delighted with Mr. Biddle's company, and though she pestered him endlessly, he never seemed to tire of her questions.

"Would you show us the engine room? What do all the whistles mean? Is there a place to wash our clothes?"

Embarrassingly, she wasn't even afraid to ask for the privy!

As Captain Dorr predicted, two days later the *Veracruz* made port in Nicaragua at San Juan del Sur. Several crew members went ashore for a load of coal to fuel the next leg of the voyage. While Mother and Lizzie retired to their quarters for a brief rest, Molly and Joanna found a spot on the upper deck to watch the proceedings.

The job was almost finished when Molly noticed an odd disturbance arising from the hill beyond the wharf. She poked Joanna's side and pointed toward the noise.

"Do you see those men? What are they doing?"

A contingent of armed soldiers came charging downhill from the village, yelling and firing shots toward the ships anchored in the harbor. The crewmen still on shore began diving into the shallow water and swimming for their lives toward the steamer.

Captain Dorr and the chief engineer had been talking by the wheelhouse, but their heads jerked up sharply at the sound of gunfire.

"What's happening here?" yelled the captain.

Apparently caught off guard, he began spouting words no lady would dare repeat. Then he took command of the situation.

"Zounds, men!" he bellowed. "Arm yourselves and ready the cannon. All on deck take cover, now!"

A volley of musket balls whizzed toward the boat. Molly winced when one lodged in a nearby railing and sent splinters flying.

"Jo," she called, "are you all right?"

"Yes, but we need to hide."

"This way!"

She grabbed her sister's hand, and they scrambled to the other side of the deck and slid behind a pile of wooden crates.

Before the men could react to orders, the crew on a small brigantine at anchor next to the *Veracruz* took aim at the men on shore. Cannonballs sprayed the hillside, and the soldiers scattered for cover.

Captain Dorr took advantage of the pause in fighting.

"Weigh anchor!" he yelled.

"Heave away! Lively now," Mr. Biddle cried.

The boat pulled away from the wharf to escape harm's way. Passengers cautiously emerged from their hiding places, and Molly and Jo slowly poked their heads out to look around.

"Are you young ladies all right?" asked Captain Dorr with a look of concern.

"Yes, sir," Molly said. "It was quite a scare, but we're fine now."

"You handled the situation well, Miss McIntyre. Not every traveler knows what to do in such alarming circumstances."

Joanna brushed the dust and wood splinters off her skirt. "My sister is quite capable, Captain Dorr," she said calmly. "You can always rely on her to manage a challenge."

Molly looked at her with surprise. Was this the same sister who constantly feared disaster?

Having heard a commotion, Mother and Lizzie appeared from their quarters, but everything was over so fast that they missed all the action.

"Why didn't you tell us?" Lizzie complained.

"There wasn't much to see," Molly said. "It was over practically before it began."

"It's a miracle no one was hurt," Mother said.

Mr. Biddle arrived to give the captain a report on the status of the *Veracruz* and its crew.

"There be only minor damage, sir. Nerves rattled, but no injury."

Now a group of passengers approached Captain Dorr to demand an explanation for what had happened.

"Please accept my apologies," he said. "We unwittingly anchored next to a vessel commanded by Colonel William Walker, the Tennessee privateer. It was our misfortune to be caught in the crossfire between Walker and the Costa Rican army."

"The fellow's a notorious mercenary," said a man who was still clearly upset.

The captain nodded grimly.

"He had the audacity to declare himself president of Nicaragua in an attempt to make it his own slaveholding colony. Now he's trying to take over all of Central America. He's creating havoc throughout the region. General Blanco is making a valiant effort to bring Walker to justice, and I don't doubt that brazen filibuster will be made to pay with his life for the trouble he's caused."

Most of the passengers were satisfied with Captain Dorr's explanation, but not Mother. "Captain Dorr, can you guarantee our safe arrival in San Francisco?"

He bowed deeply and said, "Ma'am, I promise to do everything in my power to deliver you and your family to our destination unharmed."

Her voice softened ever so slightly. "Well then, thank you."

She really had no choice but to accept the situation. It was impossible for her to know whether the incident at San Juan del Sur could have been avoided. What could she do but take him at his word?

Thankfully, the rest of the week remained uneventful, giving Molly time to write. Danger could be thrilling, and dangerous experiences were fun to write about. Perhaps her first play would include a shipboard battle:

Pirate: Surrender, you spineless sluggard! I'll take your boat and all its booty too!
Captain: Over my dead and drowned body, you cowardly dog!
Pirate: Never mind the gold, I'll have the girl. She's the sauciest minx ever I spied!
Captain: Impudent scoundrel! Hold your tongue or I'll tear it out by the roots!

She wasn't just relating facts. These were characters and scenes of her own invention, and creating such stories swiftly became a daily habit.

The *Veracruz* sailed north along the mainland, left the Mexican coastline behind, and crossed the Sea of Cortez. Here the breezes were warm and gentle, and the translucent waters were unspeakably blue. Molly was sure there couldn't be a more beautiful place on earth.

Captain Dorr and Mr. Biddle came onto the upper deck on a day when Mother and the girls were out enjoying the view. The captain pointed to a thin line of land off in the distance.

"Ladies, that's Baja California up ahead. Once we've rounded the peninsula, it'll be straight north to San Francisco."

"California!" Lizzie clapped.

"Yes, we're getting closer now. But first we must pass the *Isla de Cedros*. It's an island covered with cedar trees—*cedros* in Spanish. Please excuse me, ladies. I must leave you in Mr. Biddle's care."

"Them's treacherous rocks up ahead," Billy said. "But no worries. The cap'n knows these waters better than any man on the Pacific. He'll get us by, safe and sound."

Molly leaned against the railing. She gazed across the water and spotted a pod of gray and white dolphins playing in the ship's wake.

"Look," she cried. "Over there!"

The creatures launched themselves high in the air, pirouetting like acrobats, turning and twisting in playful circles before slapping down into the water again. Moments later, a tall spray of seawater appeared some distance beyond the dolphins. Suddenly, an immense, graceful form shot straight up out of the water. The whale was quite close to the boat, and it splashed back into the ocean with a startling crash.

"Goodness, that was huge!"

"Aye, 'twas a gray whale, Miss Molly," said Billy.

"What were those blotchy things all over its body?"

"Oh, them be barnacles, gettin' themselves a free ride."

Two more of the whales, one much larger than the first, surfaced nearby.

"See the youngster?" Billy said. "The mother's trying her best to keep her calf away from us."

The whales disappeared below the waves, then resurfaced far in the distance, and the show was over.

***

An occasional steamship or foreign brig signaled a passing greeting as the *Veracruz* continued north. Flocks of gulls followed in the ship's wake, flying fish skirted the water's surface, and brown pelicans traveled in long, straight lines overhead. When the birds spotted fish in the transparent waters, they dove down with a splash to scoop up a meal.

By now, Mother had forgiven the captain for their close call off Nicaragua, and whenever he had a moment to spare, he stopped to answer questions and talk about the places they passed.

"Good day, Captain Dorr," she said one day. "I was wondering, could you tell us the name of the island up ahead?"

"That is the southernmost Channel Island, San Clemente. We'll be passing a string of islands now. Next is Santa Catalina, then San Nicolas, Santa Barbara, and so on. The last of them is San Miguel, named for Saint Michael."

"It sounds like a litany of the Catholic saints," Mother said.

A warm smile crinkled the corners of his brown-gold eyes.

"You're absolutely right. Spanish explorers claimed this land for Spain hundreds of years ago. They gave saints' names to many of the places they came upon."

"So," said Molly, "are we nearly there?"

"It won't be much longer now. We still have to pass a set of rocky islands covered with seabirds. They're known as the *Farallons*—the Spanish word for cliffs. When we enter San Francisco Bay you'll see a military outpost on a little island they call *Alcatraz*—Spanish for pelicans."

By the time they reached the Farallon Islands, Baja California's warmth was only a distant memory. Most of the passengers went below deck to escape the wind, but the girls didn't dare miss anything. They stood on the upper deck and watched as the *Veracruz* slipped through the turbulent waters of the narrow, fog-shrouded opening known to sailors as the "Golden Gate."

Once inside San Francisco Bay, the thick clouds lifted and parted to reveal a tiny, rocky island fortified with iron cannons and ringed with tall stacks of cannonballs.

"That must be Fort Alcatraz," Molly said. "I see the stars and stripes waving from the citadel. Goodness, look at all the people on the docks up ahead!"

Flags of every seafaring nation flew from the hundreds of boats at anchor in the harbor. The *Veracruz* drew slowly into port, met by a cheering crowd waving white handkerchiefs. After weeks of travel, they'd finally made it to California.

Chapter Twelve

California

1859

Passengers jammed the upper decks, calling greetings to friends and strangers who were waiting on the wharf.

"Hey there, ahoy!"

There was excitement in the air, and Molly thrilled to the sights and sounds of docked ships, clanging deck fittings, and snapping ropes. But then a burly, broad-chested man began shoving his way through the throng, trying to be the first person off the boat. She felt a hard push, then saw him jostle a short, thin fellow with a young boy in tow.

"Whoa, watch yourself," someone next to her said.

"Move over, sir, you're in my way!" the burly man scowled.

The man with the boy gave him an angry glare.

"Look here, mister. Everyone will get their turn."

"Stay with me, girls," Mother said nervously.

Molly felt a tightness in her chest. She took Lizzie's hand and walked with her on tiptoes, trying to keep Mother and Joanna in sight.

San Francisco didn't seem at all like the cities she'd seen in the magazine illustrations.

This was a noisy, boisterous place with rough-looking men on the docks—sweaty, unshaven laborers in faded linsey-woolsey shirts, canvas trousers, and leather suspenders; boatmen in high rubber boots and loose sack coats; slick, oily-haired rovers wearing soiled frock coats and worn-out shoes.

"They don't look like our neighbors back in Danville," Lizzie said.

"No, that's true. Still, despite appearances, they're likely good, hardworking men trying to earn an honest day's wages. Maybe they're immigrants like ourselves."

These men are like actors on a stage, Molly thought. *Each worker, sailor, and wanderer with his own costume and part to play.*

Back home, the air smells of honeysuckle and tobacco leaves. Here it's tar, fish, and something much sharper. Ambition, maybe?

With the immediate rush to depart the ship over, Mother found them a place to stand and get their bearings. Spotted seagulls and black cormorants screeched and squawked. The tall-mast ships creaked and moaned in their moorings, rocking back and forth in the shallow, brackish water near the docks. Beyond the waterfront, brick and wood buildings were scattered helter-skelter up a series of sandy hills and rocky, treeless cliffs.

The girls watched other travelers rearrange and sort their possessions. Pots, pans, blankets, and rifles poked out from every corner of their well-worn leather and canvas packs.

"It looks as if some of them are carrying everything they own on their backs," Joanna said. "Did you see the green-and-yellow parrot perched on that man's head?"

"I saw someone with a brass trumpet tied to his belt and a guitar hanging from his neck," Lizzie said.

"I think I saw him too," Molly laughed. "His face and head were hidden by his belongings. He looked like a pile of goods that had somehow grown legs!"

"I'm a little sad to leave the crew of the *Veracruz*," Lizzie said, looking back at the ship.

"I know," Molly said. "They feel like old friends by now. We said goodbye to Mr. Biddle, but I didn't see Captain Dorr. Let's go see if we can find him."

The crowd had thinned considerably, and the girls quickly spotted the captain standing near the end of the pier.

Molly went up to him and said, "Thank you, sir, for all you've taught us. We'll miss you."

"Not at all, Mary Catherine. I've been happy to help."

Mother came to join them and said, "We owe you our thanks, Captain. You and your crew ensured our safe arrival. You kept your word."

"It's been my pleasure, Mrs. McIntyre," he said, then hesitated for a long moment. "I hope you don't think it forward to ask, but have you reserved lodging for the night? As you can see, it will be dark soon. I'd be honored to help you find suitable accommodations."

Molly thought she saw Mother's cheeks turning rosy pink, but it might have been the late afternoon sunlight.

"You are most kind, Captain, but that isn't necessary. My nephew Caleb has arranged temporary quarters for us. I am sure we can make do until he arrives to accompany us to Sacramento."

With a slightly formal bow, he nodded toward Molly.

"Take good care of your mother, young lady."

"Don't worry, Captain Dorr. I will."

He started to go, but Mother quickly held out her hand.

"Thank you, Captain," she said. "I—we won't forget you."

Turning away quickly as if to avoid saying goodbye, she lifted her chin and aimed her gaze at the road ahead.

"Now girls, we must find a porter to collect our cases."

A few departing passengers stood on the docks, and the muddy, unpaved streets remained clogged with horses, mules, and carriages.

Pushcarts were still available for hire, and Mother said, "There's a man who looks trustworthy. Let's ask if he's willing to transport our bags."

The porter signaled that he was for hire. Mother showed him the prescribed address, and he motioned for them to follow. By now, the daylight had faded. Gas lanterns lit the darkening streets as they headed up the hill away from the waterfront. Gladly, it was only a short walk before the porter deposited their bags in front of an abandoned ship's hull.

"Here we are, ma'am."

"Oh my, this—this can't be right, sir. You must be mistaken."

"Sure, ma'am, 'tis your hotel. This be the *Niantic*."

"Mother," Molly said, "this looks like a boat."

"That's so, miss," the man chuckled. "This ol' whaler were beached here in forty-nine. Its crew headed to the gold country and never were seen ag'in. Tis not the only ship turned into lodging. There be hundreds of such boats 'round here. Most of 'em buried, covered up in sand."

"I hope it doesn't sink," Joanna muttered under her breath.

He pushed open a narrow entryway cut into the ship's hull, led them into a small chamber lit by a single tallow candle, and stacked their things against a wall.

"Thank you for your assistance," Mother said.

She handed him a coin, which he immediately pocketed.

"I'll be off then." He tipped his hat, pulled it down over one deeply lidded eye, and was gone.

A slim, bushy-haired boy not much older than Lizzie slouched on a low, three-legged stool near the door. He looked up when they entered, wiped his nose on a dirty shirtsleeve, and nodded at Mother.

"Good evening, young man," she said, straightening her shoulders in an effort to appear more confident than she actually felt. "My name is Mrs. David McIntyre. Mr. Caleb Handley is my nephew and he has arranged for our stay here. My daughters and I require safekeeping for our baggage and clean beds for the night."

The boy checked the register he held on his lap. He picked up the candlestick, motioned them up a set of rickety stairs, and led the way down a dim, damp hallway. Stopping in front of a low wooden door, he chose a heavily rusted key from among several on a large iron ring, swung open the door, and set the candle on a knee-high bedside table.

"Here be your space for the night," he announced.

In the meager light, Molly made out four narrow beds stacked right and left against the wood-plank walls.

"There's food to be had, for a fee," the boy said.

"Thank you, young man, but I am afraid we are too exhausted to eat," Mother said.

"Suit yourself. Be sure to lock the door. Key's on the nightstand," he said, and backed away.

Molly dropped onto one of the two bottom bunks, unlaced and removed her boots, stretched, and yawned. The room smelled of salt, tar, and the sea, but no matter. For now, she only wanted to sleep.

***

Late the following morning, she awoke to the sound of Caleb Handley's booming voice. "Welcome to California, Aunt Sarah."

It took a few moments to realize where she was, but then she spotted Joanna peering at her from the hallway.

"It's time to get up. Caleb and Rebecca are here, so try as best you can to make yourself presentable, then come join us for breakfast."

Molly supposed she must look a mess. She quickly brushed and pinned her hair, then looked for a relatively clean dress to pull over her shift. She hadn't a single unstained item left to wear, but when her cousins met her with hugs and happy tears, a disheveled appearance no longer seemed important.

"We figured you'd all be hungry," Caleb said, "so we picked up a fresh loaf of sourdough from Boudin's. They have the best bread in the city."

Rebecca unwrapped the still-warm bread and broke it into big, crusty chunks for everyone to share. When Molly caught a whiff of the yeasty fragrance, she suddenly realized she was famished. Moments later, only a few crumbs were left.

"Cousin Molly," Caleb said, "Rebecca is going to help Aunt Sarah make arrangements for your belongings to be sent to the riverboat. Meanwhile, I've offered to give Jo and Lizzie a brief tour of the city. Would you care to come with us?"

"I'd love to! I'll get my hat and shawl."

They stepped out onto Market Street, and Molly pulled her wrap tightly around her shoulders. Kentucky summers were languid, hot, and humid—nothing like this cold, damp San Francisco fog. Lumber, rocks, and loose bricks littered the gravel pathway, and she soon learned that crossing these streets meant taking a serious risk. One might easily fall into a muddy pothole, collide with a passing mule wagon, or be hit by a loaded handcart.

"Be careful where you step," Caleb said, raising his voice to be heard over the noise of hammers and saws. "There are brand-new buildings going up all over town."

Molly said, "Goodness, Caleb, so much is happening here."

"There is a lot now, but little more than a decade ago this place was a quiet, remote village called Yerba Buena. A few Mexican soldiers guarded the trading post and presidio at the opening to the bay, and native men and women lived at the mission and worked for the priests, but there wasn't much else to see. Then gold was discovered, and men came pouring in from around the world. Suddenly, the little Spanish mission town was the American city of San Francisco."

Sawyers, bricklayers, teamsters, shopkeepers, delivery boys, and workmen of all sorts filled the streets, but scarcely a woman was to be seen. Some of the men they encountered whistled or stared rudely at the girls, and Molly bit her lip and scowled when one man used the worst sort of language.

"Haven't those unmannerly fellows ever seen a lady before?"

Caleb shrugged. "I'm afraid this isn't the best town for young women. It can be dangerous, especially for a girl who dares to venture out alone. But I guarantee you, it will change. Someday San Francisco will be one of the world's great cities."

"Hmmm. I'd say it has a lot of growing up to do."

Caleb continued praising the city and pointing out the new buildings going up, but the raw energy of the place left the girls unsettled. They were careful to stay close to him for the rest of the tour.

On Sacramento Street, Molly noticed a large gold-lettered sign above the entrance of a wide, impressive building.

"The *What Cheer House*," she read aloud. "What sort of place is that?"

"Oh, it's a well-known room and board establishment. Very respectable. It even has a lending library for residents."

Joanna perked up.

"A library? May we go in?"

"Goodness, no. It's only for men."

This wasn't the answer Joanna wanted to hear, and Molly wasn't happy about it either.

"Sorry Jo," she said. "They must not realize that women can read."

"The proprietor's rules are strict," Caleb said. "His establishment caters exclusively to men. Women aren't allowed on the premises and alcohol is strictly forbidden. Still, it's one of the few places in San Francisco where a single man can have his clothes laundered and enjoy a hot bath."

"I see," Molly said. "That does sound civilized. Speaking of which, I was hoping to see one of the city's theaters. Are there any nearby?"

He pulled a watch from his vest pocket and checked the time.

"Mcguire's Opera House is over on Washington Street. I'm afraid the others are also across town. Sorry, Molly, we can't risk missing the boat to Sacramento."

She hid her disappointment. She'd really like to visit one of those theaters someday, maybe as the playwright. Hopefully soon.

***

"Hurry, Caleb," Rebecca said. "We must find a place where we can sit together. I want Aunt Sarah and our cousins to tell us everything about their travels."

Their little group boarded yet another steamer, this time headed upriver to Sacramento. When they were settled, Mother and the girls launched into a detailed account of their journey.

"You had quite the adventure," Caleb said. "I'm glad you made it here safely."

"We've been most fortunate," Mother said. "Now, Caleb, won't you tell us more about Sacramento?"

"Well, Aunt Sarah, the town is growing faster than you'd ever believe. Just now, workmen are breaking ground on the new Capitol Building. I'm told it will look much like the National Capitol in Washington, D.C., but this one has a big difference. Our dome will be gold-plated with precious metal mined from California rivers and hills. And there's big news coming out of Nevada Territory. We've found a new, extremely promising silver vein near Virginia City. Some say the value of the strike they call the Comstock Lode might be greater than the one at Sutter's Mill."

"Cousin Caleb," said Molly, "does Sacramento have a theater anywhere?"

"Or a library?" Joanna added hopefully.

"Well, not exactly. A few wealthy men subscribe to a private library association. Supposedly, their books will be available to the public someday. As for theaters, there's wild entertainment in the saloons and drinking tents along the riverfront. Definitely not the place for proper young ladies!"

Rebecca's eyes widened until he quickly added, "So I've been told."

Molly was beginning to understand the situation. Western theater had an undesirable reputation, and respectable theaters wouldn't be easy to find. Frontier song and dance shows catering to the lonely miners were likely to feature scantily clad chorus girls and bawdy variety acts.

She'd have to decide later how to reconcile her plans for writing plays with the realities of life in California. In the meantime, there was another question on her mind. It was one she'd had since leaving Kentucky.

"Cousin Rebecca," she said, "we're such a long distance from civilization. Has it been difficult for you, living so far from home and everything you've ever known?"

Rebecca scooted close to her husband and took his hand in hers.

"Molly, when I lived in Kentucky, I thought Sacramento was a world away. But I don't feel that way anymore, not as long as I'm with Caleb. Once you settle down, I know you'll love it here too."

Molly needed a place to think. As the steamboat continued its push upriver, she found a quiet spot to be alone, sat down, and put pencil to paper.

California isn't as scary as I thought, but it's challenging for sure. Kentucky's dark woods and lush green fields were kind and comforting, but these gold-dusted hills seem to expect more from me. They ask big questions and offer immense promise if I'm willing to work to find the answers.

It was close to nightfall when the boat docked at Sacramento's *embarcadero.* Most of the riverside shops had already shuttered, but loud noises and lively music rose from saloons across from the landing. Some of their fellow travelers headed into the bars, others picked up their bags and knapsacks and hurried away, presumably to lodge in local boardinghouses or perhaps with family and friends.

Mule carts stood nearby, waiting to transport visitors, and Caleb hired one to take them to a quiet street several blocks from the river. After a short ride they stopped in front of a narrow, red-brick walkway that led to a simple, two-story house with white lace curtains in the windows and a pot of petunias on the front porch.

"Here we are, Aunt Sarah," Caleb said. "I hope you like it."

Swinging open the door, he ushered them inside. Immediately to the right of the entry was a set of carved wooden stairs that led to the upstairs rooms. To the left, a doorway opened into a small front parlor furnished with an upholstered loveseat and sofa. A thickly braided, multicolored rag rug covered the hardwood floor and six cane-backed straight chairs circled an oak dining table with a crochet lace tablecloth and a round crystal bowl full of flowers.

"How perfectly charming," Mother said. "Girls, isn't this lovely?"

Joanna was already across the room.

She peered at a wood-framed picture on the parlor wall and said, "Look, Molly. Caleb and Rebecca brought your drawing with them all the way from Kentucky."

Molly had assumed she'd never miss their fat house cat. But seeing her pencil sketch of Peony almost made her cry.

"Our house isn't big," Rebecca said, "but it's more than enough for the two of us. We really don't use the upstairs. The small bedroom is for you, Aunt Sarah. The one next to it at the top of the stairs should be large enough for the girls to share."

"Housing isn't easy to come by around here," Caleb said. "There's no point in letting extra space go to waste. Most people we know invite relatives and friends to live with them, at least when they first arrive."

"We are so very grateful," Mother said.

"Not another word, Aunt Sarah. You are family."

Caleb and Rebecca are amazingly generous, Molly thought. *It can't be easy bringing four new people into their home. But almost everyone here is starting out new. Kentucky is in our past, and California is our future. This is where new stories begin.*

Chapter Thirteen

Sacramento

1860

Molly was eager to explore her new surroundings, but the first day had to be spent cleaning, sorting, and arranging their belongings.

"It will be hard for three of us to share this little room," Joanna said.

"One small closet and a bureau," Lizzie groaned. "It's a good thing I didn't bring much with me from home."

"We're lucky to have such a nice place to live," Molly said. "Let's each take a drawer and stuff our things in as best we can. I'm taking the top one. The two of you can fight over the rest!"

During supper that evening, Rebecca said, "Caleb, are you free to walk downtown with us tomorrow? I'd like your help showing Sarah and the girls around their new home."

"I can accompany you as far as Collis Huntington's hardware. I have a meeting there in the morning with Theodore Judah. He seems to think there's a way to put in a railroad over the Sierra Nevada mountains."

He explained how Collis Huntington and Mark Hopkins had made their fortunes selling supplies to miners and now, along with Leland Stanford and Charles Crocker, were trying to find a way to build a railroad across the continent.

"While you're at your meeting," Rebecca said, "we'll stop in at Miss Wingate's Millinery. I want Sarah and the girls to see her latest creations. I'm sure she must be the most talented hat maker in the entire state."

That night Molly was too excited to get much sleep. How could she, with a whole new world waiting for her? This was a brand-new place to explore, and who could guess what sort of rousing adventures lay ahead? Sacramento wasn't New York, but it was definitely more thrilling than Danville. The most exciting thing that ever happened back home was when Phoebe Springer fainted in church while the choir sang "Rock of Ages".

She woke with the morning sunrise and drew back the window curtains.

"Lizzie, Jo, wake up! You have to see this absolutely perfect day."

Mother was already downstairs helping Rebecca with breakfast, and the girls ate quickly, helped clear the morning dishes, and got ready to go.

Caleb was singing the town's praises almost before they reached the street.

"The American and Sacramento rivers merge just north of here," he said. "That makes this a superb central location for the state capital. The rivers have an unfortunate habit of overflowing their banks on occasion, but otherwise the setting is perfect."

Molly took a deep breath of the clean autumn air. She could see why Caleb loved this place so much. Tall cottonwood trees lined the streets, and their yellow leaves shimmered like gold nuggets in the late September sun. His enthusiasm was infectious, and when she looked at California through his eyes the future seemed limitless.

"Caleb," she said, "isn't that the wharf where the steamship left us the other night?"

"Yes, that's the embarcadero up ahead, but we'll turn left on Second Street. You'll find that all the roads beyond the waterfront are laid out in an orderly grid of letters and numbers. It's quite helpful, because this town's growing like Topsy. We're already as big as Lexington, if not bigger."

Molly supposed this was true, but Sacramento didn't look much at all like Lexington. This city was vibrant but raw, with muddy streets smelling of horse manure and a saloon on every corner. The wrought-iron balconies and floor-to-ceiling windows reminded her a little of New Orleans, but here the buildings looked as if they'd been thrown up fast, like circus tents, and were just as likely to come down in a strong storm.

Loaded wagons rolled by, kicking up dust on the street, and a blacksmith's hammer rang from a building farther down the block. At the sound of heavy leather boots on the boardwalk, Molly turned to see two men with unkempt beards, soiled, rumpled work shirts, and worn canvas pants.

They crossed the road, and she said softly to Caleb, "Those are scruffy-looking fellows."

"The men going into the assay office?"

"Yes, they look as if they've spent the night in a haystack."

"In this town, you can't ever tell a man by appearances. They could be poor as paupers or rich as kings, with their pockets full of gold dust or nuggets ready to be weighed."

Caleb paused to point out a new red-brick building next door to the iron and carriage works.

"The Hook and Ladder Association just finished building our new firehouse. Lots of wood houses went up cheap and quick during the Gold Rush, but unfortunately, they burned down just as fast. Now everybody wants buildings made of stone or brick."

He stopped in front of a large, two-story building where shovels, brooms, pitchforks, and sledgehammers were stacked outside the door, and Molly read the sign above the entrance.

"*Huntington, Hopkins & Co.* May we go in?"

"Yes, but here is where I must leave you. My meeting is upstairs."

Inside the store, a bald-headed salesclerk emerged from behind a tall stack of burlap sacks.

"Good day, ladies. Let me know how I can help."

Heavy hemp rope, rubber hoses, leather straps, and lightweight hand tools hung from iron hooks screwed into the rafters. Horseshoes, mule fittings, jars of stove polish, animal traps, kitchen implements, and household cutlery filled every inch of space.

"I've never seen so many different kinds of things for sale under one roof," Molly said.

"Yes, miss. All you'd expect to find in a hardware store, and more. Coal, iron, and steel downstairs."

"Thank you, sir, we're just looking," Rebecca said to the clerk before ushering them back outside.

"There isn't much of interest in there, Aunt Sarah. You'll find Miss Wingate's hat shop much more enjoyable."

Molly sighed. She would have loved to see more, but all in good time. And sure enough, the following months brought new and interesting experiences every day of the week.

"Mother and I came upon the most wonderful grocery today," Joanna said one afternoon.

She set a burlap bag full of spring onions, carrots, and asparagus on the kitchen counter.

"These vegetables look wonderful," Molly said. "Wherever did you find them?"

"Only a few blocks from here near the Chinese laundry. Mother says the produce at Mr. Ling's shop is so fresh, we won't ever need to plant a garden."

Back in Danville, Molly had never met anyone from China. But in Sacramento she met people from all over the world. There was always someone or something to write about, and she settled into the habit of entering notes in her journal every evening.

People of all sorts call California home. They say this valley belonged to native tribes for longer than anyone knows, but then Spaniards came and claimed it for themselves. Mexican governors ruled the land until America won the war with Mexico and took it away. Then the Gold Rush brought men from across the globe to work the mines, and soon Chinese immigrants and Yankee settlers were planting farms and orchards....

***

In early April, Caleb came home with astounding news.

"A Pony Express rider arrived in Sacramento today with a letter for Governor Downey from President Buchanan. It seems impossible to believe, but the message was posted in St. Joseph, Missouri only ten days ago."

Could this be true? It had taken their family two months to get to California and a wagon train needed four months or more to cover the distance. The world was changing so fast that a new way of life arrived almost before Molly had time to notice.

A few weeks later, she was at work in the kitchen when Mother came looking for her.

"You need a break, dear. Finish what you're doing, then let's take a walk down to the river. This day is too beautiful to be spent entirely indoors."

Molly was glad for an excuse to go outside. A slight spring breeze rustled the fresh sycamore leaves, and all sorts of wildflowers were in bloom. They walked slowly, stopping now and then to admire the bright blue lupine and brilliant California poppies.

"There's a little trail around here somewhere," Molly said. "It leads to a spot overlooking the river."

"Yes, I know where you mean."

The narrow, seldom-used path led through a tangle of blackberry brambles and wild currant bushes. A covey of quail skittered deep into the brush, a woodpecker hammered holes on the trunk of a sprawling oak, and a boat whistle sounded in the distance. Reaching the river, they found a clearing near the water's edge and sat to rest on a sycamore log.

"What a delightful view," Mother said.

"I enjoy watching the riverboats," Molly said. "They remind me of the adventures we had on the way from Kentucky. Honestly, Mother, didn't you wonder whether we'd ever make it?"

"Maybe," she said, smiling. "Anyway, that's over, and now we're settled."

They gazed silently at the silver river, each in her own thoughts.

After a minute or so, Mother said, "Molly, I'm sure you realize that we can't rely on Caleb and Rebecca forever. It's time for you to consider your future. You need to marry, and soon."

"There just aren't many bachelors around here with interests like mine. I think I landed on the wrong side of the continent."

"Perhaps," Mother said. "But we are here, and you must face reality. You do not have the means to pursue whatever life you desire. Miss Wingate managed to open up her own millinery shop, but most unmarried girls aren't so lucky. All too often they end up working as nursemaids or laundresses. Or, God forbid, entertaining drunken miners in a riverfront saloon."

"I only hoped to find someone who thinks a little like me. Someone who shares my ideas."

"What if we ask Rebecca to help?"

Molly sighed. Mother was not going to let the matter drop.

"All right. Let's ask Rebecca."

***

"Molly is already eighteen years of age," Mother told Rebecca. "I'm afraid she'll never meet anyone suitable. I hope it isn't too late for her."

"Don't worry, Aunt Sarah. With so many bachelors in Sacramento, she is sure to find a perfect husband."

"Not if she doesn't begin to socialize. I wonder, would you be willing to help her?"

Rebecca's eyes lit up at the thought of becoming a matchmaker.

"I do know quite a few neighbors. I could easily introduce her to some of our more eligible single men."

Rebecca agreed to take Molly as her protégée. At last, Mother's plans were set in motion.

"Remember, Molly, you must always try to look your best," advised Rebecca. "We will have to refresh your wardrobe, then attend to your hair. Rows of braids pinned behind the ears are currently very fashionable."

"I brought my best printed waist with me from Kentucky," Molly offered.

"Excellent. They are still in style, and I will lend you my paisley-print India shawl."

Once Molly's appearance met with her cousin's exacting approval, the two young women began regular strolls through the neighborhood. As they walked, Rebecca pointed out every bachelor she thought might make a good marriage prospect.

One afternoon, she discreetly motioned for Molly to stop.

"Smile," she said in a low voice. "Here comes Seamus Tracey. The man made a small fortune in the goldfields. Sadly, his wife died last winter and left him with four motherless boys."

A hollow-cheeked man limped toward them from across the road, focused his watery blue eyes on Rebecca, and said mournfully, "G'day, Mrs. Handley."

"Good day to you, Mr. Tracey," Rebecca said brightly. "Allow me to introduce my husband's cousin, Miss Mary Catherine McIntyre. She's recently moved here from Kentucky."

He began to eye Molly up and down.

"Pleased to meet you, sir."

She looked down at her feet, trying to ignore the fact that he seemed to be shopping for a new filly. Also, he smelled like he'd been brined in a barrel of pickles. Her stomach roiled at the thought of marrying such a sour-faced fellow.

"How are your darling children, Mr. Tracey?" chirped Rebecca.

"Not the same since their mother left us, Mrs. Handley."

"The poor dears. I'm sure they miss her excellent cooking. By the way, Mr. Tracey, you really should taste Mary Catherine's soda bread. It is exceptional."

Molly made a face.

"Oh dear. Will you excuse me? I can feel a tiny rock in my shoe."

Sitting on a low stone wall, she leaned down and slowly tended to her shoe.

I don't mind meeting a widower, she thought, *but I'm not looking for a job as a cook. Besides, love and respect are a thousand times more important than money. I'd rather fuss with this pebble all afternoon than talk about soda bread with Mr. Pickle-breath.*

Seamus Tracey continued walking slowly and awkwardly down the street. Molly stood up, smoothed her skirts, and breathed a sigh of relief.

Rebecca nudged her gently.

"He's actually quite nice. You could do worse, you know."

Molly grimaced.

"I realize you mean well, Rebecca, but a man with four boys isn't looking for a wife. He needs to find them a nanny."

Rebecca was trying to help, but what could she be thinking? Doors might open if she married someone wealthy like Mr. Tracey. Still, she hoped his sons missed their mother for more than her cooking.

On another day, Molly and Rebecca were strolling down Merchant Street when a smartly turned-out carriage passed them by. The driver's tailored livery and polished harnesses perfectly matched the beautiful team of coal-black horses. A red-bearded gentleman in the passenger seat sported a fine black suit, and the beautiful companion at his side wore an elegant dress in the deepest ruby-red velvet Molly had ever seen.

"There goes Governor Downey," Rebecca said. "Isn't he fine-looking? Caleb says he's very personable. A born politician—extremely ambitious and quite the charmer."

"Was that his wife in the carriage with him?"

"Why, yes. I've heard she's a Californio from a wealthy Los Angeles family. I wonder who does her hair? It was most elaborate, and so lovely!"

"*Californio?*"

"It means her Mexican ancestors settled in California before it became a state."

"Oh, I see," Molly said, thinking of what it must have been like long ago, before the Gold Rush changed so many lives.

"Don't you wonder what it's like being married to the governor? She's probably always busy entertaining politicians and so forth. I've been told her dressmaker is the best in Sacramento. I suppose you need stylish clothes if your husband's a politician."

"I imagine she has to practice smiling politely while the men talk politics," Molly said. "I'm not sure that would be much fun!"

Does a playwright need to look stylish? If so, I might need to pay more attention to Rebecca's advice on what to wear. Oh well, since I have yet to actually write a play, I'll worry about it when the time comes....

***

Despite attending countless Saturday soirees, Sunday picnics, and all the church socials organized for the young and unattached, none of the men she met stirred Molly's interest. There were always more than enough bachelors at these get-togethers, yet she refused to pay them any notice.

"I saw Seamus Tracey last Saturday," Rebecca announced one morning. "He had his new bride with him. She's quite the beauty, and I must say, he's never looked better. They've hired a cook and a nanny for the boys, and she has already begun plans for a splendid new house. The pair of them look happy as pie!"

"Good for them," Molly said genuinely. "I wish them well."

Still, the news was slightly upsetting.

I suppose Mother and Rebecca think I should have given Mr. Tracey more of a chance. I don't know, maybe they're right. I hate to disappoint, but marriage and family may not be in the cards for me. And if they are, shouldn't I try to end up with someone I actually like?

Rebecca was not the type to give up once she'd embarked upon a mission. Caleb had valuable connections, and he had promised to help his cousins, so she decided to enlist his assistance.

"Caleb dear," she said sweetly, "I need your help with introductions for Mary Catherine. We simply must find her an acceptable match."

Although he had guessed this was coming, he nonetheless gave her an innocent smile.

"Me?"

"Yes, darling. Your cousin needs to meet someone special, and you know so many exceptional gentlemen. Are there any upcoming events Molly might be invited to attend? Perhaps you could find a way to speak to the governor?"

"Governor Downey?"

"Of course. He might recommend one or two social gatherings for her."

Caleb rubbed his chin thoughtfully. "As it so happens, I have an appointment with the governor next week. If you'll remind me, I'll mention it to him. Perhaps Mrs. Downey would be able to help."

Rebecca was thrilled, and she was not about to let her husband forget.

***

As it turned out, Caleb's meeting with John Downey was quite the success. In late spring, a few weeks after Molly's nineteenth birthday, Señora María Jacinta Downey invited Rebecca, Molly, and Mother to tea.

The governor's gracious two-story residence was close to the center of town. White roses bloomed on either side of the front walkway and large pots of red geraniums flanked the main entrance. There were other beautiful homes in the neighborhood, but this one had a special sense of dignity and decorum.

"My, this house is impressive," Mother said in a hushed voice.

"It is one of the loveliest in the city," Rebecca said.

Molly pushed a wisp of hair back from her face and smoothed her skirt. "Is my dress too casual?"

"No, dear. You look perfect."

Rebecca presented her calling card, and a servant ushered them into a dark, wood-paneled entry room. Sunshine poured through the tall stained-glass windows of an adjoining hallway, framing the petite but powerful figure of Señora María Downey. She wore a high-collared dress of emerald wool, a color that perfectly complemented her dark complexion and warm brown eyes.

"Buenas tardes, Señora Handley," she said with a kind smile. "How lovely to meet you. Please come in."

Rebecca gave her a deep curtsy. "Mrs. Downey, please allow me to introduce my husband's aunt, Mrs. Sarah McIntyre, and her daughter Mary Catherine."

"Señora McIntyre and Mary Catherine, it is a great pleasure. My husband tells me you are new to our state. I want to hear about your travels, but first, may I offer you a cup of tea?"

Sitting at her finely polished mahogany table, they sipped hot, fragrant tea from delicate bone china cups, sampled an array of savory biscuits and sugary cakes, and spent the entire afternoon talking, laughing, and sharing stories.

"I am an Angeleno," María said, "born in *el pueblo de Nuestra Señora la Reina de los Ángeles*—the town of Our Lady, Queen of the Angels. Los Angeles was a perfect place to grow up. My cousins and I played like a pack of puppies. The street vendors, especially *Tío* Pedro, were always annoyed when we ran barefoot through the market!"

She laughed, took another sip of tea, and smiled at Molly. Molly smiled back, trying to picture this elegant woman as a pig-tailed girl chasing chickens and geese through the dusty fruit stalls.

"But then I had to grow up and learn to practice my manners. My husband and I met only a few years ago, when I was but fifteen. He was so gallant and handsome!"

"Do you miss your family?" Molly asked.

"Yes, but I write to my parents often, and they send me news of my brothers and sisters."

"I love writing," Molly said. "Letters, stories, and little skits and plays to perform with my sisters."

"Really? Do you ever attend the theater?"

Molly was unsure how to answer. Since lewd minstrel shows dominated western theatrical venues, a woman's good name could be tainted if she dared enter a theater. Mrs. Downey did not seem critical, but she chose her words carefully.

"Respectable entertainment is hard to find, so I haven't actually had many chances."

She smiled and said, "I understand. I would very much like to attend one of William Shakespeare's plays, but like Sacramento, Los Angeles has no formal playhouses. I hope someday the governor and I may visit a theater in San Francisco."

"That would be grand," Molly said. "Honestly, my greatest hope is to write for the stage. I think the world needs more stories written by women, don't you? With any luck, I'll have my own play produced someday. The idea may be foolish, but I think almost anything can be achieved if you only dare try."

Mrs. Downey gave her an encouraging nod. "Yes, Mary Catherine, I agree."

Chapter Fourteen

Senator Pacheco

1861

Molly thought of María Downey often in the weeks that followed their meeting. She knew that María's world had changed dramatically after the Mexican–American War. The Treaty of Guadalupe Hidalgo brought the region peace, but more than half of Mexico's territory had been ceded to the United States. Two years later, California was a state, and the American ways of doing things were decidedly different. Now, María was like a foreigner in her own land. Still, she was gracious, kind, and cordial to Americanos, and she treated Molly like a friend.

"I do hope something comes of our get-together with Señora Downey," Mother confided to Rebecca. "I don't understand why it is taking so long."

"She's just waiting for the right man. No doubt he'll come along soon."

Then, in April 1861, Caleb delivered alarming news.

"It's what we all dreaded. Word has just arrived by Pony Express that Fort Sumter has been attacked. Local men are forming a volunteer regiment to head east in support of the Union Army."

Mother threw her hands up with dismay. "Our country will be torn apart. I only pray that Kentucky will be spared from the fighting."

"And for our friends and families to be safe," Rebecca added. "But the war won't affect us here, will it, Caleb?"

"It can't be avoided entirely. Even though California has pledged allegiance to the Union, there are plenty of people in our state who will side with the Confederacy. Still, no one wants this war. I predict that it won't last long."

The news left Sacramento in a quiet, somber mood, and Rebecca had few opportunities for matchmaking. But life had to go on. Months passed, and since the war showed no sign of ending anytime soon, social gatherings began to appear once again.

In November, a letter arrived by the afternoon post.

"Molly, it's a note from María Downey."

"Really? What does it say?"

Mother opened the envelope and read the formal invitation out loud.

"Governor and Mrs. Downey request the pleasure of your company at an evening reception honoring Senator Romualdo Pacheco of San Luis Obispo.

With kind regards,

María Jacinta de Jesús Downey.

Oh, and here's a handwritten note from Mrs. Downey:

Senator Pacheco has recently returned from an extended stay in England. I am certain he would enjoy meeting you, and especially Mary Catherine. Please do us the honor of attending."

Molly wasn't sure what to say. What could she possibly have in common with Senator Romualdo Pacheco? Still, it would be lovely to see María again.

"What do you think, Mother?"

"Why, of course we'll go, dear. We'd be delighted to accept."

Rebecca immediately saw the event as an important opportunity for Molly. Besides, she and Caleb were also invited, and she was thrilled with the prospect of meeting the senator.

"Oh, my word!" she said. "Romualdo Pacheco is handsome, dashing, and altogether quite magnificent. He is said to be fluent in several languages and is very much the aristocrat. He has close friends and acquaintances among the English nobility. In fact, while on an extended stay in London last year, he was presented at the court of Queen Victoria!"

Caleb rightly assumed that Rebecca had a lot more to say about Senator Pacheco. He settled into his favorite chair and lit a cigar.

"I believe he's from Santa Barbara," she continued, "or perhaps San Diego. Somewhere in the state's southern region, if I'm not mistaken. Anyway, his ancestors arrived in California with the early Spanish explorers. The entire family is well-regarded. Did I mention he is not married?"

Mother raised her eyebrows and was suddenly eager to hear more. Rebecca now had everyone's full attention. She was so excited that she had to stop and catch her breath before resuming the story.

"Caleb," she said, "have you heard about the senator's mother? One of her sisters—Benicia, I believe—is the wife of the famous general, Mariano Vallejo, and another sister is married to Vallejo's brother, Salvador. Apparently, the Carrillo sisters have family members spread all over the state."

"Yes, that's true."

Caleb paused to put his cigar in a nearby ashtray.

"Pacheco's mother is said to be a remarkable woman. It seems she once had an interesting encounter with Major General John Frémont. One of her many relatives was sentenced to death for siding with Mexico during the war with the States. The man was about to face a firing squad when she approached Frémont in an attempt to intercede on his behalf. The general was so impressed with her eloquence that he halted the execution on the spot."

He smiled a little sheepishly.

"I've met Pacheco myself, actually. He told me about his youth, growing up on a southern California rancho."

"Why didn't you say so in the first place, Caleb? Tell us everything you know."

"Well, I'd say he's a good man. Educated, highly accomplished. He grew up Mexican but is comfortable around Yankees and is as loyal an American as you'll ever meet. Pacheco's a crack shot with a rifle and a remarkable horseman. He started riding almost before he could walk. I once saw him twirl a Mexican *reata* until he made it sing. He's even known to have captured a grizzly bear with a rope."

Molly laughed at the look of amazement on Mother's face.

"Honestly, Cousin," she said, "he sounds like some sort of storybook hero. How could anyone be that extraordinary?"

"Believe me, Molly, it's all true. You'll not find another man like him in the entire state, and that's a fact."

"Well, if such a man does exist, I'd very much like to meet him."

The whole story was unbelievable. And if it was true, Romualdo Pacheco was probably horribly vain and impossibly full of himself. After all, he'd met the queen of England! Still, she'd love to know if he attended the theater while in London. Maybe he's seen a play by William Shakespeare. It couldn't hurt for her to attend Mrs. Downey's reception....

***

The cold, wet autumn of 1861 was a welcome relief after the oppressive heat of the summer. Rain came early in November, and deep snow blanketed the Sierra Nevada Mountains. The morning of the Downeys' reception dawned crisp and clear, but dark clouds formed in the afternoon and threatened another downpour.

Joanna helped Molly brush and untangle her long, wavy hair, then set to pinning it up in neatly twisted braids.

"So, Molly," Joanna said, "are you a little nervous about tonight? I would be if I were you. Maybe you'll finally get to meet the man of your dreams."

Molly gave Joanna an exasperated look and smoothed a stray hair away from her forehead.

"I wasn't the least bit anxious until now. Thank you for bringing it up."

"Everyone says Senator Pacheco is amazing. I can't wait to hear what he's really like."

"I'll be sure to let you know. He's likely to be a gray-whiskered, pot-bellied, doddering old curmudgeon. I'll probably have to hide next to the punch bowl or behind the potted palms."

Mother came into the room and began tightening Molly's corset.

"You have nothing to worry about, dear. I'm sure the senator will be charming, but there will be other young men to meet as well. By the way, you look very sweet in this rose-colored sateen."

"The skirt isn't as full as it should be," Molly said, checking her reflection in the bedroom mirror.

"Rebecca says the bodice is still in style. More importantly, you are a very bright and intelligent young lady. Remember, poise and good deportment are a woman's most attractive assets."

Molly wasn't sure whether she entirely agreed. Meeting the right person had turned out to be even more difficult than she'd expected. She was feeling the pressure to find someone to marry, and after everything Caleb and Rebecca had done for her, she wanted to make a good impression that night.

"Mother," Lizzie said, "why is Molly invited to fancy parties when Jo and I are not?"

"Jealousy is unbecoming, Elizabeth. You'll have your own opportunities soon enough."

"I'm glad Molly is meeting everyone for us," Joanna said. "You'll introduce us to the best of them later, won't you, Molly?"

"I surely will. Anyway, this will probably be a dull, stuffy event full of tedious conversations."

"Aunt Sarah, Cousin Molly." Caleb's voice rose up the stairs.

"It's time to go," Mother said. "We'll tell you all about it in the morning."

Caleb was waiting at the front door.

Helping Rebecca with her cloak, he said, "It isn't far to the reception. We shall walk."

Rebecca looked down at her lightweight slippers and soft, buttery yellow gown.

"I hope the rain has stopped," she said, frowning. "I don't want my clothing ruined."

Caleb tucked his wife's arm under his and led her through the front door onto the steps.

"Don't worry, dear. We have umbrellas."

Molly knew Rebecca liked looking her best and also knew that Caleb would not want to be late. The others were already on their way down the sidewalk, so she grabbed her cloak and hurried after them.

Horses and carriages filled the street. Some delivered party guests, others waited for a turn to pull up at the main entrance. Molly saw Caleb nod at a particularly elegant, well-dressed couple stepping out of a horse-drawn cab and about to walk inside.

"Who is that, Caleb?"

"Leland Stanford, the incoming Republican governor, with his wife, Jane."

"Isn't Governor Downey a Democrat?"

"Yes, you're right. But like most Republicans, Downey is loyal to the Union. Quite a few Democrats support the Confederates and want to make California a slaveholding state, but others, like Downey, disagree."

"What about Senator Pacheco? Where does he stand on the issue?"

"Oh, he's a staunch Republican. Still, it's best to avoid talk of politics tonight. There's no way to be sure of the political leanings of those in attendance and secessionist sympathizers are everywhere."

Raindrops began to dampen the paving stones, so Molly followed her mother and cousins inside and checked her belongings at the door.

"Do mind your posture," Mother murmured. "First impressions are everything."

Molly lifted her chin. She wasn't there to learn about California's complicated politics. This was her introduction to Sacramento society, and she was expected to meet every bachelor in attendance. If she got a chance to sample the petits fours, all the better.

Guests mingled outside the inner room where Governor and Mrs. Downey were greeting visitors. Some gentlemen wore evening coats, others were dressed in blue Union Army uniforms. The ladies wore ballgowns with very low necklines and wide, elaborate hoop skirts.

Rebecca nodded toward a slender, pale girl whose dress and matching shawl were an unusual shade of purple.

"Molly, do you see the blonde girl over there? She's wearing mauve. It's the latest color from New York, but in my opinion it does nothing for her complexion. Oh, and look, there's the guest of honor, Senator Pacheco, with Mrs. Downey."

She followed Rebecca's gaze past groups of guests still waiting to enter the hall. A man of average size and height stood between the governor and his wife. He wore his black hair brushed back from his forehead, a fashionably long mustache, and a full, thick beard that showed not a trace of gray. As the receiving line inched forward, she noticed his strong, athletic grace and unmistakable charm.

Molly had supposed the senator would be pompous, annoying, and disinterested in everyone but himself. But here was a man with a kind greeting for everyone. He never seemed to stop shaking hands or leaning in to touch an arm or pat a back. The line moved her closer, and she caught the warm scent of spice and leather.

Now, Mrs. Downey was saying, "Romualdo, allow me to introduce Mrs. Sarah McIntyre, of Kentucky, and her daughter, Mary Catherine."

"Mrs. McIntyre, Miss McIntyre."

His voice was deep, low, and incredibly self-assured.

Mother murmured a few pleasantries, and Molly desperately wanted to think of something clever to say, but nothing came to mind.

Suddenly she thought of her favorite subject and blurted out, "Senator Pacheco, when you were in London, did you attend the theater?"

His eyebrows lifted in surprise.

"Why, yes. As often as I possibly could."

"Did you visit Covent Garden?"

"I did," he laughed. "I saw several fine performances, in fact." Then, softer, "They were something I will never forget."

"Shakespeare?" she pressed, ignoring his laughter. "The comedies?"

He paused, studying her with sudden seriousness.

"*As You Like It* and *A Midsummer Night's Dream*."

Molly's heart jumped. This man had seen her favorite plays performed on a London stage! She was about to ask another question, but now Mother was poking her ribs.

"Keep on moving, dear," she whispered, "we're holding up the line."

Molly stumbled ahead, not wanting to move. Finally! A man who was handsome, intelligent, and interesting. More to the point, he'd attended the theater while in London!

"We shouldn't monopolize the senator's time," Mother said, prodding her into the next room. "Let's find your cousins."

It was ridiculous. Wasn't Mother always telling her to show an interest in the men she met? But of course, someone like Romualdo Pacheco must have dozens of women clamoring for his attention.

"I see your cousins by the refreshment tables," Mother said. "Let's go over and join them."

"There you are," she said. "I was starting to wonder. Caleb wants to introduce you to his friends, but first, you must try the almond sponge. It is divine!"

Rebecca was sampling a delicate tea cake covered with rosewater icing and decorated with a tiny sliver of candied orange peel. But for once, Molly wasn't interested in pastries. She felt the senator's gaze from across the room and had no choice but to turn and look. Sure enough, his dark eyes were fixed on her. But then, he was laughing again. He said something to María Downey, who laughed too. No doubt they were talking about her, but what could possibly be so humorous?

"Molly?" Rebecca touched her arm. "Are you all right?"

"Oh, sorry. What were you saying? Something about Caleb's friends?"

Molly knew she'd best pull herself together. Her cousins wanted to introduce her to these young men. It would not do to be rude.

Rebecca interrupted Caleb, who was shaking his head vehemently and seemed about to give his opinion on the course of the war.

"Caleb dear, here's Cousin Molly. I know you'd like her to meet…"

Molly was unable to focus on Caleb's introductions. Did Senator Pacheco think she was an ignorant, unsophisticated girl from the backwoods of Kentucky? The thought was surprisingly unsettling. She turned to look again, and their eyes met for one dizzying moment. It was all she could do to look away.

This has to stop, she thought. *I'm blushing like a schoolgirl. I'll just have to avoid him for the rest of the evening.*

***

The hour grew late, and Molly congratulated herself. Somehow, she'd successfully managed to dodge him.

"Isn't it about time we said good night?" she asked Rebecca.

"Yes, we ought to be leaving," Caleb said. "It's too bad we didn't have a few minutes to spend with Pacheco."

"It is a shame," Mother sighed. "I suppose everyone wanted a piece of the senator's time. Perhaps his friends hadn't seen him since he returned home from England. After all, he was the guest of honor. Such is the life of a politician!"

"You're probably right," Rebecca said. "Caleb, would you be a dear and retrieve our belongings while I thank Mrs. Downey for the lovely evening? Would you look at the rain? It seems we'll need our umbrellas after all. I do hope my shoes aren't ruined."

Molly had other concerns besides her shoes. She saw that her luck had finally given out.

Mother followed her daughter's gaze and said, "Look, here comes Mrs. Downey. And Senator Pacheco is with her!"

Sure enough, here he was, standing right in front of her. There was no way to escape.

"Leaving already, Miss McIntyre? I hope you'll forgive me. I wanted to speak with you again this evening, but there was so little time."

Before she could answer, Rebecca swept in with, "Yes, Senator, we really must go. We live nearby and thought to walk, but alas! The rain grows heavier by the minute."

"How unfortunate!" María Downey said. "But at least you and Romualdo were able to meet one another."

"It is a pity," he said gravely.

Then his eyes brightened.

"As it happens, I have a carriage available at the door. Perhaps I might deliver your party safely home? It would be tight quarters, but more pleasant than wet feet."

Perhaps Molly had misjudged him. She hated to be rude, and it would be nice to avoid the rain. After all, she didn't want anyone's shoes ruined. Besides, who would be silly enough to turn down the offer of a ride in the midst of a downpour?

Rebecca answered before anyone could argue.

"Senator, we'd be most grateful."

"Excellent," he said. "Now, Governor Downey must be wondering where I have gone off to with his wife. Let me return María to her husband, and I will be back with my coat."

When Caleb learned of the senator's offer, he gave Molly a wide grin.

"Well done, Cousin. It's all turned out for the best, hasn't it? We're all riding home with the guest of honor."

Mother had to agree. Wasn't Senator Pacheco an impressive gentleman? Weren't they fortunate to have chanced upon him before they started home in the rain? Now their evening clothes would be saved from certain ruin.

Minutes later, Molly found herself seated in the dim light of Senator Pacheco's carriage, tucked snugly against his shoulder, breathing warm, fragrant sandalwood and damp wool.

"Miss McIntyre," he said, "María tells me you are a writer."

Molly struggled to keep her voice steady.

"Yes, I hope to be one day."

"And you love Shakespeare?"

She hesitated, then admitted softly, "I've read nearly all of his works, but I've never actually had the chance to see one of his plays."

"We must remedy that," he said simply.

Molly swallowed hard, thankful that the darkness hid her hot cheeks.

Then, before she could say anything more, Caleb announced cheerfully, "Here we are!"

Romualdo signaled the driver to stop and leapt down to escort them to the door. Mother and Rebecca hurried up the steps and into the house, but Caleb, Molly, and Senator Pacheco stopped to linger for a moment under umbrellas in the rain.

"Thanks, Pacheco," Caleb said, offering his hand. "You saved me from a scolding, not to mention having to buy my wife new shoes."

"The pleasure was all mine, Handley. But I must ask a favor of you in return."

Caleb gave him a questioning look.

"May I have permission to call upon Miss McIntyre one day soon?"

Caleb looked at Molly.

Her throat tightened, but she managed to say, "That would be lovely."

Romualdo flashed a brilliant smile.

"Excellent! Good night, then, Miss McIntyre."

He started toward the waiting cab, then stopped and turned to wave goodbye.

"I will see you soon. Good night!"

***

At breakfast the next morning, Lizzie gave Molly an inquisitive grin.

"So, was the party as boring and dull as you expected? All doddering old politicians?"

Lizzie could be a terrible tease, and Molly wasn't quite ready to face interrogation. She wanted to hide her feelings, but it was foolish to delay. She'd have to answer her sister's questions sooner or later.

"Not exactly. Actually, it was very nice."

"So, in other words, the senator was handsome and charming? He's stolen your heart?"

"I didn't say that!" Molly protested.

"Molly was introduced to Senator Pacheco, and we may expect him to call upon her soon," Mother said, barely able to contain her satisfaction. "He wishes to accompany your sister on a stroll through the neighborhood."

Molly's face turned as pink as the bouquet of late autumn roses on the dining room table.

Joanna raised an eyebrow.

"And? What did you think of him?"

"It was only a conversation. It was raining, and he offered the use of his carriage. He is a very considerate gentleman, and I do look forward to seeing him again."

Her sister wasn't about to let her off so easily.

"Hmm. A conversation in a carriage. With a senator. In the rain. Sounds to me like the beginning of one of your plays."

Molly tried to scowl, but her laughter gave her away.

Chapter Fifteen

The Great Flood

1862

Life's events are rarely as simple as we might wish them, and Molly was not able to enjoy the senator's company as soon as she had hoped. Unusually warm showers swept in from the Pacific Ocean shortly after John and María Downey's reception. They melted an early mountain snowpack, the water rushed down the hillsides, and California's Central Valley turned into a vast new lake.

"It's a tremendous tragedy," Caleb said. "Houses, barns, fences, and bridges have been swept up in the deluge. Countless animals have drowned. Churches, stables, taverns—entire towns have floated away."

"But Caleb," Mother said, "how could such a thing happen?"

"The rivers can't contain so much water. The northern channels have crested and spread far beyond their banks."

"What about Sacramento? If the rain doesn't stop, will we be safe?"

"Earthen levees protect Sacramento from flooding. Still, I'm sorry to have to tell you this, Aunt Sarah, but I have business to attend to in San Francisco. Rebecca and I are leaving tomorrow and will be away for at least two weeks. If you need anything, be sure to send us word right away."

Worry lines appeared on Mother's face, but she nodded reassuringly.

"We'll be perfectly fine. The rain will let up soon."

Caleb and Rebecca set out early the following day. Mother stood at the door, arms crossed tightly against her chest, watching them go. She waited silently until they were out of sight, then sighed deeply.

"Don't fret," Molly said. "This storm can't last forever."

"Certainly, it can't. And we have Leland Stanford's inauguration to look forward to next month. Perhaps we'll see Senator Pacheco at the celebration."

Molly assumed the heavy rainfall had kept the senator from calling upon her. After all, who in their right mind would go out for a walk in a cloudburst? She kept hoping for a break in the weather, but the dark clouds stayed put and the showers refused to let up.

The storm worsened, and wild, gale-force winds sent leaves and branches airborne. Uprooted trees thudded and crashed onto rooftops. The roads were clogged, debris blocked the streets, and everything smelled of dampness and mud.

It rained without pause through the Christmas holidays. The new governor was to be sworn into office on January 10, but by New Year's Day, the city was in terrible disarray.

Molly went to stare out the window.

"I'm afraid we won't be attending any celebrations today. Downed trees are blocking the way and our road is covered with water."

"Ugh!" Lizzie said. "I'm tired of being stuck indoors. This horrible rainstorm! Will we ever have any fun again?"

"I'm disappointed, too, but there is nothing to be done about it."

"If we leave the house, we're sure to be soaked through," Joanna said. "Our clothes will be ruined, and we will all end up sick."

"I want to see how bad it is out there," Lizzie said, opening the door a crack, then letting out a shriek. "Eeee!"

Muddy water surged and slithered over the front steps, bringing a tide of mice and rats swarming up the stairs.

"Shut it, Lizzie!" Molly cried. "Quick, before they get in!"

She could tolerate bugs and spiders, even snakes, but rodents inside the house were too much for her to bear.

Dirty waves reached the top of the porch. Then the threshold. Then across the parlor floor. Soon it wouldn't be just mice and rats swimming for their lives. Dogs, cats, farm animals—all sorts of creatures would be searching for high ground.

"Rebecca's rug is completely soaked," Molly said. "There's no way to stop the water. We've got to get upstairs."

They fled up the narrow staircase, dragging the sopping wet hems of their skirts and petticoats. From the landing, Molly watched the parlor fill with water. Mother's knitting basket floated beside her needlepoint cushions. Rebecca's lace curtains looked to be a lost cause. What a horrid mess!

"Our neighbors have already left," Joanna said. "We have a bit of food still in the pantry but no clean water. Who knows whether anyone will rescue us? I only wish we'd stayed in Kentucky."

Outside, the roar of the storm howled and bellowed like a wild beast. The city's earthen levees groaned under pressure and were simply too weak to hold. When the levees finally gave way, it was as if an entire ocean poured through the breach. The state capital, overwhelmed with water, was quickly submerged in several feet of stinking brown muck.

"If only I had sent word to Caleb before it was too late!" Mother cried.

"It's all right," Molly said. "Surely someone will come for us."

She threw open the upstairs window and leaned out to look around. A steady, suffocating rain sheeted the shingles and plastered wet hair against her cheeks. What had been their street was now a watery, windswept canal.

All afternoon the girls took turns scanning the scene outside. Then, at last, a small boat appeared, its oars pushing through the brown floodwaters.

"Over here!" Molly yelled, waving with all her strength. "Please —help us!"

The rower used strong, sure strokes to guide his craft, skillfully avoiding fallen tree limbs and floating fence posts to reach the house. Then she saw his face. Senator Pacheco!

"Miss McIntyre," he shouted, "I'm here to help. Bring only what you must. The floodwaters are rising—we've no time to waste."

He steadied the dinghy beneath the upstairs window and tossed Molly a coil of rope. She caught it with numb fingers and pulled with all her might.

"Hold tight," he called. "I'll keep the boat steady. Hurry. One at a time."

Mother went first, clutching his arm and scrambling across the slick shingles before dropping into the rowboat.

"Careful, now."

The dinghy rocked alarmingly, but Lizzie managed to summon enough courage to scoot in beside Mother.

"Drat these long dresses," Joanna said, crawling halfway out the window.

Her petticoat caught on a protruding nail, but what did a snagged skirt matter in a situation like this? She tore herself loose and Pacheco steadied her into the boat.

Now it was Molly's turn. Letting loose the line, she tossed him the rope.

"Trust me," he ordered. "I will not let you fall."

She leapt, his arms caught her, and he pulled her close. For one breathless instant, she felt his heartbeat through their soaking wet clothes.

"Well done," he murmured, and set her firmly beside him.

Molly's chest flooded with emotion. She never imagined California would be like this. Here she was, clinging to a rope in a rainstorm, trusting a man she barely knew. But every word of praise for him seemed to be true. And though the entire city was underwater, she felt safer here, next to him, than anywhere else.

Careful to avoid the masses of floating debris, Romualdo rowed his dinghy through Sacramento's submerged streets. Out in the open current, he gave wide berth to several thick clumps of bushes. Then a huge, drifting pile of uprooted trees slammed against the bow. Had he been a lesser man, the boat might have tipped.

"Look over there," Lizzie cried, pointing to a squawking flock of unhappy chickens stranded on what was left of a henhouse roof.

A sodden cow floated by on a raft of driftwood, then came a half-submerged haystack and the bloated carcass of a fat black-and-white pig.

"It looks like an entire farm washed away," Molly said. "Is there dry ground anywhere?"

With rain dripping from his beard, Romualdo gave her a confident nod.

"The riverboats anchored up ahead are taking evacuees to San Francisco."

Once he was certain the family was securely settled on one of the boats, he said, "You'll be safe now. When you reach the city, send to Caleb for help."

Molly stopped him before he could leave.

"Where will you go now?"

"I must look for survivors. Then I hope to learn Governor Stanford's plans for dealing with this disaster."

"I don't want to think what might have happened if you hadn't come when you did. I am so grateful."

His dark eyes met hers with a long, searching look.

Then he said, "I hope the weather is more enjoyable the next time we meet. If conditions do not improve soon, I expect to end up in San Francisco myself."

"If you do," she said, her voice beginning to tremble, "I hope you will look for us. I want to thank you properly for your help today."

"Do not worry," he said. "I will find you."

Molly watched him go, thinking how much she hoped he would do that very soon.

The riverboat was crammed with desperate, waterlogged refugees. She looked around, hoping to find a spot where they could all be together.

Lizzie wore a miserable look on her face.

"I'm so cold! And this place stinks."

"Hush, now," Molly said. "Sit here next to Mother. We'll be there soon."

To be honest, she couldn't say when they'd reach high ground. The Sacramento River spread out for untold miles in all directions. The center channel was so deeply flooded that the pilot was forced to steer by the tops of cottonwood trees.

"Look over there. What is it?"

Joanna was pointing to what seemed to be a group of travelers on a wooden raft. Only, the current was moving swiftly, and they were motionless.

"Oh, my goodness, those families are marooned on their rooftops!"

The captain guided his boat close enough to rescue the stranded families. Farther on, Molly saw what looked like leafy green islands in a sea of floodwater. It turned out to be people perched like birds in the branches of submerged trees. Somehow, they too were brought on board.

Mothers and fathers held crying babies in their arms and hugged whimpering children on their cold and wet laps. Molly was soaked to the skin, thoroughly chilled, and exhausted. She never knew how she fell asleep in the midst of it all. Hours later, they disembarked at the San Francisco Embarcadero.

***

"Aunt Sarah, I came as soon as I heard."

The sight of Caleb coming toward them with an armful of blankets brought Molly close to tears. He led them to a house close to the wharf, where Rebecca was waiting with hot coffee and dry clothes.

"You poor dears! What a terrible time you've had. Let's get you next to the fireplace and warm you up."

Molly's hands shook around her cup. She hadn't realized how much she was trembling until Rebecca wrapped her in another warm blanket.

Mother shivered, rubbed her hands together, and held them close to the fire.

"Caleb, you are uncommonly good to us," she said. "I can't think where we'd be without your help."

"Aunt Sarah, as I've said many times, we are family. Now, as soon as you feel up to it, please tell us what happened."

Mother explained how they'd been caught by the rapidly rising floodwaters, rescued, and brought to safety. When she finished, Lizzie spoke up.

"Senator Pacheco was unbelievably brave. I wanted to hug him and thank him for rescuing us, but all his attention was on Molly. 'Miss McIntyre, are you comfortable? Miss McIntyre, you look chilled, let me give you my coat.'"

"Molly, the senator seems to have taken a fancy to you," Rebecca said with a laugh. "I hope you plan to see him again."

Molly felt herself flush. She only wished she knew when or if she would see him again.

Denying the truth would bring endless teasing from her sisters, so she admitted, "I'm fond of him, too."

***

Over the next few weeks, Caleb brought news of the tremendous devastation all across the West.

"Oregon, Idaho, and the Nevada territories have been hit with extensive flooding. More than ten feet of rain fell in California's

Central Valley and a new inland sea covers over half the length of the state. Thousands of cattle have drowned. Countless orchards, farms, and ranches are in ruins."

"What about Sacramento? When can we return home?"

"I'm sorry, Aunt Sarah. The capital is submerged in several feet of filthy water. Those who've chosen to stay have to row their boats around piles of waterlogged furniture and decaying animal carcasses. I'm afraid we'll be living in San Francisco for quite some time."

"Do you think the capital will be abandoned?"

"It's hard to say. It will take a tremendous effort to clean up the city before anyone can begin to rebuild. Even Governor Stanford has decided to stay away. There's talk of moving the legislature to San Francisco, at least for the time being."

The legislature could come to San Francisco! If it did, Molly might see Senator Pacheco again. She wondered where he was, and if he was safe....

Chapter Sixteen

San Francisco

1862

At last, the rain stopped. Despite the horrific flood and the ongoing Civil War, people rebuilt their lives and carried on as best they could. Mother and the girls stayed with Caleb and Rebecca in a wood-frame house they'd rented on Washington Street. The low-pitched roof, overhanging eaves, and tall, narrow windows were solid and comforting, but the foggy days took some getting used to. Still, their neighbors were friendly, and Molly found herself liking San Francisco more than she'd expected.

The long, lingering days after the flood stretched into weeks of waiting and wondering why Senator Pacheco had not kept his promise to call on her. Had she only imagined the spark between them?

"There's no point in sitting at home, hoping for him to appear," Rebecca said. "You must make time for social pleasures."

"I know I need to get out, but there haven't been many opportunities."

"Caleb and I are planning to attend Elida Vineyard's wedding next weekend. There are never enough dance partners for all the single men at these sorts of events. I know Elida would be happy if you joined us. Don't you agree, Caleb?"

"Yes, you should come. The wedding will be at the new Russ House on Montgomery Street. The building fills the entire city block from Bush to Pine. It's worth attending just to see the place."

"All right, I believe I will join you. But remind me, how is it that you know Elida?"

"Her father is what you might call an elbow relation. Maybe you've heard mention of James Vineyard? He was in the Wisconsin legislature some years back but quarreled with a fellow politician. They settled the argument with pistols, his opponent wound up dead, and James left town. He eventually found his way to California. Now he's a state senator from Los Angeles."

"Hmm. I see."

It seemed that California was the kind of place where all sorts of people created new lives for themselves.

"Wait 'til you meet the bride," Rebecca said. "She's a girl with strength and determination if there ever was one. Charles will do well with her for a wife."

"Very true," Caleb said. "Elida is the smartest and prettiest of all the Vineyard girls and Charles has been courting her for years. It's about time she agreed to the marriage."

"I take it that Charles is the bridegroom," Molly said.

"Yes, Charles DeLong," Caleb said. "Another state senator. Handsome fellow, and almost as good-looking as Pacheco. Everyone says he's one to watch. Too bad he's such a gambler. He's also known for liking the ladies a bit too much, but Elida isn't the type to put up with any of that nonsense. She'll soon have him mending his ways."

Molly supposed the wedding would be entertaining, if nothing else. Who could say what sorts of fascinating gentlemen might be in attendance? After all, she couldn't keep waiting forever, wringing her hands, hoping Act Two would begin and wondering when Romualdo Pacheco would show up at her door.

***

"Rebecca, I need help with what to wear to tomorrow's wedding. Should it be the rose-colored gown again?"

Rebecca was happy to advise Molly on her attire for the Vineyard wedding. Though in fact, there wasn't much to choose from.

"The pale pink suits you, and it is a good choice for spring," she said. "Odds are there will be lots of flowers to match your dress. And with your rosy complexion…"

A firm knock sounded on the downstairs door, and Molly looked up. Could it be…No, probably not. Still, she could hear Mother talking to a man whose voice sounded very familiar.

"Molly dear, you have a visitor. It's Senator Pacheco."

"Senator Pacheco!" Molly hissed. "I was starting to think I'd never see him again. What should I say?"

Rebecca opened the bedroom door and went to lean over the banister.

"Thank you, Aunt Sarah," she called. "She will be down shortly."

Then she whispered to Molly, "Now, don't rush down all aflutter. Try to settle yourself first. Just remember to be who you are."

Molly took a deep breath, smoothed her skirts, and checked her image in the wall mirror. She tucked away a loose strand of hair, lifted her chin, and headed downstairs. Senator Romualdo Pacheco stood hesitantly in the front hallway, hat in hand.

"Senator Pacheco, I'm so pleased to see you again. How well you look."

Where had Mother gone, and why did her voice sound so stiff and formal? It wasn't how she felt. What did Rebecca say? Oh, yes. Be yourself.

"Miss McIntyre," he said, "I am sorry it has taken me until now to call on you. You must think badly of me, but I have just arrived in town. I am to be a groomsman at a wedding tomorrow…"

Molly stood wordlessly, completely out of things to say. Goodness, she'd forgotten how handsome he was! Then again, the last time they met, he had been rescuing her from a raging flood—thoroughly soaked, nearly exhausted, and amazingly wonderful…

Romualdo shifted his hat from one hand to the other. He paused tentatively, then turned and started to reach for the door as if he were about to leave. This wasn't what she wanted!

"No, don't go. Won't you stay?"

Molly stepped forward to take his hat.

"It has been a while, but you're here now. Please, come in and sit down."

He followed her into the parlor, settled into a soft cushion on the settee, and gave her a rueful smile.

"I would have come sooner, but the entire state is a disaster. The mess is not only in Sacramento, it is all over California."

"I want to know everything. But first, let me get us some tea."

Mother had set the kettle to boiling on the kitchen stove and was arranging cups and saucers on a serving tray.

"Take him a plate of your spicy gingerbread cookies, dear. Men always love gingerbread."

Molly rolled her eyes and smiled to herself. Mother never missed the chance to stage-manage a courtship opportunity.

She brought in the tray of tea and cookies and set them neatly on the table.

Pouring him a cup of tea, she said, "Careful, it's hot. But you managed to survive a flood. I guess you can handle a little hot tea."

He laughed, and the tension in the room eased a little.

"Gingerbread is my specialty," she said, offering him the cookies before settling herself into a nearby chair. "I hope you like them. Otherwise, I'll tell Mother not to let you in next time. That is, if you happen to come again."

"That is the last thing I would want. I mean, I do hope to visit again."

"Hmmm. So, tell me, where have you been?"

Once Romualdo started talking, his story poured out.

"I headed south as soon as the roads were passable. I had to check on my family, but the bridges were washed out and detours made travel difficult. It was not as bad in San Luis Obispo as in some of the other places I passed, but still, I worried for my mother. My stepfather died last October. Since then she has had only my brother to help her."

"Oh, I'm sorry. I, I didn't know."

"Of course not."

He looked away for a moment and took a deep breath before continuing.

"I am the executor of his estate, with responsibility for carrying out his will."

Molly nodded. Although she wasn't exactly sure what that might mean for him, she wanted to be sympathetic.

"That must be a lot to take on."

"It will be several years before everything is put in order. I am trying to salvage what I can of property my stepfather owned around San Luis Obispo, San Simeon, and Paso Robles. We had a punishing decade of drought, and now the flood has killed what was left of the cattle and destroyed much of the land."

She felt a pang of sympathy, remembering how she'd felt when her father died and the difficulties her family had faced.

"How is your mother?"

"It has not been easy for her. She has had many losses, and now there are immense bills to pay. In time she could lose her home near San Luis Obispo, the *Rancho de los Osos*."

"It must be very hard."

"Yes. But I do have some good news. With Sacramento still underwater, the legislature is moving to San Francisco. I will be living close by, at least for now."

"My goodness, the capital has been flooded for over two months already!"

"And still the water has not drained away."

He gave her a quick grin.

"Did you hear how Governor Stanford arrived at his swearing-in ceremony? He had to take a rowboat to the Capitol building. When he returned to his house the water was so high, he had to climb in through the second-floor window."

Molly tried to suppress a giggle.

"I shouldn't laugh. After all, we were in much the same situation ourselves. It's just so amusing to picture the governor trying to crawl through a tiny window."

Romualdo leaned back and gave a hearty laugh.

"You are right. It was quite a sight."

The gingerbread and warm tea seemed to have helped him relax. Or maybe it was something else. Maybe he felt as comfortable with Molly as she did with him….

"Tell me," she said, "by any chance, is it Charles DeLong's wedding you're attending tomorrow?"

"Why yes. How did you know?"

"A lucky guess. Elida Vineyard is a relation of ours. I'm planning to be there too."

"Then I will see you at the wedding."

"Yes, I will see you tomorrow."

***

When the cousins arrived at the Russ House the following day, Molly spotted Romualdo right away.

"There he is," she said, "with the other groomsmen. Do you think we should go over and say hello?"

109

"No need for that," Caleb said. "Here he comes now."

Romualdo had been watching for them. Excusing himself from his companions, he strode directly across the marble-floored entrance hall.

"Miss McIntyre, Mr. and Mrs. Handley," he said, "it is very good to see you."

"You're looking well," Caleb said, shaking his hand. "No worse for the wear after all the trouble in Sacramento. And I must thank you, Senator. I'm forever in your debt for rescuing my aunt and cousins from the floodwaters."

"Not at all, Caleb. Bringing Miss McIntyre with you today more than repays any debt you might have owed. But the ceremony will begin any moment. May I escort you to your places?"

Romualdo offered Molly his arm and led her and her cousins to seats close to the front of the room.

"You will have an excellent view from here," he said, then added softly to Molly, "Miss McIntyre, will you do me the honor of joining me for the festivities after the ceremony?"

"It would be my pleasure."

"I shall look for you then."

Rebecca had been right about the flowers. Molly's dress was almost the same soft shade as the gowns worn by Elida's four bridesmaids. Delicate, pink-tinted roses, carnations, and lilies spilled from the white porcelain vases displayed around the room, and pale pink carnations sprouted from the men's lapels.

The bride and groom recited solemn vows before the Archbishop, and after carrying out his duties as a groomsman, Romualdo rejoined Molly and her cousins.

"It was an excellent ceremony," Caleb said. "Short and to the point. Do you have any idea when the food will be served?"

"Caleb!" Rebecca scolded. "Do try to behave."

"I agree with Caleb," Romualdo laughed. "It is time to eat."

The Vineyards had spared no expense for their daughter Elida. Two hundred guests filed into the hotel's lavishly appointed banquet room. There they encountered sterling silver platters heaped with ham in aspic jelly, cold chicken and smoked beef tongue. Tall pyramids of macaroni salad towered over whole roasted turkeys stuffed with plump Pacific oysters. The champagne flowed freely, the orchestra played waltzes, quadrilles, and reels, and all the while, Romualdo stayed close by Molly's side.

During a pause in the music, he went to get them each a glass of wine, and Molly found herself standing near the bride.

"Mrs. DeLong," she said, "this is a lovely wedding. You and Charles make a very handsome couple."

Elida glanced at Romualdo, who was now in deep conversation near the punch table.

"As do you and the senator."

Leaning close to Molly and keeping her voice low, she added, "A bit of advice, Miss McIntyre. Life won't be easy with him. Men like ours live for excitement."

"Thank you, Mrs. DeLong, I'll keep that in mind."

Exactly the sort of man she'd been hoping to find.

The band struck up another waltz, and Molly and Romualdo took to the ballroom floor. Suddenly, acutely aware of his hand resting lightly against her back, she let herself forget all but the music and the joy of being held in his arms.

***

Sacramento remained almost uninhabitable for another two months. The legislature stayed in San Francisco, and Romualdo called upon Molly whenever he could. Mother encouraged the senator's visits. Her eldest daughter finally had a suitable beau, and an exceptional marriage prospect at that.

When Romualdo offered to take Molly and her sisters for a walk through the neighborhood, Mother agreed without a moment's hesitation.

"It is a beautiful day," she said. "Enjoy yourselves."

The younger girls dashed up the slope to the top of Nob Hill, leaving Molly and Romualdo to follow at a slower pace.

"You're very quiet," she said, holding her bonnet back against the wind. "Is the hill too steep for you?"

He laughed. "I may be older than you, but I still have some life left in me. Do you want to race?"

"Not in these skirts. You have an unfair advantage."

They reached a ledge overlooking the harbor and sat down to take in the view.

"Tell me more about your writing," he said. "You mentioned that you are working on a story about coming here from Kentucky. Is it finished?"

"Not quite. But honestly, I don't know if I'll ever find a magazine to take it. California is so far from the East Coast, corresponding with a publisher on the other side of the continent takes forever. It would have been easier if we still lived in Kentucky."

"It must have been difficult to leave so much behind."

Molly talked about her father's death, and how the impending war made Mother want a new life for their family.

"I understand," he said. "It is hard to recover from such a loss."

"Yes. Now you've heard my family story. I want to hear yours. The whole of it—not just the romantic, amazing Senator Pacheco version."

He stooped to toss a pebble. "You would find it sad."

"I like sad stories," she said. "They make people more interesting. If you don't tell me, I may make up something scandalous."

That earned her a reluctant smile, and he began to speak of his father's death. The rebellion, the bullet through the heart.

"My father was a soldier, an aide to the Mexican Governor, Manuel Victoria. He rode with him south to Los Angeles and met up with rebels at Cahuenga Pass. A coward named Avila shot my father in the back. I was only a few weeks old."

"So, you never knew him," she said softly. "That must have left a hollow impossible to fill."

He nodded once, surprised at her directness.

She would not let him fall back into silence.

"And your mother? How did she cope?"

"It was not easy for her. She was only nineteen, a widow with two little boys."

His voice grew steadier, and he spoke of his childhood in Santa Barbara.

"For the first few years we lived at the home of my godfather, Don José de la Guerra, *el Gran Capitán*. He taught me to ride a pony and twirl a lariat. '*Aldito*,' he would say, 'Practice with *la reata* every day, and someday you will be better than your brother Mariano.'"

"And are you?" she teased, trying to lighten the mood.

"Better than Mariano?" he laughed. "Some would say yes."

"Aha! You are competitive," Molly said. "You will be on my team when we play charades."

Romualdo laughed, then said, "Do you see that rig approaching the wharf? My stepfather, Captain Wilson, had two like it. When I was seven, he put my brother and me on the *Don Quixote* and sent us to live in Honolulu."

"The Sandwich Islands? Why so far away?"

"The captain believed in the importance of a good English education, but no such school existed in all of Alta California. His ships made regular stops in the islands, and the schoolmaster of the Oahu Charity School was a fellow Scotsman. So off we went."

"You must have been so homesick!"

"Yes, I was. My brother and I spoke no English and our teachers knew no Spanish. I did not see my mother for more than five years."

Molly felt the sadness in his voice.

"I can only imagine how hard that must have been."

"It was not all bad. Mariano and I learned to swim like the fish. My classmates were of mixed race—the sons of foreign sailors and Hawaiian mothers—and other schools refused to take them. They taught me the local language, and I learned English and French. But I nearly forgot how to speak Spanish!"

A brisk breeze swirled Molly's skirts and tugged at her ribbons. He reached out, gently brushing the ribbons back from her cheek. Then he seemed to remember himself.

"I see your sisters up ahead," he said. "Shall we join them?"

"I suppose we should," she said reluctantly.

Romualdo stood and offered her his hand.

We come from completely different worlds, she thought. *If I were to spend my entire life with him, I'd likely have still more to learn....*

***

A few days later, Romualdo brought Molly unwelcome news.

"The war seems far away," he said, "but it is causing serious trouble in California. It is not just minor scuffles between pro-Union men and a few Southern sympathizers. The Confederates are after our

113

gold and silver. If they get their hands on it, the tide of war could turn against us."

"But California sides with the North," said Molly. "Can there be that many secessionists here?"

"Yes, unfortunately. Dangerous numbers of them. There may even be warships lying in wait along the Pacific coastline. One of our men overheard a schooner captain bragging about his plans to capture Fort Alcatraz. When Navy sailors seized his ship, they found cannons, ammunition, and fifteen Confederate soldiers hidden aboard."

"What did they do with the rebels?"

"They are behind bars on Alcatraz Island."

Molly shuddered. The fort's prison cells were inescapable, cut into solid rock and surrounded by icy, shark-infested waters.

Romualdo's expression darkened.

"We believe the Confederates have hidden a stockpile of weapons south of Los Angeles. If they are not found, the Union could be in grave danger. Californios have formed a native cavalry, and Governor Stanford has commissioned me brigadier general. We ride tomorrow."

Molly looked down at the folded hands in her lap, then lifted her chin.

"You're leaving again?"

"I'm sorry, Molly. It is my duty. I have pledged support for the Union. Sadly, some of my relatives are rebel sympathizers. They still resent the Yankees for waging war against Mexico, and do not wish to obey American laws. They will never forgive the Union for turning Alta California into an American state."

"I suppose you are the most qualified for the job?"

He shrugged and said, "Californios know the area and the people better than anyone else."

"Well, I suppose if I am to keep company with a soldier, I must expect sudden departures. When will you be back?"

"You deserve my honesty, Molly. It is dangerous work. I may not come back soon...or at all."

Her throat tightened, but she refused to let him see the fear in her eyes.

"You'd better come back. I dislike unfinished stories."

A flicker of admiration softened his gaze.

"You make it sound as if I am a character in one of your tales."

"Maybe you are," she said. "But you'd best behave. You have yet to prove yourself a proper hero."

That made him laugh, low and warm, before he sobered and reached for her hand. He pressed it once, then got up and started toward the door.

"Where should I expect to see you again? And when?"

"I'll return to San Francisco as soon as I can. In the meantime, your family should remain here. Sacramento will be habitable again, but it may take years for the city to completely recover."

When he was gone, Molly pulled out her journal to jot down a few lines for the play she would one day write.

> *Mother: He's packing his things this very minute!*
> *Kate: Oh, 'twill break my heart if he leaves me!*
> *Mother: If you'd only listened to me, he would have*
> *remained with you.*
> *Kate: 'Tis too late. He's really going away....*

Witnesses never forgot the stirring spectacle of Romualdo's company, the First Battalion of the Native Cavalry, riding south out of San Francisco. His ragtag assortment of gamblers, ranch hands, shopkeepers, and musicians had been transformed into a splendid band of soldiers, all carrying lances with brilliant red pennants that fluttered like flames in the wind.

Molly watched them go, her heart torn but proud. Still, she was not about to sit pining at the window like some tragic heroine. She would write, she would live her own life, and she would be ready when he returned.

Chapter Seventeen

San Francisco

1862

Romualdo's advice proved to be sound. With Sacramento still in disarray, Caleb agreed that they should remain in San Francisco, at least for the time being.

There was plenty to keep Molly busy. Cleaning, washing, and cooking were household tasks all the women shared. Dressmakers were expensive, so if she wanted a new dress, she sewed it herself. Idle hours were spent writing down story ideas and filling a sketchbook with neighborhood scenes. The girls played charades in the evenings, and sometimes acted out the short skits and plays Molly wrote for the family's entertainment.

The late spring weather steadily improved, and the girls were eager to explore their new surroundings. Mother, however, objected to her daughters roaming the streets without the protection of an escort.

"We shall be perfectly fine," Molly insisted. "San Francisco is becoming more civilized every day. Besides, walking is excellent exercise, especially up and down these hills."

"It isn't proper for young ladies to venture out alone," Mother said.

"I'm twenty years old, Mother. I can look after Joanna and Lizzie. Actually, the three of us will look after one another."

It took some time, but at last Mother began to see that a little fresh air might be healthy for her daughters. She could no longer deny their growing independence. They were capable young women. Surely a little adventure during daylight hours would be acceptable.

So, one bright June morning, the sisters set out for the heart of town, each with her own purpose in mind.

"I want to visit Davidson & Lane's Dry Goods store," Lizzie said. "Rebecca says they carry the latest Parisian styles. I so wish I could buy something new. A hat, or at least a pair of shoes. Why must I be the youngest? Everything I own is hand-me-down."

"You're lucky to have so many choices," Joanna said. "I'm perfectly satisfied with my clothes, but it's been forever since I've had something new to read. I'm going to look for a good bookshop."

"Let's head for Portsmouth Plaza," Molly said. "The town center should have something to please us all."

She tucked her notebook and pencil firmly beneath her arm. One never knew what sorts of characters might appear on the streets of San Francisco. Sure enough, as they approached the square, Molly stopped to take in an amusing sight.

Two short, stout women were crossing Kearny Street. Dressed head to toe in elegant black silk widow's weeds, they strutted and preened like a pair of prize bantam hens. Elaborately beaded, netted, and feathered black hats teetered atop neatly coiffed hairdos, and their dresses exactly matched from collar to hem. Even the way they lifted their skirts to cross a mud puddle looked identical.

"Over there," Molly whispered, suppressing a laugh. "Have you ever seen such a pair?"

"Do you think they're twins?" Joanna asked.

"They do look alike. Let's try to find out."

The girls followed the ladies into a narrow shop tucked between the Merchants' Exchange and Piper's Pharmacy. They smiled politely at the proprietor and began admiring the display of beribboned bonnets and flower-trimmed hats.

"This one is adorable," Lizzie said. "I'm sure I saw something like it in Rebecca's latest fashion magazine."

"The yellow daisies are a charming touch," said Joanna, "but I prefer something simpler. What do you think of this wide-brimmed straw?"

"I love the blue velvet ribbons," Molly said, glancing toward the counter.

While her sisters *oohed* and *aahed*, she turned her attention to the conversation between the shopkeeper and her look-alike customers.

"Be sure the spray of leaves on those roses matches," one of them commanded. "They must be turned just so."

She picked up a silk flower, bent the stem between her fingers, and looked up to be sure the salesclerk understood.

"Yes, Miss Viola," the clerk said crisply. "Both hats will be exactly the same."

"All right then. Please get it correct this time. She is Viola. I am Lily. Do try to keep our names straight."

"I'm the one with the dimples," Viola added helpfully. "Otherwise, we're identical."

"Of course," the shopkeeper murmured, flustered.

Her eye darted toward Lizzie, who had perched a bright green satin bonnet on her head and was admiring her reflection in the counter mirror.

"I'll be right with you, Miss."

Turning back to the twins, she said, "Miss Lily, would you pardon me for just a moment?"

"She's Lily. I'm Viola," the first woman corrected again.

"It's quite all right," Joanna said, stepping in to spare the poor clerk. "We're only looking today."

"I don't know why she can't make an effort to remember our names," Lily muttered. "Come along, Viola. This girl seems more interested in window-shoppers than paying customers."

The sisters swept out, their black skirts swishing in perfect unison.

Molly walked over to the shopkeeper and said, "I'm sorry. It seems we've cost you a sale."

"Don't worry, they'll be back. They enjoy confusing me."

……....………….."How can anyone tell them apart?"

"It's not easy, that's for sure."

Later that evening, Molly described the curious sisters to her cousins.

"They wore perfectly matching leather boots and gloves, black silk crepe dresses, and identical jet earrings. Even their voices sounded alike."

"I've seen them downtown," said Rebecca. "They always dress the same. They carry matching black parasols and stroll through the neighborhoods as if they owned the city."

"Everyone knows about those twins," Caleb added. "They were married to brothers who struck a rich vein of gold back in '51. Unfortunately, the men quarreled over a card game and wound up in the Hangtown graveyard. Both widows were left with a fortune."

"How dreadful," Molly said. "But we couldn't help laughing all the way home, thinking of the sorts of tricks identical twins could play. I have an idea for a little play about them. I believe I'll call it *Nothing But Money.*"

"Speaking of interesting characters," Caleb said, "have you met Joshua Norton yet? You'll find him holding court on a downtown street corner, dressed in a military uniform with a feathered hat, proclaiming himself Emperor of the United States. He's forever lecturing passersby on his grand schemes—bridges, railways, even a tunnel across the bay to Oakland."

"We haven't seen him," Molly said. "Perhaps the next time we are out."

"Not to change the subject, Caleb," Joanna interrupted, "but do you know where I might find a good bookstore? We didn't see one today."

"You should try Anton Roman's new shop on Montgomery Street. I'm told it's the city's finest shop for books."

Joanna's eyes lit up, and Molly knew where they'd be going next. She wondered when her sister had grown so at ease in California. When had Joanna stopped anticipating danger around every corner? Perhaps she was a westerner at heart....

***

Later that week, the sisters set out for Roman's bookstore on Montgomery Street. They'd nearly arrived at the shop when a noisy ruckus stopped them short.

Lizzie was immediately alarmed.

"What's all that commotion?"

"Something strange is happening," said Joanna.

It wasn't the raucous laughter and honky-tonk piano music one could expect coming from a saloon, nor did it sound like an ordinary bar fight. Molly edged closer and peered cautiously around the corner.

A gang of angry men stood in the middle of the street, shouting at a wagon belonging to the city dogcatcher. The man was forcing two yelping, snapping mongrels into a steel cage.

"What do you think you're doing?" yelled one of the infuriated men.

"No strays allowed on city streets," the warden yelled back, then slammed a lock on the cage, climbed up to take his reins, and urged his horse forward.

The crowd followed after him, hurling bottles and profanities. A couple of the men aimed a barrage of rocks at the dogcatcher's wagon, but he was too far out of range.

"You'll hear from us," a burly man yelled, shaking his fist. "Those dogs aren't mutts. They're the best rat catchers in the city!"

Molly knew the dogs. Everyone in San Francisco did. The black-and-white Newfoundland was named Bummer, and the scrappy yellow mixed-breed beside him was Lazarus. Bummer had once rescued Lazarus from a savage fight with a bigger dog, then nursed him back to health. Since then, the two were inseparable. Beloved barroom guardians, they roamed the streets, begging for scraps and keeping the alleyways around neighborhood bars from swarming with rats.

When the girls returned home, they described the scene to Caleb, and he let out a low whistle.

"The barflies on Montgomery Street love those animals," he said. "My guess is that dogcatcher will have the devil to pay."

The sisters fretted over Bummer and Lazarus for days, until finally, Caleb brought home news of their fate.

"The Board of Supervisors held a public hearing today. After testimony from a parade of irate citizens, they've decided to make a special exception for Bummer and Lazarus. A resolution's been passed to give the dogs free rein of the city."

With so much to see and hear, Molly's notebook filled steadily. Sometimes, when she reread her notes, she came to the thrilling, improbable conclusion that her writing was getting better.

***

It was over a year into the country's Civil War, and life in California carried on. Molly regularly reminded herself not to pine, though she did check the street now and then, just in case a certain cavalryman happened by.

President Lincoln had good reason to worry about security in the West. Particularly in Southern California, where rebel loyalties ran deep. The Native Cavalry confiscated a small cache of weapons hidden near Los Angeles, then rode across the desert to guard the Colorado River and southern Arizona. Romualdo and his fellow Lancers did not return until late September.

The San Francisco summer had been wrapped in its usual dense fog, but when Romualdo came home the sun broke through the gloom. Molly couldn't wait to tell him her news.

"A New York magazine might want to publish one of my stories," she said, holding up the letter she'd received that morning. "With a few changes here and there, the editor may decide to print it."

"Excellent, Molly! I am of the opinion that readers will love your writing."

"I hope you're right," she said. "I am going to work on it straight away."

"I only hope you'll save some time for me," he teased. "My brother Mariano is coming next week. If the weather allows, we will go sailing on the bay. I would like you to join us."

Molly barely hesitated.

"May we ask Caleb and Rebecca too? They would love it."

"Of course," he said. "The *Consuela* is moored at Mission Cove. She is a fine sloop—fast when the wind is right, but steady enough for an afternoon cruise."

***

The day dawned clear and bright, with a brisk breeze perfect for sailing. Molly and her cousins took the city omnibus to Mission Cove and Romualdo greeted them at the dock.

"Oomph, this is heavy," Caleb said, setting down a large wicker hamper. "We've brought enough food to feed the Union Army."

Romualdo laughed and waved toward a man working on deck.

"Come, I want you to meet my brother, Mariano."

Mariano was clearly a rancher, not a politician. His tanned skin was deeply creased by years spent out of doors. His eyes were kind beneath a wide-brimmed hat, and Molly liked him at once.

"I'm afraid I'm more landsman than sailor," Caleb said, "but I'll help however I can."

"*Gracias, amigo*," Romualdo said with a grin. "We have it handled."

Within minutes, the brothers had guided the *Consuela* out of her berth. She caught the wind and went skimming across the glittering water of San Francisco Bay.

"Prepare to come about," Romualdo called. "Watch the boom!"

The sail swung sharply with the canvas snapping in the wind, and Rebecca squealed as a spray of saltwater splashed across the deck.

Molly grabbed for the rail.

"It's freezing!" she laughed, shivering.

Thankfully, Romualdo had thought ahead and brought waterproof mackintoshes for the ladies. Caleb was thoroughly soaked, but he didn't seem to mind. He grasped the railing with one wet arm and held Rebecca tightly with the other.

"Hold on, my dear! Here we go!"

They turned again. The wind was gentler now, and they glided smoothly past Alcatraz Island and across the bay toward Sausalito. Molly was having fun now.

"Would you like a turn at the helm?" he asked.

"If you'll teach me."

He firmly guided her hands on the wheel.

"There. That's right, steady as she goes."

Rebecca reached into the picnic basket and brought out the ham sandwiches, pickled vegetables, and a few slices of Molly's ginger cake. The sea air had sharpened their appetites, and the hamper was soon empty.

"Mariano, you must tell me," Caleb said, "Where did you and your brother learn to handle a boat like this?"

"Has Aldo not mentioned our time on the *Ayacucho* and *Don Quijote*? After five years of school in Honolulu, we spent six more years as apprentices on our stepfather's merchant ships. We learned how to use the trade winds and to navigate by following the stars. My brother kept an accounting of our shipments from *Alta California* and South America to the Pacific Islands."

"So, you worked the Pacific trade route?"

Mariano nodded.

"In Valparaiso, we exchanged cowhides and tallow from the California ranchos for Chilean saddles, bridles, and shoes. Then we set sail for Honolulu, where we traded finished goods for silks and spices from the Orient. These we sold back in California before repeating the cycle."

"Those voyages taught us more than business," Romualdo added. "We learned how to recognize an honest fellow or spot a thief."

"I see," Caleb chuckled. "No wonder the Republicans want to nominate you for state treasurer. You know how to keep books—and how to read men."

Romualdo smiled modestly.

"Let us just say I have learned to be cautious."

Mariano slapped his brother's shoulder and said, "There is no better man for the job."

"Thank you for your confidence, Mariano. Right now, I need some practical help. It is time to tack."

The boom swung again, laughter filled the air, and the *Consuela* cut a graceful path back toward the harbor.

After they docked, Rebecca and Molly lingered on the pier while the men secured the sails.

"I must say," Rebecca said, "that man is quite the catch. He's clever, kind, and clearly captivated with you. Can you picture yourself as the wife of a politician? You'd meet everyone in California who matters, or at least those in power. Who knows, Molly? You could be married to Romualdo someday."

"Oh, Rebecca."

Naturally, she'd thought of it. But what sort of role would she have to play in his life? She hoped that marriage, if it came, wouldn't mean giving up on her own plans for the future.

When they were ready to leave, Romualdo walked with Molly to meet the Market Street omnibus.

"I am happy you met Mariano," he said. "And I hope you enjoyed sailing."

"Very much so. It was a perfect day."

She reached up and tucked a lock of loose hair behind her ear.

"I loved meeting your brother. And I want to hear what you decide about next year's election."

"You will be the first to know."

Chapter Eighteen

An Important Question

1863

With Sacramento still recovering from the flood, the California legislature recessed in April and would not meet again for several months. This gave Romualdo, Molly, and her sisters ample time to explore the city of San Francisco.

A favorite picnic spot was at Fort Point, near the narrow throat of the Golden Gate. Here they could sit with a simple lunch of sausages and buns and watch the steamships and sailing vessels pass through the turbulent currents between ocean and bay. They also loved the beach south of town. They'd take a streetcar to the city's edge, then walk for miles along the shore, searching for seashells and sand dollars. There was always something interesting to find.

One day in May, they were strolling the beach by the water's edge when Romualdo said, "Look here, Lizzie, hold out your hands."

The receding tide had left a wavy line of bubbles in the sand. Digging swiftly into the wet surface, he brought up a handful of tiny crabs and dropped them into Lizzie's cupped palms. They wriggled in the sandy grit, trying frantically to escape.

"Oooh! They tickle my fingers," she squealed, and let them fall back into the surf.

They all laughed at the sight of the little creatures scuttling for safety and madly burrowing themselves back into the sand.

On the way home, Lizzie leaned close to Molly.

"I love Romualdo," she whispered. "If you don't marry him, I believe I will."

Molly gave her sister a quick hug. It seemed she wasn't the only one who'd fallen under his spell. Romualdo had charmed her entire family.

Then, in June, Romualdo surprised Molly with tickets to the theater.

"John McCullough is starring in *Hamlet* at Maguire's Opera House. It is the most elegant theater in the city, and he may be the finest actor in the West. I hope you will agree to come with me."

Molly had always longed to see the play, but Mother would likely object to Maguire's notorious reputation. There were whispers about a separate entrance for unaccompanied ladies, "fallen women" who were said to entertain single men in private boxes. Though the opera house occasionally offered respectable performances, many shows were shockingly risqué. An actress had once ridden a horse on stage, and she'd been clad in nothing but a flesh-colored body stocking!

In the end, it was an easy sell.

"Your father might never have approved," Mother said, "but you will be with Senator Pacheco. If Caleb and Rebecca agree to accompany you, I suppose it's all right."

So, Molly attended her first Shakespeare play. The performance was magnificent, and when the final curtain fell, the audience gave the cast their enthusiastic approval.

"John McCullough is extraordinary," she said. "Should we go backstage to congratulate him?"

"It is worth a try," Romualdo said.

"Good luck," Caleb said. "He'll be mobbed by a horde of admirers. We'll wait for you here."

"You are probably right. But if you and Rebecca do not mind, we will attempt it."

He took Molly's hand, and together they hurried through a side passageway to the theater's backstage. They wove their way through a musty maze of brightly painted scenery, curtains, ropes, and the remnants of past productions. Racks of elaborate costumes lined the walls—red and green velvets, blue and yellow satins, delicate laces, and heavily embroidered brocades. The air was thick with dust, greasepaint, and the smell of well-worn fabric.

"There he is," Romualdo said, nodding toward a small throng gathered in the corridor.

"Caleb was right," Molly whispered. "He's surrounded. I doubt we'll have a chance to speak with him."

Then she heard a deep, sonorous voice rise above the chatter.

"Please excuse me, friends. It is time I removed my tights!"

Laughter rippled through the crowd as the actor bowed with a graceful flourish and made for the dressing room. Before he could disappear through the door, Romualdo stepped forward and extended his hand.

"Mr. McCullough! A masterful performance, sir!"

He gave them an inquiring look.

"Thank you, friend. Most kind. Forgive me, have we met before?"

"My name is Pacheco, Romualdo Pacheco, and this is Miss Mary Catherine McIntyre."

Molly curtsied slightly, trying not to appear too star-struck. She'd never met a famous actor before, and this one was tall, powerfully built, classically handsome, and not at all standoffish.

"Mr. McCullough, you were absolutely marvelous. It is an honor to meet you."

"Miss McIntyre, the honor is entirely mine. But now, if you'll pardon me, I really must..."

And at that, he was swallowed up by another laughing mob of well-wishers.

"Oh, Romualdo," Molly said, watching him go. "He's just the sort of dashing, romantic character I'd love to write about. I wish I could write a play for him."

"You should, Molly. It would be a great success."

If only there was a way to make it happen. She loved Romualdo's optimism, but in reality, the prospects were dismal. She'd once imagined California a backward frontier, but now she knew better. Irish-born John McCullough learned his craft on Broadway beside renowned thespians like Edwin Booth. Like many others, he'd headed for the Sierra Nevada mining camps to refine his craft, then wound up in San Francisco. Now local theaters rivaled those of London and New York.

Newspapers like *The Californian* and *The Golden Age* rarely employed women and hardly ever published their poetry. Books and plays were seldom published west of the Rockies, and correspondence with publishers on the East Coast could take months. She regularly performed private readings of her work for family and friends or within the local ladies' literary salons. But these were short scenes, dialogues, and sketches—not full-fledged productions. Not yet.

"I appreciate your confidence," she said. "What about you? Have you decided whether to run for state treasurer?"

"Yes. The thing is, I will be obliged to travel the state and meet with voters. It means having to be away for several weeks."

"Oh. Of course."

She wanted to be encouraging and hoped he didn't hear the disappointment in her voice.

"How wonderful! I'm thrilled for you. The people will love you."

"We will see. I am sorry to have to leave you."

Mother was dismayed at the news of Romualdo's plans.

"Must he go now, just when you were becoming so well acquainted?"

"He won't be gone forever," Molly assured her. "He must meet with as many voters as possible if he hopes to win. He'll be back before the election."

"I do hope he plans to propose soon," Mother said, giving Molly a searching look. "Has he hinted at his intentions?"

She shook her head.

"Not in so many words."

Lizzie rolled her eyes.

"Aren't you afraid he'll forget you while he's gone? If I were away so much, I believe I'd find someone else to keep me company."

"Fiddlesticks!" Molly said sharply. "He's not a flighty fussbudget like you, Lizzie. He's a man with a strong sense of purpose. He'll be back as soon as he's able."

"Really?" she teased. "Are you sure?"

What a horrid pest. Lizzie would have added another jab, but Joanna spoke up before she had the chance.

"Romualdo's responsibilities are increasing with every week that passes. No doubt, while he's away, he'll realize how much he wants and needs Molly by his side. Just wait. We'll see them married before the year is out."

***

Romualdo campaigned up and down the California coast, and with Governor Stanford's backing became the Republican nominee for state treasurer. He also had strong support among Californios. If elected, he would be the first native-born Californian and the first of Mexican descent to win statewide office.

When he returned in early August, Molly met him at her door with a wide, welcoming smile.

"I'm so glad you're back," she said.

It was all she could do to keep from throwing her arms around him and giving him a kiss. After all, respectable young ladies didn't do such things.

"Molly, you do not know how I have missed you," Romualdo said. "There is much I want to say, but I have only a few moments now. Would you spend the day with me tomorrow?"

"Yes, of course, but I—"

Mother suddenly appeared at the doorway.

"Why, Senator Pacheco, you've returned."

"Mrs. McIntyre, the very person I hoped to see. May I have permission to take Molly to lunch tomorrow? I know of an excellent restaurant at Land's End."

She smiled knowingly.

"Yes, that would be agreeable, provided you return her home before dark."

"We will take the new toll road," he promised. "Far faster than jolting along by the dunes. We shall be back by sunset."

"That sounds lovely," she said. "Now, won't you stay for tea? I want to hear all about your campaign."

He glanced at his pocket watch and frowned.

"I wish I could, but I am expected at the governor's office and already I am late. Molly, I shall call for you before noon tomorrow."

She watched from the doorway as he strode down the street, then laughed and waved when he turned and called back, "Be sure to wear a warm wrap."

***

The scene at Land's End overlook was nothing less than spectacular. Heavy waves crashed against the dark basalt cliffs and a freezing wind sent sprays of salt water high into the air. Long-necked cormorants dove headfirst into the ocean, fishing for a meal of anchovies or sardines. Picnickers carried baskets and blankets and wandered the bluffs above Ocean Beach, searching for the perfect spot to sit while guarding their hats, kerchiefs, and parasols from the stiff ocean breeze.

Molly raised her voice over the roar of the breakers.

"I'm glad you warned me to bring a warm coat!"

"It is cold, isn't it? Come, let us hurry inside."

Romualdo slipped his arm over Molly's shivering shoulders and guided her down a flight of carved granite steps to the great door of the Cliff House Restaurant. The *maître d'* led them to a small corner table with a breathtaking view of the sea.

"Romualdo, this is so beautiful," she said, gazing off to the distant horizon.

"I hoped you would like it. I wanted this day to be special."

He ordered oysters and champagne, and Molly gazed out the window, thinking how much her life had changed in the four short years since she'd left Kentucky. She'd left for California with little more than hopes and dreams, and San Francisco had turned out to be an exciting, vibrant place, rich with stories, theaters, and fascinating people.

Romualdo broke the silence.

"Tell me, how is your writing coming along?"

"I've had no progress in getting published," she admitted. "But I haven't lost all hope. I'm full of new ideas for stories and plays. I'd love to have you read what I've written."

"I would be honored."

"What about your campaign?" she asked. "Did everything go well in the south?"

He laughed and said, "I am fortunate to have many relatives. With eleven aunts and uncles on my mother's side and more cousins than I can count, I expect strong support among Californios."

"Be serious, Romualdo. The election is only a few weeks away."

"I have Governor Stanford's endorsement, which carries some weight. We will see if he can convince everyone else to vote for me."

Then his tone softened, and he reached across the table to take her hand.

"Molly," he said, "There's something I must say."

Her heart gave a startled leap.

"Yes?"

"I missed you deeply while I was away. I have realized that I want you always in my life. I hope you feel the same."

"I do," she said, her voice quiet but steady.

"Then, will you marry me?"

For a moment, the ocean's roar dimmed to a distant hush. These were words she'd longed to hear since the day they'd first met. There could be only one answer.

"Goodness, yes! Of course, I will."

Kentucky twilight lingers soft and long into the evening, but on the Pacific Coast, darkness falls swiftly at the instant the sun drops into the ocean. Molly wished the day would last forever, but they were expected home by dusk. And truthfully, she could hardly wait to share her news.

Chapter Nineteen

Los Pachecos

1863–1864

In August 1863, during the campaign for state treasurer, Romualdo formally asked Mother for Molly's hand in marriage. She granted it at once. Why wouldn't she? Senator Pacheco was an exceptional match for her daughter. Mrs. Sarah McIntyre proudly announced her daughter's engagement, and the wedding was set for Saturday, October 31, Romualdo's birthday.

The world seemed to grow smaller every year. Though a trip across the nation still took several weeks, California seemed closer to the East than ever before. The Pony Express had been replaced by telegraph lines, and news could cross the continent in an instant. Molly was overjoyed when a Western Union telegram arrived on the eve of her wedding.

CONGRATULATIONS LOVE JOY BEST WISHES STOP
LOUIS AND MARY

Molly set the slip of paper aside and sighed. "I wish Uncle Louis and Aunt Mary could have been here. It's been so long since we've seen them. I know they would love Romualdo if they could ever meet him. And I'm sorry Father never had the chance to know him."

"Your father would be very proud," Mother said softly. "Still, we can't let yesterday's regrets shadow today's blessings. Your wedding will be perfectly beautiful."

She forced a smile and handed Molly a flat package wrapped in thin white tissue.

"A small gift."

Molly carefully undid the wrapping.

"White gloves! Oh, Mother, thank you."

"You needed a new pair," said Mother, blinking back tears. "You may wear my Brussels lace shawl as a veil, if you like. Just to borrow, naturally. Joanna and Elizabeth will want it for their weddings one day."

There was no way Molly could afford to have a new dress made for this one event. She had resigned herself to wearing one already in her wardrobe, but Rebecca came to the rescue.

"I have a nearly new gown of cream-colored silk," she said. "It should fit you perfectly. Did you know, Queen Victoria wore white when she married Prince Albert? Now every girl wants a white dress for her wedding."

Molly thanked her with a warm hug. How could one not appreciate Rebecca? She knew the appropriate attire for every occasion.

At last the wedding day arrived. When the carriage drew up to the doors of St. Mary's, Caleb offered his hand to help Molly out, then motioned toward the cathedral's entrance.

"There he is, waiting for you."

Romualdo stood framed beneath the Gothic arch at the top of the steps. At his side were his brother Mariano and a tiny woman dressed head to toe in black. A delicate *mantilla* of Spanish lace framed her dark hair, and only the faintest trace of silver showed at her temples. At fifty-one years of age, *Doña* María Ramona Pacheco y Wilson was still formidable and strikingly beautiful.

Romualdo came to greet Molly and her family, then turned to his mother.

"*Madre,*" he said, "allow me to introduce Mrs. Sarah McIntyre."

Doña Ramona extended her hand graciously. "*Con mucho gusto,*" she said, her accent kind but dignified. "It is a great pleasure."

Mother curtsied and murmured a polite greeting.

"And this," said Romualdo, "is Molly."

"I am so happy to meet you," Doña Ramona said with a slight bow and a warm, welcoming smile.

Molly had worried Romualdo's mother might disapprove of her son's choice of a bride. After all, she was a newcomer to California with little to show for herself beyond good manners and determination. Yet Doña Ramona's smile was reassuring, her eyes were friendly, and her voice was gentle. In that moment, Molly knew all would be well.

The families spoke quietly on the church steps, waiting for the parish priest to summon them inside.

"It is time," he finally announced. "Please come in."

It was a modest wedding. Few of Molly's relatives lived nearby and her mother did not have the means to stage a grand affair. Still, the small group of family and friends who witnessed the ceremony were happy to share the couple's joy.

When the vows were said and the newlyweds left the church hand-in-hand, Romualdo pulled Molly close and whispered, "Mrs. Pacheco, I am so happy."

After the wedding, Caleb and Rebecca hosted a joyous breakfast reception, and in the midst of the celebration, Mariano got up to raise his glass.

"Ladies and gentlemen, *señoras y señores,* may I have your attention? I am Mariano Pacheco, the older, far better-looking brother of our new state treasurer!"

The room erupted with applause and laughter.

When it had quieted, Mariano said, "I assure you, my friends, that you will never meet a stronger or braver vaquero than my brother. But we must congratulate him today for capturing a treasure greater than all the gold in California. To the bride and groom!"

He hugged his brother, glasses clinked, and voices rose in cheers.

"Hurrah for Pacheco!"

Then, before anyone could protest, Romualdo swept Molly into his arms for a kiss.

When the guests began to take their leave, the newlyweds said goodbye to Molly's family, then to Mariano and Doña Ramona.

"I wish we could stay longer," Romualdo said, "but we must leave for Sacramento. Work waits for me at the capital."

Doña Ramona took Molly's arm and said, "My son has chosen a fine woman to marry. I pray for God's blessings upon you both."

"Thank you, *Doña* Ramona. I hope to visit you someday at the *Rancho de los Osos.*"

"May that day be very soon."

***

"Molly, I have important business in San Luis Obispo," Romualdo said a few months after the wedding. "I would like us to make the journey together. Will you come with me?"

She needed no convincing. Molly was eager to see the countryside, and she was curious about life on a California *rancho*. After all, it was the world that had shaped her husband's childhood. She also knew how heavily his family problems weighed upon him. His stepfather's estate remained unsettled, Mariano's health was failing, and *Doña* Ramona had too many burdens to carry alone.

"Of course, I'll come," she said. "When do we leave?"

"As soon as weather allows. It seems that George Hearst wants to buy a tract of my mother's land. Once her holdings at Cambria and San Simeon are sold, the *Rancho de los Osos* will be nearly all she has left."

"Why does she want to sell?"

Romualdo frowned.

"It is not that she *wants* to sell. Under Mexican rule, our ranches were open and unfenced. No one worried of boundaries and deeds. But now, American courts demand that Californio ranchers produce records to verify ownership. The process is time-consuming and expensive."

"So, she needs money to pay the lawyers?"

"Yes. The years of drought, followed by the floods, have destroyed our cattle herds. Little is left to sell except the land itself. Yankee lawyers descend on us like vultures, and taxes and legal fees nearly ruin us."

"Is there any way I can help?"

He shook his head, smiling faintly. "All I truly need is to have you with me."

***

The journey from San Francisco to the landing at Avila took two days by coastal steamer. A wagon brought them from the harbor and through San Luis Obispo to a road leading further south. There, the air was warm and scented with sage.

"Our land begins here," Romualdo said as they turned west toward the ocean. "We will be there soon."

The way led through a soft, verdant valley and followed a clear stream lined with thirsty willows and lush, yellow-green grasses. A pair of gray foxes stared curiously before darting into a dense growth of coyote brush. The road closely followed the streambank, and their horses startled a flock of mallards into a whirl of wings. Higher up the slopes, skittish black-tailed deer grazed among the granite boulders and eyed the travelers warily. After all, these animals were a favored meal of mountain lions and grizzlies, and it was the Ranch of the Bears.

After a few miles, Romualdo turned the horses north. They climbed a gently sloping hill and passed a small sheepfold near the creek, a barn for farm animals, and corrals for the horses and mules.

Doña Ramona's two-story adobe held a commanding view of the countryside. Vegetable and flower gardens grew close to the main buildings, wooden shutters framed the open windows of the upper rooms, and surrounding patios opened onto a small vineyard and an orchard of figs, pomegranates, and olives.

Their wagon stopped in the central courtyard, the great wooden door of the house opened, and Doña Ramona herself came out to greet them.

"Molly, *Aldito*! How good to see you! Come in, queridos, come in."

Molly returned her embrace.

"Romualdo did not tell me this would be so beautiful!"

"You must be tired from your journey. Take time to rest before the evening meal. Then we shall have time to talk."

"*Muchas gracias, Doña* Ramona."

"Molly! *¿Hablas español?*"

"I am learning, little by little. Romualdo is teaching me."

"We shall practice while you are here," she said, smiling. "Now, come with me. Your room is ready for you."

Molly was grateful for the coolness of the building's thick adobe walls. She sat on a low leather stool, pulled off her dusty boots, stretched her tired legs, and looked around.

Although the room was of modest size, high ceilings and pale plaster walls made it seem airy and bright. Crisp white linens and plump goose-feather pillows dressed the canopied bed and a blue-and-white porcelain pitcher sat on the washstand beside a bowl of fresh, ripe oranges. In one corner, a small wooden altar bore a gold-framed image of the Virgin of Guadalupe, a beeswax taper in a silver candleholder, and a string of dried herbs and flowers.

"Aldo, this room is lovely," she said. "Will you show me around the grounds tomorrow?"

"I wish I could," he said, unbuckling his long overcoat and setting it over a chair. "I have meetings with the lawyers in the morning. My mother will show you the rancho. You will be in good hands."

***

Molly awoke to the sound of birdsong and the scent of wood smoke drifting through the open window. She'd slept soundly and was surprisingly hungry. Following her nose to the dining room, she discovered Romualdo and his mother sharing a breakfast of *chorizos, tortillas,* and fresh hen's eggs.

"*Buenos días,* Molly," Doña Ramona said. "*Por favor,* come join us."

"I wondered when you would finally wake up," Romualdo laughed. "You must try the *champurrado.* When I was a boy, it was my favorite treat."

Doña Ramona filled a cup with steaming hot, chocolate-rich cow's milk thickened with masa. Molly took a sip and smacked her lips.

"This is delicious. Will you teach me how to make it?"

"Of course," Ramona said. "It is easy. But you must stir it with patience—like life itself."

Romualdo laughed again and said, "My mother is full of wisdom."

He pushed back his chair and stood up to go.

"*Madre,* I must leave for town. I will be gone most of the day. Will you kindly take care of my wife?"

"We shall be so busy," Ramona said with a twinkle, "we may not notice you are gone."

Molly began to gather the breakfast dishes, but Ramona stopped her with an upraised hand.

"Alma will tend to this. It is a beautiful morning. Let us go into the garden."

Molly followed her through the arched doorway and out into a sunny patio. A low wooden gate opened into a brilliant, spring-blooming space. She stopped and took a deep breath—the air was full of flowery perfume.

Deep-purple morning glories trailed over whitewashed adobe walls. A tangle of blue fiesta flowers mingled with orange poppies and pink flowering currant. Honeybees, collecting loads of yellow pollen, buzzed lazily among the blooms.

"How absolutely charming," Molly said.

"It gives me joy," Ramona replied. "And I must tell you, *mi nuera,* I am happy to see my son so content."

They strolled arm in arm along the gravel path, and as they walked, Molly answered Ramona's questions about her journey from Kentucky.

After a while she said, "What was it like for you, growing up in San Diego?"

Ramona gave her a gentle smile.

"The *casa de Carrillo* was a lively place. Ours was a large family and we welcomed all sorts of people to our home. Soldiers, politicians, foreign traders, neighbors, relatives—they all came for conversation, and to hear my father play his violin.

"I was only thirteen when I met Aldo's father. He was a soldier from Mexico, an aide to the new governor. So tall and handsome in his military uniform! I thought him the most gallant man I had ever seen, and we fell in love."

"You were so young!"

"Yes, and my parents made us wait a full year before granting us permission to marry. I was the first in our family to wed, even before my sister Josepha eloped with Henry Fitch. But that is a story for another time. There were thirteen of us—I had six brothers and six sisters. Perhaps my father was worried over how many mouths he had to feed."

Molly smiled at the thought of her own mother having to find husbands for seven girls.

"We were married in the mission church of San Diego de Alcalá," Ramona went on. "I wore a red silk gown and my mother's ivory comb, and with orange blossoms in my hair I felt like a Spanish princess.

"*Rancheros* came from as far as Los Angeles to witness our vows. They arrived wearing black velvet jackets, riding handsome, high-stepping horses with silver bridles and finely tooled leather saddles. What a sight they were!

"After the ceremony, Governor Echeandía himself led a procession through the streets of town. The tables in the patio of our adobe overflowed with fruit, sausages, and wine. My father roasted a whole steer in the courtyard. How the smell of rich meat on the grill made my mouth water!

"Then we had a grand *fandango,* with music and dancing in the village square. The men in *sombreros* and wide-legged pants stomped their black boots to the rhythm of the music, and red sashes flashed as they twirled. Young girls in colorful skirts swirled around the men, little children played among the dancers, and the old folks laughed and clapped in time to the songs. They were probably thinking of their own weddings from long, long ago."

"What a grand celebration that must have been."

"We were very happy."

Ramona's voice trailed away, and she rose to turn toward the house.

"It grows warm. Shall we go back?"

Molly heard the quiet sorrow in her voice and wished she knew how to help. Ramona had endured the loss of two husbands and years of hardship. It was impossible to understand her pain. Being there, listening to her story, was all she could offer. Following her into the house, she thought how this woman's life told the history of California itself.

***

The next morning, Romualdo left early for town, but Molly didn't mind. She was glad to spend more time with his mother.

"It is such a pretty day," she said. "Might we walk again?"

"Of course," Ramona said. "I will show you the orchard."

They followed a rocky dirt path beyond the adobe to a small grove of lemon and olive trees. There was a sweet scent of citrus air and the garden was alive with humming insects. The gravel crunched beneath their shoes, and a pair of quail darted out from the brush ahead. Molly smiled and watched their little bobbing top knots until the birds disappeared behind a clump of tall grass.

The women stopped to sit on a low stone bench in the filtered shade. The morning breeze was cool, and Ramona shifted in her seat, trying to find a bit of warmth in the morning sun. Molly noticed a bright glint of light shine from the thin chain at Ramona's throat, and thought of the story she'd heard the day before.

"Doña Ramona," she said, "the silver cross you always wear—was it given to you by someone in your family?"

Ramona reached up to finger her delicate necklace.

"It belonged to *mi abuela*, María Feliciana Arballo. She was among the first women to come from Mexico and settle in Alta California."

"Then, your family has been here for a very long time."

She nodded and said, "My grandfather, Juan Francisco López, was a soldier who came to California with the explorer Gaspar de Portolá. My grandmother followed Juan Bautista de Anza's army through the desert to California, and *Padre* Serra gave her this cross soon after she arrived in San Diego."

"Padre Serra," Molly said softly. "*Fray* Junípero Serra, the Franciscan priest who built the missions?"

"The same. He was a holy man, but stern. He brought native people to the missions and taught them our prayers, our ways, and our language. Many died or fled to the hills. Some say he brought salvation; others say he brought only sorrow."

Ramona's eyes darkened, and a long pause settled between them, full of ghosts.

After a while, Molly asked, "Weren't the missions huge ranches, with thousands of cattle and sheep? What happened to them?"

"The church was never meant to own them forever. When Mexico won its independence from Spain, the new government took the land from the priests and gave it to our citizens."

"Is that how you came to own it?"

Ramona nodded again.

"The governor granted vast acres to Californios. But then the war was lost, and California became an American state. Gold was discovered, and adventurers came from around the world. We could not stop so many from moving onto our land. Now our people, the *gente de razón,* are far outnumbered by newcomers. Most of what was once ours is lost."

Ramona gazed beyond the orchard toward the valley, her face composed, her mind somewhere far away. Molly sat with her in silence, thinking about the stories she'd heard, the all but forgotten tales of Old California. Perhaps one day she would find a way to tell them so they could always be remembered.

Chapter Twenty

The Californios

1864

After supper, Doña Ramona excused herself for the evening and left Molly with Romualdo and Mariano before the great stone fireplace. The oak logs hissed and popped, chasing the chill from every corner of the room. At first, the talk was of ranch accounts and needed repairs to fences and wells. But as the fire burned down to glowing embers, the men relaxed and began to reminisce about their youth.

"Molly," said Mariano, leaning forward with a gleam in his eye, "has anyone told you the story of my brother and the grizzly bear?"

She shook her head.

"Not properly. I should like to hear it from you."

He rubbed his hands together and settled back with a satisfied smile.

"Then you shall have it now, from a witness who was actually there."

"My brother loves this story," Romualdo said, pretending to yawn. "It will take a while, Molly. Make yourself comfortable."

She tucked a thick wool throw over her knees and settled deeply into her chair. Mariano stood up, took a stick of wood from a stack near the hearth, and added it to the fire. The flames blazed up, casting a warm amber glow across his face. He took a deep breath and began.

"It was the autumn of 1849, not long after my twentieth birthday, when Aldo was only eighteen. We had just returned to Rancho de los Osos from the Sierra Madre. Fortune hunters still combed the hills for gold, but like most Californios, we soon had our fill of prospecting.

"Early one morning, well before dawn, Aldo roused me from my sleep. He had found footprints in the soft ground outside our adobe. 'Hurry,' he said. 'There is a huge grizzly nearby. If we are quick, we may reach him before he is too far up the mountain.'

"I threw on my clothes before I was altogether awake. I scarcely had time to pull on my boots before we were into our saddles. Aldo and two vaqueros were already ahead of me. Reaching them, I saw the tracks myself. I tell you, Molly, they were the biggest I have ever known."

"Allow me to explain," Romualdo said, breaking in. "Our livestock was in danger, and a brazen animal so close to our *hacienda* was a danger to our lives. Now, Mariano, go on."

"The horses sensed the animal first," Mariano continued. "They balked, unwilling to go further. Then we saw him."

Mariano waved an arm toward an imaginary hillside.

"The bear was erect and motionless, waiting in the dry brush halfway up the mountain. It was as if he dared us to come closer.

"Aldo did not hesitate. He had no fear of the beast and had not lost his skill with a lasso. His horse was nervous, but he kept him steady, stood high in his stirrups, and unleashed *la reata*. The rope flew straight and fast like an arrow shot from a bow. When it caught the bear's huge right foreleg, the beast let out a tremendous roar. Our horses trembled beneath us, but we followed my brother's lead and threw our ropes to catch and secure the hindfeet and the other front paw. Inch by inch, we dragged the snarling, hissing animal down the hill and into town."

Mariano dropped his arms as if to mark the end of the story, but Molly had to know what happened next.

"Goodness!" she said, her eyes wide. "What became of the creature?"

Mariano laughed.

"Our stepfather loved to antagonize the mission priests. He staged a bull-and-bear fight in the town square, right in front of the church. On Sunday morning, no less! After holy mass, the worshipers were met with a raucous crowd of half-drunken revelers gathered around the bull ring, yelling and cursing at the animals and one another."

"What happened then?"

"I do not recall whether the bull or the bear won the contest," Mariano said with a grin. "But I will never forget how angry our mother was when she saw her husband collecting money from onlookers, taking bets on which animal would win. I do not believe she ever forgave him."

"I hope the story has not upset you," Romualdo said. "Pitting a wild bear against a fighting bull is a brutal, bloody sport. But in those days, there was little entertainment to be had. Men looked for whatever excitement they could find."

Molly pitied the animals, but still, she had to smile. She loved seeing the brothers together like this, enjoying each other's company and sharing stories vastly different from any she had ever known.

Romualdo spent the next morning with his mother and brother, reviewing accounts and assessing their finances.

After lunch, Ramona said, "Enough work for today, Aldito. Molly must see the ocean. Take the gray mare and my two-wheeled cart."

"There's an old road leading to the bluffs," Romualdo said. "I know of a good spot to watch the sunset."

They followed a narrow, well-worn path past the ranch hands' quarters, corrals, and outbuildings, and beyond the flower garden's rough, prickly pear fences. The cart sent clouds of dust into the air, and large stones and potholes made it slow going for their little horse, but they finally reached a set of rocky cliffs high above the beach.

While Romualdo cared for their horse, Molly walked to the edge of the bluff. Blue-black swallows rode the ocean wind, sweeping in and out of hundreds of nests clinging to the muddy ledges. Looking down, it took her a moment to realize that the brown, gleaming boulders heaped on the beach were not rocks at all, but massive sea creatures.

"Aldo, come look at these enormous sea lions. They look like giant slugs!"

He came to stand beside her, shading his eyes from the sun's glare.

"Those are elephant seals. The big ones are not just lounging on the sand. They are actually guarding their harems."

As he spoke, a gigantic bull roared, reared up, and lunged at one of the smaller animals. The interloper had come a little too close to his family. It backed down and moved away.

"An old bull will fight to protect his family," he said.

"I see his battle scars," Molly said. "I wonder how long he can hold on."

They found a patch of sand against the bluff and sat together, watching the sky turn brilliant colors. Sunlight broke through the clouds, and ribbons of pink, orange, and violet shimmered across the wet sand.

Molly was quiet for a long time before Romualdo turned to her.

"What is bothering you, *querida*? It seems you have something on your mind."

"I was thinking about you and your family," she said. "And Mariano's stories. He said you abandoned the goldfields soon after you arrived. Why? What happened there?"

He took some time before answering.

"Those were difficult days. Californio*s* were among the first to hear about the gold in the hills. It was only a day or two away on horseback for some, and many came home wealthy. Then Americanos swarmed the mining camps, and everything changed. It mattered little who we were or how long our families had lived here. Our skin was brown, and our language was Spanish. They called us 'greasers.' It was not safe to stay, so we came home. We still had our land, after all."

"And now even that is nearly gone," Molly said.

She felt his loss keenly. There had been a wild freedom in that vanished time. What would the world look like without it?

He drew her close with one arm and shielded his eyes from the last rays of the sun.

"Do you see how fast the sun sets?" he said. "The time of the ranchos is disappearing like the sun at the end of a beautiful day. But there will always be another dawn, and we can always hope for a better tomorrow."

Chapter Twenty-One

Weddings and Babies

1864–1867

Father's death and the threat of war had led Mother to take the greatest gamble of her life. Leaving Kentucky hadn't been easy, even with the help of her brother Louis. She had risked bringing her daughters down the Mississippi River and across the Gulf of Mexico and the Caribbean Sea, then taking them over the Isthmus of Panama to board a steamer on the Pacific coast. It was a bold, perilous adventure. But that was all behind them now. California was their new home, and Molly had the perfect husband. Her family had found peace at last.

Nevertheless, Mother could not stop worrying.

"Lizzie is outgoing enough," she told Molly one afternoon. "She'll likely do well for herself, but Joanna is another story altogether."

"There's plenty of time," Molly said. "She's only just turned twenty."

Frowning, Mother folded her hands in her lap.

"Her head is always buried in a book. If she doesn't start taking notice of the world around her, it may be too late."

"Wouldn't you rather have her wait for love than rush into a match that's a mistake?"

"I am only considering your sister's future. I don't want to pressure her into a loveless marriage, but not everyone is as lucky as you, my dear."

Molly saw some truth to Mother's concern. Joanna wasn't a lively charmer like Lizzie, who attracted attention wherever she went. Jo was more introspective and thoughtful. Men noticed her, to be sure, but hers was a quiet grace. She was more contented with reading than attending social occasions. So, when Joanna at last showed an interest in someone, it took them all by surprise.

It was a blustery February evening when Caleb's friend, Mr. Enoch Wilson, arrived for Sunday supper looking like a half-drowned housecat.

"Hurry in," Caleb said as the door blew open. "It's nasty out there, isn't it?"

"Sorry to arrive like this," Enoch said, sending water droplets flying as he shook his hat.

He looked ruefully at his damp trousers and dripping wet overcoat.

"I caught the worst of it between here and Market Street. Seems I've gotten quite a drenching."

"Looks like you did," laughed Caleb. "At least your boots are dry."

"Oiled with mink fat," Enoch said good-naturedly. "Best water repellent there is. Though I must confess, I should have remembered my umbrella."

"You're fine," Caleb said. "Come in and meet my family. I'll be back in a flash."

Molly and Romualdo emerged from the parlor to greet Caleb's guest.

"Welcome, Mr. Wilson," Molly said. "We're glad you were willing to brave this dreadful weather."

"A few raindrops don't bother me," he said with a modest smile. "I'm grateful to be invited. This is a welcome change from the boardinghouse."

Lighthearted laughter floated in from the kitchen and Enoch turned to look.

"It sounds like someone's having a good time."

"That will be Molly's sisters, Lizzie and Joanna," Romualdo said.

"The food smells good," Enoch said appreciatively.

"Supper will be ready soon," Molly said. "You and my husband can take some time to get acquainted while I tell the others you're here."

Caleb returned from hanging Enoch's coat to dry and led him over to the parlor fireplace.

"Mr. Wilson, you seem like an enterprising fellow," Romualdo said. "Are you new to San Francisco?"

"Not so new," he replied. "I left Virginia in '48, planning to farm up in the Willamette Valley. That didn't work out. I came down to try for gold and saw I could make a fair business selling supplies to miners. Better than digging for ore. Now I run a dry-goods store on Market Street."

"His shop is thriving," Caleb said. "And he has ambitious plans for expansion. Ah, here come the ladies."

Caleb rose to make introductions.

"Mr. Wilson, allow me to present my wife Rebecca, my Aunt Sarah, and my cousins Joanna and Elizabeth McIntyre."

Mother was immediately alert and took in Caleb's visitor with a practiced eye, assessing every detail. Enoch was a sight older than her girls, tall and freckled, with bushy auburn hair and a curly, reddish-brown beard. But he was neatly groomed, wore clean trousers, and owned a well-fitting jacket. He looked healthy enough, despite a slightly crooked smile, and his eyes were astonishingly blue. More importantly, his gaze was not fixed on Lizzie. From the very first, he belonged entirely to Joanna.

"Elizabeth, dear," Mother said meaningfully, raising her eyebrows to be sure she had Lizzie's full attention. "Come with me, please. I need your help in the kitchen."

Lizzie obeyed, but not without a glance back at Enoch. She really would have preferred to stay. But no matter. He hardly seemed to notice her.

Enoch, meanwhile, took a seat beside Joanna and gave her a friendly smile.

"It's a great pleasure to meet you, Miss McIntyre."

"Likewise, Mr. Wilson. Caleb tells us you became acquainted with one another while residing at the What Cheer House on Sacramento Street."

"The very same," he said. "We both made use of its lending library."

The golden flecks in Joanna's dark eyes sparkled with interest, and her voice held a new warmth.

"You are a reader, then, Mr. Wilson? What sort of books do you favor?"

"I'm partial to the works of Mr. Dickens, but of late I've been reading Jules Verne. What an imagination that man has!"

"Have you read *Great Expectations*?"

"Just finished it last week," Enoch said, his blue eyes twinkling.

They talked nonstop during dinner, discussing the merits of their favorite books. Enoch paused momentarily to praise Rebecca's good cooking—the broiled kidneys were exceptional, and he truly enjoyed the boiled lamb with caper sauce. Otherwise, he seemed barely aware of the meal. All his attention was on Joanna.

Later that evening, after the rain had stopped and their visitor had taken his leave, Rebecca caught Molly in the hallway.

"I believe Mr. Wilson quite enjoyed Joanna's company," she said with a knowing smile.

"I noticed," Molly said. "He certainly was in no great hurry to leave."

Romualdo joined them and added, "I have a feeling we'll be seeing much more of Mr. Enoch Wilson."

As predicted, Enoch became a frequent caller. He came each Sunday evening, rain or shine, often bringing a small gift—a book, a box of candies, or a bouquet of hothouse roses from the flower stand on Montgomery Street. He was kind to everyone, and his manners were impeccable.

Mother began to show tentative signs of approval, and true to form, she wasted no time inquiring into his credentials. He appeared to be a first-rate prospect for Joanna, yet important questions remained.

"Caleb," she said one day, "your friend Mr. Wilson seems like a fine man. But tell me. At his age, why doesn't he already have a wife and family?"

Caleb set aside his newspaper.

"He was married once," he said quietly. "He crossed the plains with his young bride on a wagon train bound for Oregon Territory. She fell ill along the way, with fever, perhaps, and lost the child she carried. Enoch had to bury them both before they reached the Snake River. He's never forgotten them."

Mother pressed a hand to her chest.

"Such a tragedy."

Caleb nodded.

"He heard how fast San Francisco was growing and it sounded promising, so he came and set up a store. That's when we first met.

Enoch's done well for himself, but I think he's been lonely for some time now. He's a good, decent man. He'd make Joanna a good husband."

Indeed, Enoch's kind attention seemed to draw Joanna out of her shell. She laughed more readily, took greater care with her appearance, and no longer spent every spare moment immersed in her books. They courted through the winter and into the spring, always with proper company. They sometimes walked together to Mr. Roman's bookshop, or perhaps they would visit the gardens at Strawberry Island. By early March everyone in the family was sure their engagement was only a matter of time.

"I do hope he proposes soon," Mother whispered to Molly one evening. "They have waited long enough."

"He is just working up his courage," Molly said. "He's not the impulsive sort."

Then, one Sunday afternoon, while the family lingered over tea, Enoch asked to speak privately with Mother. Everyone knew what that meant. By the time the china cups were cleared, plans were underway for another wedding.

Enoch and Joanna married in the spring of 1865. Mother's Brussels lace shawl came out again, as did Rebecca's cream satin gown.

"I'm so glad the wedding happened when it did," Molly said to her sister, then groaned and stretched her hands across her bulging belly. "In another month, I won't be able to fit into this dress."

"I'm so excited for you," Joanna said. "What do you think? Will it be a boy or a girl?"

"Romualdo says he wants a daughter, but I'd rather like it to be a boy. After living with girls all my life, having a son would be a refreshing change."

***

Shortly after Joanna's wedding, word came of Robert E. Lee's surrender to General Grant at Appomattox. San Francisco's church bells rang out, cannons boomed over the harbor, and flags unfurled from the city's rooftops. At last the terrible war was over.

149

Molly, now heavy with child, stood next to Romualdo, watching fireworks shoot across the bay.

"At last," she said, "our children will grow up in a place where everyone is free."

"Yes," Romualdo said, slipping his arm around her shoulders. "But the country's wounds are deep. President Lincoln has plenty of work ahead."

Tragically, the nation's joy was short-lived. Less than two weeks later, horrible news flashed across the telegraph lines. President Abraham Lincoln was dead.

"It came over the wire early this morning," Romualdo said. "He was at Ford's Theater with Mrs. Lincoln when John Wilkes Booth shot him in the back of the head."

"Booth?" Molly repeated, stunned. "Edwin Booth's brother? How could this be? They're a family of actors, not assassins."

Romualdo shook his head.

"It makes no sense at all. The world has lost a great, great man."

San Francisco went into mourning. Crepe hung from every door, church bells tolled, and even the rowdiest saloons fell silent for a day. Molly felt as though the light had gone out of the country just as it had begun to shine again.

Still, life went on, as it always must, and in August, Molly gave birth to a baby girl.

"She is lovelier than the most beautiful morning of spring," Romualdo whispered, gazing at the tiny babe in Molly's arms. "We will call her Maybella."

***

The baby was Sarah McIntyre's first grandchild, and she was eager to help however she could. Still, Molly's responsibilities seemed endless. As wife of the State Treasurer, she had luncheons to attend and receptions to plan. In addition to her many social obligations, the cooking, baking, cleaning, laundry, shopping, sewing, mending, and gardening still had to be done.

Society's expectations almost put a stop to her writing, but Romualdo saw her frustration and offered a ready solution.

"Molly," he said, "the city is full of people looking for work. You must hire someone to help."

Severe hardship had brought droves of European immigrants to San Francisco. Having escaped famine and persecution, they were more than willing to do almost any sort of paid labor. Many hardworking women took jobs as household maids or servants.

Within a week, Molly had hired a young woman to help with the household chores. Nancy Creadle was a sturdy and cheerful redheaded girl with a charming Irish brogue.

"She asks twenty-five dollars a month, plus room and board," Molly told Mother.

"That's a fair price, but isn't she Irish?"

"I know, a lot of folks won't hire Catholics, but we really don't mind. As you know, Romualdo's family is Catholic. Besides, Nancy promises to keep her religious beliefs to herself."

Nancy proved to be a great blessing. She swept the house, beat the rugs, and dusted the furniture every day of the week. On Mondays, she pumped water from the backyard well and set it to boil in a large copper kettle, then washed and scrubbed the family laundry before hanging it on the clothesline to dry. On Tuesdays, she heated a heavy iron on the kitchen stove and pressed dampened shirts and petticoats until they were wrinkle-free.

With Nancy's help, Molly found the time she needed to write. She sketched ideas for skits and plays and hoped her stories would one day find a ready audience.

In the meantime, Little Maybella was the center of everyone's attention. But that was only until the following spring, when Joanna gave birth to a baby boy. He was an adorable blue-eyed redhead like his father Enoch. Now, with two grandchildren, Sarah's life was nearly perfect.

"Truly," she said to Molly, "there's not much else I could ever want. Except, well, to see Lizzie settled and married with her own babies."

"I'm glad to know children make you happy," Molly said, "because you're about to become a grandmother again."

"Another baby? With Maybella scarcely a year old?"

"Yes," Molly said with a grin. "We're both hoping for a son this time, and if it is a boy, we'll name him Romualdo. But since Yankees can never say the name correctly, we intend to make it simple and call him Waldo."

Chapter Twenty-Two

Montana Territory

1868–1870

"He won't let go," giggled two-year-old Maybella as she tried to extract her finger from Waldo's determined little fist.

"Your brother is strong like your father," Molly said. "Exactly like him. Dark, handsome, and always looking for something to eat."

Romualdo laughed and held their son firmly in his arms.

"I believe he takes more after his mother. He is lively and bright and insists on staying up all night."

"Speaking of staying late," Molly said, "what's your opinion of Lizzie's beau, Henry Miller? Bankers don't usually keep such hours, but Mother said he didn't leave until after ten o'clock last Saturday night."

"Do you believe he plans to propose?"

"Mother hopes so. Henry is good-looking and a dapper dresser, and he has a steady income. She thinks he's an excellent prospect for Lizzie."

Henry Miller, another of Caleb's friends, was well liked by everyone, and Lizzie had never been happier. Within weeks, their engagement appeared in the San Francisco newspapers.

Mrs. Sarah McIntyre of Danville, Kentucky, announces the betrothal of her daughter, Miss Elizabeth Leticia McIntyre, to Mr. Henry Robinson Miller of Sacramento. A spring wedding is planned.

Molly and Joanna's weddings had been modest affairs, but Lizzie said she wanted something more elaborate. After all, Henry's father was a well-to-do banker, and his many friends and relatives were expecting invitations.

"I hope Mother won't mind," Lizzie said. "Henry plans to invite several business associates."

"Will you wear Rebecca's white satin gown?" Joanna asked.

"No, it was lovely for you and Molly, but it doesn't suit me. Henry's mother knows a seamstress who makes the most fabulous wedding dresses. We have an appointment to see her next week."

"Mother will want you to wear her Brussels lace veil," Molly reminded her.

"I know. But it's terribly old-fashioned."

"She'll be disappointed if you don't use it," Joanna said.

Lizzie shrugged, unconcerned.

"After my wedding, Mother will have everything she's ever wanted—all three of us happily married. She should be perfectly satisfied."

"I'm not so sure," Molly said. "It's been nearly ten years since Father died. I sometimes wonder if she isn't lonely."

"How could she be, with three grandchildren to keep her busy?"

"There are other things in life," Joanna said.

"Maybe for you," said Lizzie, "but Henry and I believe parenthood is life's greatest joy. We can't wait to start having babies of our own."

Molly folded her hands on her lap.

"Lizzie, I love my children with all my heart, but between their needs and my household duties, there is barely a moment left in the day."

"You should count your blessings," Lizzie said. "Your husband is a successful politician and you have two lovely children."

Joanna's little boy was perched in his mother's arms, but he began to squirm and reach for the floor.

"Arthur is being fussy," she said.

"Let me take him," Lizzie said. "My nephew and I are going on a nice walk together."

Molly watched them go off hand in hand, then sighed deeply.

"Don't mind Lizzie," Joanna said. "You've always wanted more from life than the rest of us. You'll find a way to make it happen."

"I hope you're right."

She turned to study her sister.

"What about you, Jo? With the children keeping us so busy, we can't visit like we used to. Tell me, are you and Enoch happy?"

Joanna glanced down at her folded hands before looking up again.

"Enoch is a wonderful husband. We love each other, and we love little Arthur."

"You seem distant, though. Are you sure everything is all right?"

"Well, business has been awfully slow, and San Francisco's economy isn't what it once was. Enoch says there's a huge demand for supplies in Montana Territory. You must have heard—they've discovered gold and silver in Helena. They say Last Chance Gulch is the new Mother Lode."

Molly's eyes widened.

"Jo, you can't mean—you aren't thinking of moving there?"

"Enoch believes it will be a great opportunity for us."

"He cannot be serious. A stagecoach is the only reasonable method of travel to Montana, and the roads are infested with outlaws."

"Oh, Molly," Joanna said. "Do you remember when I was afraid to leave Kentucky? California turned out far better than we ever could have guessed. Maybe Montana will be the same."

Molly threw up her hands.

"Montana is not California. The towns are little more than mining camps, and snow closes the roads for much of the year. We might never see you again!"

"Then pray for me," Joanna said quietly, "because Enoch means to go."

It was an astonishing turn of events. Molly's cautious, fearful sister had become the brave and adventurous one. Molly couldn't let it go. She tried to dismiss it as idle talk, but knew that once Joanna had made a decision, no one could do a thing to change her mind.

Soon after Lizzie's wedding, Enoch and Joanna broke the news to Mother.

"Molly, did you know about this?" Mother cried. "Please explain it to me. Why would your sister want to live in such a place? And they're taking little Arthur with them!"

"They've made up their minds, Mother. There's nothing we can do to change their plans. Trust me, I've tried."

So, Enoch filled his wagon with provisions for a new dry-goods store in Helena, Montana. Joanna packed what she could and readied her family for the journey north.

Molly blinked back tears. All she could do was pray that it would turn out for the best.

"I want no excuses, Joanna," she said, "do you hear? You must promise to write. Every scrap of news. You must tell me everything."

"I promise."

***

Joanna was true to her word.

July 1868: Montana is lovelier than I can describe. I only wish you could see it! The rivers run fast and clear, the sky goes on forever, and the mountains make me want to sing. The weather can change in a blink—snowflakes fell on our Independence Day picnic! Enoch's business is thriving. Everyone stops for supplies at his store near Last Chance Gulch. They say there's so much gold in Helena, there's a millionaire on every corner. It just might be true!

August 1868: Enoch's been awfully busy, and now he's elected to the territorial legislature. It meets down in Virginia City, more than a hundred miles away. I don't know how he can possibly do it all....

September 1868: The weather has turned. Last week, Arthur and I were picking huckleberries near Prickly Pear Creek. An early snow this week left drifts so deep the wagons can't get through. Write soon and give my love to everyone.

Then the letters stopped.

"Nothing for weeks," Molly said. "Why doesn't she write?"

"They are sure to be in good health," Romualdo said. "Snow has likely closed the mountain passes. The mail may be delayed until the thaw."

"I suppose you're right."

His assurances didn't stop Molly from worrying. She kept a close watch on the mailbox, waiting impatiently for a note from Joanna to appear. Then, at last, the letters came again.

April 1869: It's finally spring! There's wild asparagus down by the river, and the rhubarb I planted last fall has sprouted in my little garden. Enoch's boots are always caked with placer mud, but he stays out of the saloons and gambling halls, and we are happy....

May 1869: The weather has begun to warm, the wild roses will bloom any day, and I have exciting news. Tell Maybella and Waldo they'll soon have another cousin.

Joanna's latest news only added to Molly's worry. Montana Territory was rugged and remote. Women gave birth at home, often alone. But the dangers of childbirth were considered a woman's lot in life, and far too many never lived to see their babies.

September 1869: Our little daughter arrived on the tenth of the month. We named her Mary Elizabeth, after you and Lizzie. All went well, owing to the help of a skillful midwife named Peg. Her husband has a claim up on the gulch, and both were enslaved before the war. But she's willing to deliver every baby in the camp, no matter whether the mother is black or white....

March 1870: Influenza swept through the mining camps last month. The children and I are well, but Enoch still feels poorly, and his body shakes with a terrible cough....

Joanna's husband did not outlast Montana's cold, harsh winter. His illness turned to pneumonia, and he died on the first day of spring.

When he first set out across the American continent, Enoch Wilson was a young man with bright hopes for the future. He met with tragedy, had to bury his wife and newborn child, yet found a way to start again. Joanna was left a young widow, but her children inherited precious gifts: a pioneer's strength of character and the great ability to love.

In May, when the frozen ground had thawed, Joanna gave her husband a proper burial in the Helena cemetery. She sold all she could salvage, packed up little Arthur and Mary Elizabeth, and began the long, sorrowful journey home to San Francisco.

Chapter Twenty-Three

Joys and Sorrows

1870–1871

Molly and Lizzie rode up Filbert Street in a horsecar packed with shoppers. It was winter, and the day was miserably cold and wet. Molly shivered, pulled her wrap tight against the wind, and listened to her sister's complaints about life in San Francisco.

"I don't know how much longer I can put up with it," Lizzie said. "I've repeatedly told Henry how I worry about living here, and now we have our baby to consider. The city has grown entirely too fast. And those terrible earthquakes! Mr. Pickering's pharmacy was almost destroyed three years ago. The poor man was lucky to get out alive. I don't want to think what might happen if another, stronger quake comes along."

Molly clutched her packages with one arm and used her free hand to grip the leather strap dangling above her head. The cobblestone streets were slick with drizzle, and the horsecar jerked back and forth, wheels lurching and clanking against the steel tracks. The draft horses struggled to pull the heavily laden car. It was hard to keep their footing on such a steep hill, and the click and clack of iron horseshoes on the stone pavement only added to the racket.

Molly tightened her hold on the strap, leaned close to Lizzie, and raised her voice to be heard over the noise.

"Caleb says they plan to install a cable car on Clay Street."

"Newfangled inventions won't make the city any safer."

"At least they'll keep the streets cleaner. Less manure to step around."

Lizzie sniffed. "Even so, I think our family should move to Oakland."

"All that way across the bay?"

"It's not so far. Henry can take the ferry to his office each morning and still be home in time for supper."

Molly understood Oakland's rural appeal. Wide-open fields and magnificent groves of live oaks gave the children plenty of space to play. The houses going in near Lake Merritt's shoreline would be a quiet respite from San Francisco's noise and bustle.

"Great things are coming to Oakland," Lizzie said. "They've finished putting in the railroad, and there's a brand-new train station at 16th and Wood. We'd be well connected to the rest of the country. The town's fast becoming the most important—"

"Whoa! Hold on!" someone shouted.

"Look out," the driver cried. "We're slipping!"

He slammed down hard on his brake, but it was no use. The horsecar began sliding steadily backward down the hill.

"Out! Everyone, out!"

A woman shrieked, and panic broke loose. Frightened passengers leapt from the car and scrambled to escape. People were shouting frantically, searching for loved ones, tripping over the belongings now scattered across the cobblestones. A man's shoulder slammed into Molly, her skirts became tangled around her legs, and her knees hit hard on the pavement.

"Lizzie, where are you?" she screamed.

"Over here," Lizzie shouted. "Are you hurt?"

Molly struggled to her feet and rushed to throw her arms around her sister. Then she saw the horsecar. It was sliding backward down the rails, rolling slowly at first, but quickly gaining speed. The poor horses were still attached to their harnesses, and she covered her ears to block out the horrible shrieks of injured animals.

Lizzie clung to Molly and whispered, "I don't want to look."

They both turned away to avoid the spectacle of the wreckage. Unfortunately, they could not escape the dreadful noise when everything crashed in a jumbled heap at the bottom of the hill.

***

Lizzie could not get the accident out of her mind. She told Henry the story over and over, wanting to be sure her husband understood how awful the experience had been for her.

"You might understand my distress if you'd been there when it happened. I was afraid for my life! What if our little Henry had been in the car with me? Oh! I dare not think of it!"

159

Lizzie's anxiety did not abate, and her husband eventually warmed to the idea of moving.

"Very well, my dear," he said. "It's time we found a house in Oakland. But what about your mother? She's been such a help with the baby. Would she be willing to leave Molly and Joanna's families behind in the city?"

"Mother dotes on our little boy. She'll come with us. You'll see."

As it turned out, Mother needed little convincing.

"When your sisters see how lovely Oakland is," she said, "it's only a matter of time before they decide to follow us across the bay. They both know my heart's greatest desire is to have us all together."

As always, Mother was right. Soon after the Millers settled in Oakland, Joanna followed. She used her savings from Enoch's store to rent a little house in the very same neighborhood.

Romualdo was next to suggest the move.

"Molly, perhaps we should join them across the bay. San Francisco is not the best place for our children. They should grow up near their cousins, surrounded by family."

"But I love it here," she said, "and more respectable families are moving into the city every day."

She also wanted to stay close to the theaters. Even though bawdy, risqué stage performances were still standard fare, mainstream entertainment was becoming easier to find every day. How could she ever become a playwright, living out in the countryside, surrounded by orchards and dairy farms?

"The Central Pacific finished putting in the Long Wharf on the East Bay shore," Romualdo went on. "They are adding new railroad lines in every direction. Oakland will not stay rural for long. One day it is bound to be the commercial hub of the western states."

This sounded more promising. Oakland's weather was better than San Francisco, and train travel was far more convenient.

"Very well," she said at last. "I suppose it isn't so far away. But you must promise we'll attend the theater as often as we possibly can."

Romualdo promised, and Molly started looking for a house near Lake Merritt. In a short time, she found just the right one, close to the Millers, next door to Joanna. Mother could barely contain her happiness.

"After all we've been through, we are together. Our family is truly blessed."

Mother was right, again. Life was close to perfect, so far as Molly was concerned. They'd had their share of tragedies, but it was all behind them now. Everyone had to worry about smallpox, of course, and there was always the threat of typhoid or scarlet fever. But thus far, thank the good Lord, their family had been spared.

One morning, Molly found Romualdo and Waldo together in the backyard, fastening a pair of cattle horns to an old tree stump with a length of rope.

"Aldo, whatever are you doing?"

"I am about to teach our son how to lasso a steer."

"You realize he's only five years old."

"Old enough to learn how to properly throw a rope. I was lassoing calves when I was his age."

Waldo chased a squirrel across the grass. Romualdo fastened the horns securely to the stump. Molly smiled despite herself.

"Come here, son," he called.

Eager to please his father, Waldo ran to where Romualdo waited with the coiled lariat.

"Now, hold the loop out in front of you like this," Romualdo said. "Give it a nice, even swing."

Waldo tossed the rope and hit the target squarely.

"Did you see, Papa? I did it!"

A wide smile spread across Romualdo's face.

"Perfect, son. You are a splendid vaquero."

Molly knelt to hug her little boy.

"Excellent, Waldo! You made it on your very first try."

Joanna and her son Arthur came around the corner of the house, and Waldo ran to greet them, holding the lariat out to his cousin.

"Arthur! Did you see me rope the cow? Do you want to try?"

The boys took turns tossing the lasso, missing the mark as often as not. They soon lost interest in the game and moved on to the more challenging work of catching the squirrel. Waldo might have captured the poor animal if it hadn't scurried up a nearby tree trunk. But the boys were only momentarily disappointed, because then they spotted Maybella coming out of the house with a rag doll in her arms.

"Come on," Waldo yelled, and the boys ran off to terrorize his sister.

"Those two are like brothers," Molly said.

"It's good to see them together," Joanna said. "I'm so glad you moved here."

"So am I. Oakland has turned out to be a good fit for us. Romualdo takes the train when he needs to be in Sacramento, and I can catch the ferry into the city."

"Have you joined Ina Coolbrith's writers' group?"

"It's been a while, but yes, I go whenever I can."

Ina Coolbrith's literary salon at her flat on Russian Hill drew the city's aspiring writers as well as celebrated authors like Joaquin Miller, Ambrose Bierce, and Samuel Clemens.

"Ina is a remarkable woman," Joanna said. "Did you know she's helping Bret Harte edit the *Overland Monthly*? At last, we have a magazine being published in California!"

"Yes, I've been reading her wonderful poetry," Molly said. "Bret Harte is a scallywag, but his short stories are making him famous all over the country. By the way, I plan to attend Elizabeth Cady Stanton's lecture in the city next week. Would you like to come?"

Before Joanna could answer, Romualdo spoke up from where he stood on the porch.

"We should all stay out of San Francisco for a while. The hospitals are overwhelmed. First, it was the smallpox epidemic, and now diphtheria. It is frightening to hear how many children have died."

Molly frowned.

"Sanitation must be the problem. On warm days, the stench from the gutters is unbearable. I'm sure it's the open sewers and blocked drains that are spreading pestilence."

"Perhaps," he said, "but it is not for certain. No one knows what causes these diseases. Doctors may even be passing the illness from one patient to the next."

"Okay, then. We'll wait."

***

No one could say for sure how the tragedy fell upon their family. One of the children had a runny nose, then everyone had coughs and sore throats. Molly helped Mother administer teas and apply mustard plasters, but they did little to help. Everyone was sick. But for Waldo, it was far worse. A fiery rash spread over his little body, a high fever and chills overtook him, and toxins inflamed his throat. He could no longer swallow, then he couldn't breathe. Although the doctors were called, there was nothing to be done.

Life holds times of unbelievable joy, and at other times, the suffering is nearly too much to bear.

On the morning of her son's funeral, Molly woke in confusion. What was causing this crushing weight? Then it all came back in a terrible rush. Waldo was gone. She buried her head in the bed pillow and lay still for a long while, wishing away the pain.

The bedroom door opened, and she heard a gentle voice say, "Your clothes are on the chair, dear. Joanna set them out for you last night."

"Yes, Mother. I remember."

"Everyone is waiting in the parlor. The undertaker will be here soon."

She climbed out of bed, splashed water on her face, brushed her hair, and slowly and deliberately willed herself into the heavy black mourning dress. Finally, she tied her bootlaces, stood up, and forced herself to face the day.

Romualdo was the sort of man who tried to hide his grief and be strong for others. But when he gathered her in his arms, Molly felt his body shake. Little Maybella clung to her skirts, and she reached down to hold her close.

"It seems impossible now," Mother said quietly, "but one day you'll find your tears are spent. There will be nothing left to cry."

The undertaker's black horses waited outside the house. Caleb helped Romualdo lift Waldo's white coffin into the back of the wagon. A second black carriage and team of four brought the family to the entrance of Mountain View Cemetery.

"The road is too narrow," Romualdo said. "Let me help you down, Molly. We will walk from here."

Hand in hand, they followed the funeral wagon through the ornate iron gates. Thick, wet fog shrouded the scores of neatly spaced gravestones. A gravel path on the right led across a wide, green field, then wound up and around a series of steep hills. The trail narrowed as they reached the top, and here the wagon stopped.

Romualdo stepped forward to lift the little casket from the back of the wagon.

"My brave son," he whispered.

Waldo was laid to rest on a quiet slope above Oakland's canopy of ancient oaks. The fog lifted, and the mourners could see white-sailed ships on San Francisco Bay. Beyond the bay, far in the distance, was the city itself. Farther yet was the vast Pacific, the ocean that first brought Molly's family to California.

Molly moaned, rocking back and forth, as if the motion could comfort her broken heart.

It was all painfully beautiful.

Romualdo took her arm, and together they walked slowly down the hill.

Chapter Twenty-Four

Betrayed

1873–1874

"Tell me a story, Mama," Maybella murmured, fingering her soft woolen blanket while struggling to stay awake.

"It's late, sweetheart," Molly whispered, gently brushing the hair from her daughter's forehead. "Time to say good night."

"Just one story, please! A little one."

Molly was tired but couldn't bring herself to tell her daughter no.

"Very well, Bella. One story. Do you know the legend of the beautiful Queen Califia?"

Maybella shook her head, eyes heavy with sleep.

"No? Well, then, my dear, I will tell you all about her."

"Long, long ago, there was a magical island far beyond the distant oceans, to the right of the Indies, and close to the fabled Garden of Eden. This land was unimaginably rich, with an abundance of gold, silver, and precious stones. A good and wise queen ruled the realm, and can you imagine? Every one of her subjects was a woman. They were powerful, fearless warriors who kept fierce, lionlike eagles called griffins as companions. And though no man lived among them, yet these women were mighty and content. The queen's name was Califia, and her island was called California."

Maybella's eyes had begun to flutter, then shut. But now Molly was wide awake, musing over the fantastical tale of chivalrous knights, courageous women, and imaginary beasts. She'd read the old story by Spanish writer García Rodríguez de Montalvo, the one explorer Hernán Cortés and his men had loved. When they sailed west from Mexico and landed on the Baja Peninsula, they believed they'd found Montalvo's fabled island and named it California.

Careful not to wake her daughter, Molly climbed out of bed and went in search of her husband.

"Romualdo," she said, "I have an idea for a book. Please tell me what you think."

He listened intently as she described a stirring tale of romantic adventures and courageous, exciting escapades.

When she had finished, he said, "Molly, I love it. I cannot wait to see this story in print."

Something about Califia's legend had sparked Molly's imagination. Was it her strength and courage? Or was the writing merely a way to escape her own sorrows? Whatever the case, as she began to write, the pen flowed with a life of its own.

It was long past noon, and though early in May, the sun beat fiercely down upon the white-sailed Spanish galleon, the only vessel to be seen for miles around....

Montalban, by Mrs. R. Pacheco, impressed the New York publishers. It was a novel inspired by medieval Spanish romances and infused with lively tales of Old California, just the sort of story to engage eastern readers who hungered for adventures set in the American West.

"I have exciting news," she told Mother. "They've accepted my manuscript. The publisher says it has great dramatic possibilities. It might even make an interesting play! I am finally about to become a real author."

Sarah McIntyre hugged her daughter.

"Wonderful, Molly! I could not be prouder. I always knew you'd become a famous author someday."

At this, all Molly could do was smile.

***

While Molly pursued her writing, Romualdo put his energy into politics and his star continued to rise. He was admired across the state as a Californio who supported business, stood for national unity, and believed in the importance of public schools. His background and experience appealed to a wide range of voters, so it was no surprise when Republicans nominated him to run for lieutenant governor.

"Molly, you haven't said much about the upcoming election," Mother remarked one afternoon over tea. "Is everything going well for Romualdo?"

"I believe so. We're leaving for Southern California soon. He wants me along with him on his campaign. He says everyone asks to meet the candidate's wife."

Sarah signaled her pride and approval.

"All the newspapers are praising him, and it's no wonder. Your husband is not merely another politician. He's a California native son, soldier, *ranchero*, and bear fighter, no less! I certainly hope he appreciates you, Molly. It can't possibly hurt that he has a beautiful, talented woman at his side."

Molly tucked a stray lock of hair behind her ear.

"Oh, Mother," she laughed. "Aldo and I know how lucky we are to have one another. I do all I can to support his career, and he helps me find the time to write."

***

By 1873, rowdy, immoral crowds were seldom seen in San Francisco's best theatres. Only a few years earlier, playhouses were among the favorite gathering places for loud, uncouth men who drank too much and engaged in all sorts of unmentionable activities. But women and families followed the men who came for California's wealth. They enriched and refined the region, and now, respectable, clean-living citizens could enjoy a play without ruining their good reputations.

One autumn night, the well-known novelist Mrs. Romualdo Pacheco was out on the town with her husband, California's new Lieutenant Governor. The couple had tickets for a performance of *The Comedy of Errors* by William Shakespeare. The actors in the play's cast were among the city's most popular, and the story's premise—identical twins separated at birth, mistaken identities, silly mix-ups—was the sort of thing they both enjoyed.

Molly felt exceptionally fashionable that evening. She was sure that even Rebecca would have approved of her ensemble. The wide, bell-shaped hoops and cotton crinolines of days past were thoroughly out of date. She'd chosen to wear a slim skirt of deep, russet red silk that was bustled and draped in the latest mode and trimmed with multiple layers of gathers, ribbons, and pleats.

She stole a glance at her husband. Despite a few traces of gray, his black mustache and long, full beard had him looking as stylish as any of the younger men serving in the state legislature. Without a doubt, the two of them made a handsome couple.

"I can hardly wait for the show," she said. "The reviews have been excellent."

"McCullough promised us seats in the front row."

"I'm glad you spoke to him. Tickets have been selling out week after week since he took charge. This is the most successful show house in the city."

"Perhaps the entire country. It seems everyone is willing to spend money on entertainment these days."

San Francisco's California Theatre was truly spectacular. Painted murals at the Bush Street entrance featured scenes of the bay and the surrounding mountains. Fluted Grecian columns and elaborately carved floral designs decorated the interior walls. Rainbow-hued, opalescent pendants hung from coffered ceilings, and state-of-the-art limelight fixtures illuminated the stage. John McCullough's fame as an actor attracted the world's most highly acclaimed performers, and altogether, it made for an outstanding venue.

Romualdo slipped his arm around Molly's waist. "We have much to celebrate tonight, *querida.* The election is behind us, and your first novel is a triumph. And I have a surprise for you."

"A surprise?"

"I gave McCullough one of your scripts to read."

"Aldo!" Molly gasped. "What did he say?"

"He said he might be interested in producing one of your plays. Why not? *Uncle Tom's Cabin* and *East Lynne* are plays written by women, and they are both wildly popular."

"Do you have any idea how long I've waited for a chance like this?"

"Indeed, yes, I think I do," he laughed. "McCullough wants to meet with us after the show."

Molly fidgeted on the edge of her seat all through the performance.

What would Mr. McCullough say? What should she say to him?

Then the show was over, and she was seated in a reception room off the lobby, face-to-face with the charismatic theater manager.

"Lieutenant Governor Pacheco, and Mrs. Pacheco," he said with his usual charming smile. "I trust you enjoyed the performance?"

"It was superb, Mr. McCullough," Romualdo said.

Molly nodded and said, "We are both tremendously fond of Shakespeare, and the actors were excellent."

Once they'd exchanged a few pleasantries, the manager's eyes focused on Molly.

"Tell me, Mrs. Pacheco, what was your opinion of Belle Pateman's portrayal of Lady Macbeth last season?"

"I thought she was magnificent. It's clear why she is such a popular leading lady."

McCullough smiled.

"I completely agree. Belle wrote to say she is considering a European tour this spring, but I believe an original play, one written to showcase her many talents, might convince her to return to San Francisco for another season."

Molly hardly dared guess where this might be going. She reached for Romualdo's hand and held it tightly.

"What does—what does Belle think of the idea?"

"Oh, she's most enthusiastic."

He paused, then said with a dramatic wave of his hand, "Mrs. Pacheco, I want you to create a new play with Mrs. Pateman in mind. It will mark your debut as a serious playwright, and Belle's triumphant return to our fair city."

McCullough leaned back in his chair with a self-satisfied smile.

"What do you say, madam? It will be your debut offering with the California Theatre. Do you accept the challenge?"

Molly steadied her voice and lifted her chin.

"Mr. McCullough, I shall set to work immediately."

"Congratulations, Molly," Romualdo said as they left the theater. "A play written for the famous English actress Belle Pateman, no less!"

"Yes, I am delighted beyond measure! But what direction should the script take? Belle is a talented, versatile actress, and San Francisco audiences are exceptionally demanding. They'll want to see the full range of her abilities."

"How about a drama of mistaken identities, cruel infidelities, that sort of thing?"

"Perhaps. She is well-versed in comedy and can portray a romantic heroine as easily as an evil villainess."

"Whatever you do, be sure to add a tragic ending. They are always popular."

"I still can't believe it's true! It will be a challenge, that's certain, but it's a challenge I'm ready to take. I can't wait to get started!"

When she told her sisters, Joanna said, "Molly, this is most excellent news! I could not be more pleased for you."

"Such an honor," Lizzie said. "I only hope people don't think you were chosen because of your husband's position as Lieutenant Governor."

"Oh, Lizzie," Joanna said, glowering at her sister. "Can't you just be happy for Molly? She has wanted this for so long."

"It's fine, Jo," Molly said. "Let them think Romualdo pulled strings for me. I'll show the naysayers. I'm determined to be a success without anyone's help."

***

"It is well written," John McCullough said after reviewing an initial draft. "What will you call it?"

"*Betrayed,*" Molly said. "Because in the end, everyone is."

"Hmm, an interesting title. I think Belle will be pleased with her character's complexity. Once we have her approval, we'll start with costumes and set design. Rehearsals will begin as soon as she arrives from New York."

Only a few weeks later, Belle Pateman returned to San Francisco amid a torrent of fanfare and publicity. Molly's play was the first of the new season, and posters appeared on every street corner.

Betrayed
Featuring the Sensational British Actress
Mrs. Belle Pateman
An Original Drama in Four Acts
Written by Mrs. R. Pacheco
Wife of California Lieutenant Governor Romualdo Pacheco

On opening night, patrons packed the house with excited anticipation. Molly and Romualdo arrived early and entered the foyer just ahead of a small crowd of theatergoers.

"This show is bound to be marvelous," they heard a woman say to her companion. "Belle Pateman and Mary Pacheco. An inspired collaboration!"

"Both of them are exceptionally talented," said her friend. "We're lucky to have tickets. I hear it's a sellout."

"Just listen to what they're saying!" Romualdo said. "This is your moment, Molly."

"Let's sit in the back row," she said nervously. "I want to watch the audience's reaction."

The curtain finally rose, and Belle entered center stage. She acknowledged the thunderous applause with a deep, dramatic bow. San Franciscans expected yet another stellar performance from the celebrated Mrs. Pateman, and they roared their approval.

Belle appeared to have the audience under her spell. At first, all went well. But as the play progressed, Molly's excitement turned to stunned confusion. Something was terribly wrong.

"What is she doing?" Molly whispered, horrified.

Belle's rhythm slipped. Her delivery was overly exaggerated, and her lines fell flat. The supporting cast glanced at one another, bewildered. They missed their cues, there were snickers from the crowd, then laughter erupted in all the wrong places.

The theater began to empty at intermission. Only the most loyal patrons stayed through the final act. The applause, when it came, was polite at best.

Betrayed closed after a single night. The morning papers were merciless, and Molly read the notices in dumb disbelief.

"Mrs. Pacheco's script was never to my liking," Mrs. Pateman *was heard to say. "I merely wished to humor the management. I shan't make that mistake again."*

"*Betrayed*," Molly said bitterly. "Have you ever heard of a title more fitting?"

Romualdo tried to be encouraging.

"Do not take it so to heart. There is always a lesson to be learned."

She laughed bitterly.

"I've learned that my career as a playwright is over. Never, never again will I expose myself to such public humiliation."

"Balderdash, Molly," he said gently. "Most people never hope to accomplish what you've done. If your first play was not a success, it need not be your last. You are an enormously talented writer. Someday we will see your plays produced in New York City, perhaps even London. It will happen for you. I am absolutely sure of it."

Molly looked up at him, grateful for his love and support, but wondering if Lizzie had been right. Maybe she should surrender her dreams. Still, somewhere deep inside, she knew she could never give up.

Chapter Twenty-Five

The Governor's Ball

1875

After fourteen years of construction work, California's Capitol building was nearly complete. Formal gardens graced the Capitol grounds and stately American elms lined a new bridle path. Tall, straight Italian pines grew in orderly rows outside the main entrance. Inside, massive carved-wood doors led to assembly chambers furnished with hand-hewn black walnut desks. Everything was ready for Governor Newton Booth's gala opening celebration—the Governor's Ball.

"Molly, what on earth are you planning to wear?" Rebecca demanded.

"Something that won't make me look like every other politician's wife," Molly said lightly. "But don't fret, there's plenty of time. We have until December."

"The best dressmakers are bound to be engaged with other clients. Considering your husband's position, I wouldn't wait another day."

"I'll order a new gown, I promise."

Molly understood Rebecca's point. As Lieutenant Governor, Romualdo was a favorite of people throughout the state. He'd rightly claimed the spotlight. His career was on the rise, and even if *Betrayed* had been a total disaster, she still had an important role to play as the wife of a popular politician.

Rebecca recommended a reputable seamstress, and Molly placed an order for a sophisticated silk brocade ball gown in a flattering shade of midnight blue. It showed her figure to the best advantage, with a close-fitted waist, a skirt that gracefully swept the floor, and a bodice trimmed with beads that shimmered like stars. After all, she'd chosen the role, why not dress the part?

Still, the situation gnawed at her. She'd always pictured herself center stage, not merely a member of the supporting cast. She loved him and would do anything for him, but in the end, how much did he truly rely on her?

On the evening of the big event, Molly descended the stairs in all her finery, with a delicate mother-of-pearl fan fluttering in her gloved hand.

"*Querida*," Romualdo said softly, "you grow lovelier every day."

"Whether true or not, thank you for saying so."

He helped fasten her new white ermine cape over her shoulders and kissed her gently. "I wish I did not have to share you with anyone else tonight."

"I feel the same," she said. "But we don't dare keep your admirers waiting."

They hailed a hired carriage for the short ride to the Capitol, but the way was so clogged with horse-drawn cabs that it was close to impassable. Horses snorted and pawed the cold ground while elegantly dressed partygoers spilled out onto the walkways and into the building.

"We will walk from here," Romualdo told the driver.

He helped Molly out of the coach, and together they made their way down a tree-lined path to the front entrance.

"Governor Booth should be nearby," he said. "We are expected to join him for the opening procession."

Molly spotted the governor and his entourage near the front staircase. But before they could reach him, she heard people shouting, "Pacheco! Hurrah for the lieutenant governor," and within moments they were surrounded by supporters eager to shake her husband's hand. She pulled her cape close against the cold and waited patiently while Romualdo greeted his enthusiastic admirers.

After a few moments, she touched his arm and said, "Forgive me for interrupting, but I believe the grand march is about to begin."

"You are right, *querida*," he said. "*Por favor, mis amigos.* Please excuse us. We will see one another again soon."

The elite of California society lined the Capitol steps to watch Governor Booth and his party ascend the great staircase that night. They followed him inside, where flickering gas lamps lit the corridors and blazing fireplaces warmed the legislative chambers. Scarlet hangings covered the walls of the Senate, and the Assembly chambers were draped in soft sage green.

Ladies in gorgeous evening gowns strolled the halls in a carefully calculated display of wealth and status. Mellow-toned velvets, silks, and brocades, bejeweled wrists and fingers, elaborately carved pink-shell cameos, delicate Spanish lace *mantillas,* tall, ivory hair combs—every item of clothing was chosen to impress.

Long banquet tables adorned with bouquets of English roses, Oriental lilies, and chrysanthemums stretched the length of the upper hallways. The Pachecos were assigned seats among the other dignitaries. Molly found herself wedged between her husband and a red-faced gentleman wearing a uniform covered with military medals. Romualdo reached over to shake his hand.

"General Stanhope! If I'm not mistaken, the last time we met was the Yuma campaign."

"Pacheco!"

The general's voice bounced off the marble walls, and his brass buttons looked almost ready to burst.

"Indeed, sir, a superb campaign, that one. This pretty young lady must be your wife. How d'ya do, ma'am?"

Molly did her best to smile politely.

"It's a pleasure, General."

"Beg pardon, ma'am."

He clutched his belly and let out a small belch.

"The doctors say I indulge in too much rich food. But what choice does a man have when he's required to attend banquets such as this?"

The wide floral centerpieces blocked Molly's view of the guests seated across the table. It was nearly impossible to converse with anyone else, so she sighed, sat back, and listened to the general launch into a long tale of family troubles.

"It's my daughter who gives me the dyspepsia, you see. No respect from the younger generation. I chose a perfectly adequate husband for her. A strong, disciplined, military man like myself. It's beyond me why she'd want to marry her brother's good-for-nothing college chum."

Molly hid a smile behind her fan. A daughter with her own ideas? How delicious! Here was a story with possibilities. General Stanhope prattled on, and Molly made a mental note to write about it later.

Meanwhile, her husband was conversing in rapid-fire Spanish with a gentleman on his left. Finally, he paused long enough for Molly to get his attention.

"Romualdo," she said, "won't you introduce me to your friend?"

"Of course, my dear. This is Ygnacio Sepúlveda. We first met years ago, when we were both state legislators. He is now Judge of the Superior Court of Los Angeles."

"Señor Sepúlveda," Molly said, inclining her head. "It is a pleasure."

"The honor is mine, Señora Pacheco," he said smoothly. "As I was telling your husband, I believe he is the natural candidate to succeed Governor Booth in the next election."

"I agree completely. And I trust he has your full support when the time comes?"

The judge gave a light laugh and turned to Romualdo.

"Pacheco, my friend, you are fortunate to have so charming a wife. Very fortunate indeed."

All politicians need time to socialize, so Molly sat by her husband's side and listened while the men discussed governmental affairs. But only until the charlotte russe had been served, the last dishes cleared from the tables, and the band began to play a waltz. At that point she refused to wait a moment longer.

"Aldo," she said, "The orchestra is playing our favorite melody."

"Señora Pacheco," he said, offering his arm, "would you care to dance?"

"Lieutenant Governor, I would be delighted."

They took the floor, and the music swelled. Molly forgot politics, the surrounding chatter, and the curious eyes upon them. Turning and gliding in graceful rhythm, she spent the rest of the evening in her husband's arms.

***

The Governor's Ball was a grand success, and Newton Booth was a popular leader. So, it was a wonder to everyone when after a few months in office he announced his candidacy for United States Senate. He won the seat, resigned as governor in the middle of his term, and abruptly left California for Washington, D.C.

The next statewide election was still several months away, and the legislature had to fill the vacancy in Sacramento. After some deliberation, they named Lieutenant Governor Pacheco to complete Booth's term of office.

176

"Can you believe it, Molly?" Rebecca cried when she heard the news. "Your husband is the new governor!"

"Of course, he is," Molly said proudly. "Romualdo is the perfect man for the job."

"But where will you live?"

"Oh, Rebecca, you make me laugh. He's only just been named governor. I haven't had time to consider such things yet."

"Well, you'd better get started. You are going to be frightfully busy. No doubt you'll be required to carry out formal duties on his behalf. At the very least, you must find proper accommodations for your family. Oakland is a long way from Sacramento."

Again, Rebecca was right. Another decision to make, another role to play. Later that evening, Molly raised the question with Romualdo.

"Now that you are governor, we really must decide where to live. What do you propose?"

"The Golden Eagle Hotel is the best hotel in Sacramento. It should do nicely."

"You want us to live in a hotel?"

"Well, yes. There is talk of building a Governor's Mansion, but nothing has come of it yet."

"What about Maybella? She can't be expected to leave her studies."

"Could she not stay with your sisters in Oakland until the end of the term?"

"I suppose Joanna could take her for a few weeks. But is the Golden Eagle safe? The Western Hotel burned to the ground only last year. I hate to think of the poor souls trapped inside."

"Do not worry, *querida*. The Golden Eagle is built of solid brick, with tin ceilings and iron shutters. It is practically fireproof."

***

On a brisk afternoon in March 1875, Governor and Mrs. Pacheco pulled up to a sprawling new building at 7th and K Streets in Sacramento. Molly stepped out of the carriage and onto the boardwalk, and two riders thundered past, their horses' hooves spraying dirt clods and gravel in her direction. The men were cracking their whips, urging their horses to go faster while a small group of onlookers cheered them on.

"Careful, my dear!"

Romualdo raised an arm to shield Molly from the flying debris.

"What on earth!" Molly gasped. "Did you see how close they came? Someone could be killed."

Romualdo appeared unfazed. His eyes were following the horses.

"They are showing off for potential buyers," he said. "If it were me, I would choose the chestnut."

Molly shook her head and said, "Horse races and piles of manure. It seems I'll need some time to get used to this neighborhood."

Before she could say more, a short fellow with magnificent black eyebrows and an officious smile hurried over to where they stood.

"Jeremy Callahan, at your service. Governor and Mrs. Pacheco, allow me to welcome you to the Golden Eagle Hotel."

He led them inside, and while Romualdo went to sign the register, Molly surveyed the lobby. Shiny brass spittoons were strategically placed beside several overstuffed chairs, and the cut-crystal chandeliers and towering parlor palms in blue-and-white Chinese pots met with her approval. The hotel did seem to be the best available option. It dominated the downtown district, and its well-appointed suites of rooms were conveniently situated close to the Capitol.

She lifted her handkerchief and covered her nose. She would have to learn to tolerate the pungent scent of fresh manure and tobacco smoke, but what else could one expect in an establishment frequented by ranchers and politicians?

"This will do nicely," Romualdo told the manager.

"Excellent, sir. The bellman will deliver your bags straight away. Oh, and Mrs. Pacheco, don't pay any mind to the Livestock Market across the way. Your rooms face the park. Have you any questions for me?"

"Yes, Mr. Callahan. Is the dining room available for private events?"

"Of course! Our excellent Oyster Saloon is located on the ground floor. I shall introduce you to the chef myself."

Molly was already forming lists in her mind. She'd need to carefully review the restaurant menu. There would be important guests to invite, seating to arrange, and—

"Pacheco!"

She looked up to find John and María Downey coming toward them from across the lobby.

"Molly, it is so good to see you," María said warmly. "And Romualdo! Did I not say you would be governor one day? Californios are overjoyed for you."

"Democrats could use a man like you," John Downey said, shaking Romualdo's hand. "Have you considered switching parties before the next election?"

"No need for that," María laughed. "Romualdo has the support of Republicans and Democrats alike. Have you not read the latest papers?"

She picked up a folded newspaper from a nearby table, opened to the editorial page, and read from it out loud.

"Mr. Pacheco does credit to the blood from which he sprang ... and has an excellent reputation for integrity, prudence, and good sense, says today's *Alta California.*

"And here, this is from the *Sacramento Bee: Pacheco will be the Republican standard bearer. "*

Romualdo smiled modestly.

"Aldo," she said, "you are clearly the people's choice."

"I appreciate your confidence, María. Let us wait and see what the Republican convention brings. In the meantime, Downey, I am planning a hunt to Mount Tamalpais next week. Will you join me?"

Molly watched him with quiet pride. Everyone saw his ability as a leader, and no one could match his mental and physical strength. Together, everything was possible.

Chapter Twenty-Six

Governor Pacheco

1875–1876

In June 1875, California Republicans gathered in Sacramento to nominate candidates for the upcoming election. Romualdo had been governor for only three months. He hadn't had time to accomplish much yet, but the voters knew and respected him. Everyone was confident his name would be at the top of the Republican ticket on Election Day.

On the day before the convention, delegates held a meeting to finalize their slate of nominees.

"Romualdo, I would like to come with you," Molly said, standing in the doorway, her arms folded.

She knew, of course, that women were not invited to join the men in their deliberations. They were not allowed to participate in politics and were expected to remain politely uninformed.

"I wish you could," he said. "Caleb will accompany me. You should not wait up for us. It is hard to say how late we will be."

"I will be awake. I plan to celebrate with you when you return."

But when the men came back from their meeting, they were in no mood for celebration. Molly had never seen Caleb so crestfallen, and the look on Romualdo's face was nothing less than alarming.

"Good heavens, Aldo, what happened?"

He didn't answer at once. Instead, he dropped into the nearest armchair and bent to slowly remove his boots. Then he sat upright, squared his shoulders, and looked at Molly with a sober smile.

"Things did not turn out as expected. They chose another man for the nomination."

Surely, she had not heard him correctly.

"You can't be serious."

"I'm afraid it's true," Caleb said grimly. "The Republicans named Timothy Phelps to head the ticket. Romualdo deferred to the wishes of his party."

"But he was clearly entitled to the nomination," Molly said, trying to hide the hurt in her chest.

"I completely agree," Caleb said. "Your husband is the most gifted politician in the state. Nevertheless, the Yankee newcomers stole the nomination right out from under him. Those scallywags have no shame. But they far outnumber Californios like Romualdo and used their votes to choose one of their own."

"But Aldo is important to all Californians, not only those of Mexican descent."

"His supporters want him to run for governor on another ticket. It's up to Romualdo, of course, but I'd say he'd have a good chance at winning."

Romualdo shrugged and stood up.

"Do not let this trouble you."

Molly tried not to cry.

"How can you stay calm after being so callously set aside? It breaks my heart to see you so poorly used."

"Let us be patient. There will be other opportunities."

The morning edition of the *Daily Alta California* tried to explain what had happened.

> *Governor Pacheco must be naturally hurt at the way in which he was treated. Called upon by all sides to accept the nomination, supported by the leading Republican papers, he came upon the scene on the day before the convention to find everything changed as by the wand of a magician. He was quietly ignored. Nothing was left for him but to magnanimously withdraw from the contest.*

"It is shameful," Rebecca said later. "Romualdo was utterly betrayed by his party. I can't imagine how you must feel."

"It is disappointing," Molly said sadly, "but not all that surprising. It seems that honor seldom wins the vote."

"Still, Romualdo remains popular, especially among Californios."

"He is governor for another five months and he still has responsibilities. We are to attend Independence Day celebrations in Monterey next month. It's meant to be an easy trip on the *Consuela*. If we set out from Mission Bay early enough, we should arrive before sunset."

"Are you taking Maybella with you?"

"Yes, and Arthur too, if Joanna agrees. The children are at the perfect ages for a sailing adventure."

"The two of them do get along well."

"Arthur has become like another son to Romualdo," Molly said softly.

Rebecca hesitated. "Ever since Waldo…"

"Yes. Four years now. So much has happened since then."

They boarded the *Consuela* with the early tide out of Mission Bay. Molly shivered and pulled her shawl close against the chill. Dense fog shrouded the shoreline, and a shrimp camp's floating houses appeared ghost-like through the thick mist. Water lapped against the hulls of wooden-sided Chinese junks anchored nearby, and the air smelled of salt and smoke. Fishermen were already at work at their nets, and soon the catch would be cooked and laid out to dry on long racks inside the camp's narrow shrimp-drying sheds.

The *Consuela* slipped quietly out of the harbor, and the fog swallowed the scene. A light morning breeze caught the sails, and Romualdo brought them through the mouth of the bay and into the open ocean. The southern current carried them swiftly down the coast, past Half Moon Bay and Santa Cruz, then across the wide, blue crescent of Monterey Bay.

Leaving the sailing to his crew, Romualdo used the time to tell the children tales of days gone by.

"In my grandfather's day," he said, "an Argentine pirate named Hipólite Bouchard raided these towns along the coast. When his ship anchored at Monterey the townspeople fled like deer into the hills. They had to watch helplessly while the brigands looted and ransacked their homes, then burned everything to the ground."

Maybella's eyes grew big and round.

"But Papa, why didn't the people fight back?"

"They never guessed such a thing could happen in such a peaceful place. Without soldiers or an army, their settlements were left defenseless."

Arthur puffed out his chest.

"I would have stopped those pirates."

"And I would have helped you," Maybella said.

"I am sure you both would make valiant soldiers," Romualdo said as seriously as he could, "but let us pray we never again have such a need."

The *Consuela* reached the southern tip of Monterey Bay just when the sun was about to set. The children leaned forward against the rails and argued over who would be first to catch sight of the town. Molly felt a sudden pang of sadness. Waldo should have been there with them.

She stood next to Romualdo, watching the sun's golden rays strike the whitewashed walls of Monterey's adobes and glance off the red-tiled roofs. Beyond the town rose a steep, shady forest of dark green cypress and pine.

"This place is enchanting," she said quietly.

She thought of everything they'd been through—losses, disappointments, victories half-won—and how she loved him. Somehow, he always believed in her, even when she didn't.

The sound of a cannon boomed across the water, and the children jumped.

"Pirate ships!" Arthur yelled, pointing toward the merchant boats anchored near the wharf.

"No, Arthur, not pirates," Romualdo chuckled. "Look at the hill high above the harbor. Do you see a wisp of smoke hanging in the air? Sentries at the *Presidio* have fired a salute to welcome us."

They neared San Carlos Beach, and Molly followed Romualdo's gaze past the stone pier to a two-story adobe close to shore.

"What is on your mind?" she asked.

"My father was once *capitán* of this fort, when the king of Spain still ruled California," he said. "That building is the old Customs House. I remember watching ships from around the world dock here. I was not much older than Maybella at the time. Monterey was capital of Alta California, and captains had to register their cargo and pay duties to Mexico. But that was many years ago..."

The *Consuela* tied up at the wharf, and a delegation of local dignitaries came forward to greet them.

"*Bienvenido a nuestra ciudad, gobernador Pacheco,*" the harbormaster said, extending his hand.

"John Cooper," Romualdo said. "It has been a very long time."

"Far too long," the man replied warmly, and turned to a woman perhaps half his age standing by his side. "Please allow me to introduce my wife, Martha."

"Governor Pacheco, it's a great honor," she said. "John often talks about your time together in Honolulu."

"I remember the days well," Romualdo said with a grin. "Our schoolmaster, Mr. Johnstone, had his hands full with all of us. But we will save our childhood stories for later. I want you to meet my family. This is my wife, Molly."

"Mrs. Pacheco," Martha said brightly, "it is a great pleasure. I so enjoyed reading your novel. Have you another book planned?"

"Thank you, Mrs. Cooper," Molly said graciously. "I have several in mind, in fact. I just haven't decided which to write first."

Martha hesitated, unsure whether she was joking or serious, then said, "Oh, of course, I understand, with your husband being the governor…"

"You must be tired from your journey," John interrupted. "You will need your rest tonight. We have a grand celebration planned for tomorrow."

***

Molly slept soundly and woke to the crowing of roosters. She'd best get up soon. A parade had been scheduled for first thing in the morning. There was only enough time for a quick breakfast of boiled eggs, sourdough toast, fig jam, and coffee before the trumpets, violins, and guitars arrived to lead the family on a march through town.

Romualdo was the guest of honor at Monterey's annual community event, and the local townspeople gave him an enthusiastic welcome. Rousing patriotic speeches preceded a festive picnic, lively music, and dancing beneath a cloudless sky.

Maybella was awed by the attention paid to her father.

"Papa," she said, "I didn't know you were famous!"

Romualdo laughed. "I can only hope to be as famous as your mother, the well-known novelist."

Molly gave him an impish grin.

"I shall take that as a challenge."

***

In November, Governor Pacheco and his family left Sacramento and returned home to Oakland. The rains had not yet set in, but the days had grown short, and the weather already felt like winter. On one of these gray, cloudy mornings, Molly and Romualdo decided to walk on the path bordering the shore of Lake Merritt.

They were silent for a time, then Molly said, "Romualdo, it has been long enough. You need to decide what to do next."

He nodded slowly.

"I have been considering what course to take, but I do not yet know if I have my party's support."

"The Republicans have not entirely abandoned you."

"No, and one betrayal does not end my career."

"You're still the most respected man in California."

He smiled and said, "We shall see if the voters share your opinion. I am thinking of a run for Congress."

"You should do it," Molly said. "You are sure to win. There is no one else like you in the state."

"Possibly. I still have the support of Californios, but I will need more than that if I wish to be elected."

"I will enjoy being married to a congressman."

"*Gracias, querida,*" he said with a laugh. "You give me strength."

He took her arm, and they continued down the lakeside path.

"You do understand," he said, "if we go to Washington, we will be away from home for months at a time."

"That is not a problem. These days the trip east takes only a week by train. Maybella will come with us. When Congress isn't in session, we'll come home, and while you're in Washington, Maybella and I will take the train to New York City. I've heard there are excellent plays performed on Broadway."

Romualdo squeezed her hand.

"An ulterior motive, perhaps?"

"Never," she laughed. "How could you think such a thing?"

Chapter Twenty-Seven

Congressman and Mrs. Pacheco

1877

It was March 1877, and Molly was helping her husband pack for the train trip to Washington, D.C. The journey would be amazingly quick. The mere five days from coast to coast was a feat thought impossible only a decade earlier. This was only a brief two-week session of Congress, so Molly and Maybella wouldn't accompany him this time. They'd wait and join him for the longer three-month session to be held in the autumn.

Romualdo was one of four Californians elected to the United States Congress, and the only Californio. No one could deny his popularity with the voters, and Molly was deeply proud of his success. Still, she couldn't stop thinking about her own desires. Dreams she'd set aside.

She tucked a pair of freshly laundered socks into one corner of his valise and sat on the edge of the bed.

"I met Matilda Bancroft at the Women's Guild luncheon yesterday," she said. "She told me how busy she's been helping Hubert with his history project. Her days are fully occupied with research, writing, and editing, and she still has the children and household to manage."

Romualdo looked up from gathering his papers.

"Bancroft is lucky to have her. If he means to publish the history of the entire Pacific Coast, he will need all the help he can get. It will take years to finish."

"I have seen Matilda's work, and she is a gifted writer. I believe she could accomplish great things on her own if she ever had the chance."

It wasn't resentment she felt over another's writing ability. Only recognition of an accomplished woman, one who chose to use her considerable gifts to bolster a brilliant husband.

Romualdo added the papers to his valise before turning to Molly.

"What about you? I hope you have not given up writing."

"Not entirely. But I don't believe I'll ever have the success I hoped to achieve as a playwright."

"You are far too talented to give up so easily," he said. "Once you set your mind to it, *querida*, you can accomplish anything."

Molly smiled softly and handed him another carefully folded broadcloth shirt. She thought of how Matilda helped her husband write his history while letting her own stories remain unwritten.

"Uncle Louis used to say, 'Never give up. Anything is possible.'"

"He was right," Romualdo said.

He closed his valise with a quiet click.

"Remember, whatever you decide, you have my full support."

She hesitated, her eyes full of mischief.

"To be honest, I actually do have something in mind. It's a comedy."

"Tell me about it."

"I'm thinking of writing a farce, a comedy of errors with identical twins and mixed-up lovers. There might be a pompous general who's dreadfully opposed to his children's wishes. Maybe a pair of foolish women who can't stop laughing and crying, and perhaps a wife with too many opinions. Purely fictitious, of course."

He grinned and said, "You know how I love comedies. Perhaps one day we will open a theater of our own. We could showcase your plays. What do you think?"

"Let me finish this one first," she said with a laugh. "But seriously, I've had another idea. You know how long I've dreamed of living in New York City. Now is the perfect time. I could rent a small apartment near the Broadway theaters. Maybella could take dance classes and I'd be able to write without too many interruptions. I know the city would inspire me, and when you aren't needed in Washington you could come and stay with us."

Romualdo tugged at his beard and quietly considered her words.

"I know it's a bold proposal," she continued. "But I fear time is passing me by. New York is the heart of the theater world, and I could learn so much, maybe finally see my work performed on Broadway."

"New York," he said slowly, half to himself. "Very well, we will find a way. Yours is an excellent plan, *querida*. Excellent indeed."

Chapter Twenty-Eight

Mrs. R. Pacheco

1879–1883

By now, Molly's travel across the country was a familiar, well-known script. The rhythm of the rails lulled her to sleep at night, and she loved early morning breakfasts in the dining car—thickly buttered Boston brown bread and hot black coffee served on crisp white linen tablecloths while the sun rose over the plains. Every trip brought memories of a far more arduous journey, the one that first brought her to live a new life in California.

"I need to meet with my constituents," Romualdo had told her. No wonder. This was his second term in Congress, and he'd been away on the East Coast for nearly a year.

"We'll all go home together," Molly had said. "Maybella misses her friends in Oakland, and I could definitely use a good visit with my mother and sisters." She didn't need to mention it, of course, but she also meant to see every new play being performed on stage in San Francisco.

Their nephew, young Arthur Wilson, waited for them at the station. He was the very image of his father Enoch—tall and gangly, redheaded, and all of fourteen years old.

"Aunt Molly! Uncle Aldo! Welcome home!"

They shared hugs all around, and Arthur loaded their luggage into a carriage for the short ride home. Molly and Romualdo wanted to hear about school, but Arthur only wanted to talk about his favorite subject, sailing.

"I'm out on the bay every chance I get, Uncle Aldo. You'll be proud of me when you see how much I've learned."

"Well then," Romualdo said, "you must show me. We will take the *Consuela* on the bay. If we are blessed with a good wind, we may pass Alcatraz Island."

"Maybe take her out to the ocean through the Golden Gate?"

"We shall see, Arthur. We shall see."

The following week was ideal for sailing. Once the morning fog had burned away, the sky opened, and a brisk breeze filled the *Consuela*'s sails. His nephew handled the ropes with surprising skill, and Romualdo was impressed.

At the end of the day, Arthur came racing through the kitchen door flush with excitement, his eyes sparkling and blue as the bay.

"Mother, Aunt Molly! You won't believe it!"

"Calm down, son. Take a breath," Joanna said. "What's this all about?"

"Uncle Romualdo wants me to help him escort President Grant's ship when it sails into San Francisco Bay!"

"It's true," Romualdo said, following through the door behind him. "General Grant is about to complete his around-the-world tour. The *Consuela* has been invited to join a flotilla to greet his ship and I'd like Arthur to join the crew. With Joanna's approval, of course."

For almost three years, American newspapers had been following Ulysses S. Grant on his travels across the globe. His meetings with foreign dignitaries had demonstrated America's growing importance as a world power and he was returning home a tremendously popular hero.

"It sounds magnificent," Joanna said. "Absolutely, Arthur should go."

"It will be quite the spectacle," Molly said. "Everyone will turn out to see General Grant."

"He is making his last stop in Japan," Romualdo said. "If all goes well, he will be here before the end of September."

September 20, 1879

When the hansom cab brought Molly home from the Oakland train depot, Maybella was there to meet her at the door.

"I'm glad you made it in time for the festivities, Mother. Everyone is already down at the harbor."

"I had to leave so much work behind in New York," Molly said, unpinning her hat and setting it on the hall bureau. "I explained to Walter the importance of family responsibilities, but he has never been very understanding."

"Maybe it's time for a different agent."

"You may be right," she said, smiling faintly. "I promised to finish Act Two of my new script while I'm here at home. I hope a change of scenery will help hurry it along."

"If we don't hurry, we'll miss the boat parade."

Molly dropped her bag beside the stairs, removed her gloves, and loosened the scarf around her neck.

"I need a minute to freshen up," she said. "You go ahead without me. I'll get there as soon as I can and look for you on the wharf."

"Okay, Mother. Try not to be too late."

Molly took a moment to watch her daughter go, then hurried upstairs. After a quick wash, she changed into a navy-and-white striped taffeta dress and short, bright red jacket, the sort of outfit she liked to set aside for patriotic occasions. It required her to wear an uncomfortable whalebone corset, but no matter, today was a special day.

The few blocks to the Oakland harbor were an easy walk. Red, white, and blue bunting decorated the neighboring houses, and American flags flapped in the cool, brisk wind. She heard strains of "Hail Columbia" and stepped up her pace. Then the muted sounds of fog horns and factory whistles led her straight to the waterfront.

"Molly, over here," Joanna shouted.

Joanna's voice was nearly lost in the music and noise of the crowd. A local brass band began a rousing version of the "Battle Hymn of the Republic," but then Molly found her sister up on her toes, scanning the harbor for any sign of her son.

"Do you see the *Consuela?*" Molly asked.

"No, not yet."

"Where's Mother?"

Joanna pointed toward the end of the wharf.

"Over there, with Captain Dorr."

Molly's eyes widened.

"Captain Dorr? From the *Veracruz?*"

Joanna laughed and said, "You've been gone for a while, Molly, and missed the big news. Mother and the captain met by chance while strolling near Lake Merritt. He's retired now and lives in Oakland. Quite close to us, in fact."

It was soon apparent that Denman Dorr had not lost his commanding voice.

"Miss Molly! Look at you, all grown up and quite the lady!"

Mother and the captain worked their way through the crowd. Just as they reached them, Lizzie's sons began yanking on the captain's coat sleeves, demanding his immediate attention.

"Henry Halstead Miller," Lizzie said, "you and Ben are to stop annoying Captain Dorr and mind your manners right this instant!"

He laughed and said, "Excuse me, ladies. It seems these young sailors require my assistance. With your permission, I must take my leave."

Molly watched them go, then raised an eyebrow at Mother.

"So, you have a new companion?"

"Yes," she said with a laugh. "Denman is an amiable friend, and we enjoy each other's company. As a matter of fact, we plan to attend a concert in the city next week."

She left to join the captain and Molly exchanged amused glances with her sisters.

"So. Did either of you ever think Mother would end up with Captain Dorr?"

"I'm sure I never imagined half of what's happened to us since we left Kentucky," Lizzie said.

With a slight smile, Joanna said, "Mother had the courage to leave home and bring us all the way across the continent. She has done everything for us. She deserves to be happy."

"I wonder if they will ever marry," Molly said.

"One can never tell," Joanna said, looking away. "Once was enough for me. I'm sure I'll never marry again."

She wiped something—it might have been a tear—from the corner of her eye. Molly sighed and slipped an arm around her sister.

"You are right," she said. "We all deserve happiness."

May 1883

The weather was particularly fine in New York that day. English roses spilled over the wrought-iron garden fences and pink hydrangea bushes crowded the public parks. Everything was in full bloom, and it was glorious.

Molly looked out her apartment window and thought back to the many hours she'd spent at the little kitchen table, lost in words. She'd sometimes even forgotten to eat until late in the afternoon. Then

Maybella would come running in from a day of classes, full of excitement over a new boy she'd met or the adorable pair of shoes she'd found on sale at Lord & Taylor's.

Romualdo put down his morning newspaper.

"We couldn't have chosen a better month to be in town," he said.

"I agree. And this day is too perfect to waste sitting indoors."

"We should walk to Union Square and take lunch at Delmonico's," he said. "On the way, I want to be sure to locate the Bijou Theatre. We cannot be late for tomorrow night's performance."

They strolled down the streets, past the rows of brownstone houses with their neatly trimmed hedges. Romualdo tipped his hat to the ladies. Most of them, like Molly, wore fancy flowered hats and carried lace parasols that looked pretty but would never withstand the rain and did little to block the sun.

The scent of lilacs drifted between passing omnibuses and horse-drawn delivery wagons. Romualdo stopped for a minute to admire a young cream-colored mare he saw pulling a one-horse chaise. The handsome driver wore a smartly cut suit to match, and the carriage was upholstered in the same soft shade of pale beige leather.

"There goes a good-looking rig," he said. "I can certainly see why you find this city so inspiring."

"Don't be silly," Molly laughed. "You must have noticed the marquee signs around here. There is nowhere in the world like New York. Every production on Broadway has at least one famous performer."

"But what about the writing? Tell me, how many of these plays truly sparkle with character and wit?"

She kept walking and ignored his comments. Then they turned the corner, and there, pasted on the theater wall, was a large, brightly colored red-and-blue playbill.

Announcing the Grand Opening of
the Original and Very Laughable Production of
Incog
A Farcical Comedy in Three Acts
With a Superb Metropolitan Cast
of Superior Merit and Excellence

Romualdo read the notice out loud, then looked at her with a teasing smile.

"The names of the leading actors and actresses are shown here in bold letters," he said. "I see those of the producers, stage manager, and director all spelled out. Oh, and look. Here is the name of the playwright, Mrs. R. Pacheco. I believe I have heard of her. She is the famous humorist from California, is she not?"

Molly's laughter rang warm and clear.

"I'm sure my father would never have approved. But Uncle Louis was right. If you try very hard and have the love of someone who believes in you, your dreams have an excellent chance indeed. They may even come true."

Author's Note

This novel began with a family memory. I was a young bride when my mother-in-law first told me the story of her great-grandmother Sarah's journey to California. The McIntyre women left Kentucky when times were deeply troubled, yet each found a new life for herself in the American West.

Molly was a girl with stories in her heart, and she ultimately realized her childhood ambitions. She became a successful playwright and was among the first American women to write theatrical comedies. She wrote several books, and her many plays were produced in dramatic clubs, lyceums, and small theaters across the United States.

Incog, her greatest commercial success, may have been inspired by Shakespeare's *The Comedy of Errors*. The lively farce of mixed-up love and mistaken identities toured across America, played to audiences in London, and was translated into German for performances in Berlin. A musical adaptation, *Three Twins*, opened on June 16, 1908, at the Herald Square Theatre in New York City and enjoyed a run of 289 performances.

Joanna Wilson never remarried after the death of her husband, Enoch, yet she managed to send both her children to college in Boston. Her son, Arthur "A.R." Wilson, graduated from the Massachusetts Institute of Technology in 1890 and went on to found successful construction companies that are still based in Watsonville, California. A lifelong sailor, he kept a racing sloop, the *Maryland G,* at the Corinthian Yacht Club on San Francisco Bay. His sister, Mary Elizabeth Wilson, graduated from Smith College, worked as an educator, and later owned and operated Berkeley's Anna Head School for Girls.

Sarah's daughter Lizzie married and raised two sons with her husband, Henry Miller, a San Francisco banker. Molly and Romualdo's daughter, Maybella, became a prominent San Francisco socialite. She married Will Tevis, whose father, Lloyd Tevis, was a fabulously wealthy nineteenth-century capitalist and president of Wells Fargo Bank.

Romualdo Pacheco was the first Latino elected to serve in the United States Congress. To this day, he remains California's only Latino governor, and according to newspaper accounts of the time, he is the only governor known to have lassoed a grizzly bear. Pacheco was an avid sailor, hunter, and outdoorsman, and over the course of his remarkable life he lived under the rule of Mexican law, Hawaiian royalty, and American presidents. After serving two terms in Washington, President Benjamin Harrison named him envoy to Central America, where he continued to work for his country.

After retiring from politics, Romualdo supported Molly's theatrical career. Together they formed *Romualdo Pacheco's Ideal Comedy Company*, which toured with her plays across California and neighboring states. In 1898, the couple opened the *New Comedy Theatre* in San Francisco. An economic downturn forced its closure, leaving them close to bankruptcy at the time of his death in 1899.

Molly spent much of her later years in New York City, where, according to writer Bret Harte, "her home was a rendezvous for artists, authors, and people who do things." She was laid to rest in 1913 beside her husband and son on a steep hill atop Oakland's Mountain View Cemetery. The spelling of her surname varies in historical records, but her gravestone reads: "Mary McIntyre, Wife of Romualdo Pacheco."

With the help and encouragement of his wife Elida, Romualdo's friend Charles DeLong went on to become American Envoy to Japan. The DeLongs moved their young family to Tokyo in 1869, bringing with them three servants, three horses, a carriage, and Elida's sewing machine.

In January 1883, María Jacinta Guirado, Governor John Downey's beautiful Californio first lady, died in a tragic train wreck outside Los Angeles. The steam engine carrying the Downeys was rounding a steep curve in the Tehachapi Mountains when it became a runaway. The cars derailed, and the train plunged down a steep ravine before bursting into intense flames. Fifteen lives were lost, and María's body was never found.

The hordes of Easterners who poured into California during the Gold Rush rapidly outnumbered native-born Californios. Their political influence faded, but familiar names such as Vallejo, Benicia,

Carrillo, and Yorba, still echo across the state, reminding us of an era vastly different from our own.

Many of the people and events of this story are real, and excerpts from her hit play *Incog* and her novel *The New Don Quixote* are used throughout the manuscript. *Romualdo Pacheco: A Californio in Two Eras,* the 1985 biography by Ronald Genini and Richard Hitchman, provided names, dates, locations, and historical insight for much of this narrative. Additional details were drawn from family lore, newspaper accounts, museum collections, and works by California historians.

This book could not have been written without the help and encouragement of family and friends. John Dorr, Mary Berg, Jane Otto, Lisa Giefer, McCall Dorr Johnson, and Beth Falkson read and reread early manuscripts and offered valuable suggestions. My thanks to them, and to everyone else who listened as Molly's story evolved and grew.

No one can be sure whether every conversation or meeting found in these pages occurred exactly as described. Yet there is no doubt that the people whose lives inspired this story possessed courage, talent, and determination.

The McIntyre women were not merely survivors. They crossed unknown frontiers and built meaningful lives in the American West. Their story reminds us that it was not only miners and politicians who shaped the California dream. Strong women, sustained by faith and the promise of a better life, believed their voices mattered and would one day be heard.

MANAGEMENT
JOS. M. GAITES
THREE TWINS
CHAS. DICKSON'S
MUSICAL ADAPTATION
OF MRS. R. PACHECO'S COMEDY "INCOG"
The
Yama Yama Man
Lyric by Collin Davis
Theatrical and Music Hall Rights of this Song are
Reserved. For permission apply to the Publishers.
M. WITMARK & SONS
NEW YORK CHICAGO LONDON PARIS
LYRICS BY
O. A. HAUERBACH
MUSIC BY
KARL L. HOSCHN

About the Author

Rose Ann Woolpert writes historical fiction based on untold stories of the American west. Her debut novel, Mrs. R. Pacheco, blends family memories with local history to bring 19th century California to life. Originally from Southern California, she currently lives in the San Francisco Bay Area where she is at work on her next book.

Follow the author at

www.historiumpress.com/rose-ann-woolpert
www.roseannwoolpert.com

www.historiumpress.com